Henry Spicer

# Judicial Dramas

Or, the romance of French criminal law

Henry Spicer

**Judicial Dramas**
*Or, the romance of French criminal law*

ISBN/EAN: 9783337394738

Printed in Europe, USA, Canada, Australia, Japan

Cover: Foto ©Andreas Hilbeck / pixelio.de

More available books at **www.hansebooks.com**

# JUDICIAL DRAMAS;

## OR THE

## ROMANCE OF FRENCH CRIMINAL LAW.

BY

# HENRY SPICER,

AUTHOR OF "SIGHTS AND SOUNDS," "OLD STYLES'S,"
"BROUGHT TO BOOK," ETC.

Periculosum est credere et non credere;
Utriusque breviter exponam rei.

LONDON:
TINSLEY BROTHERS, 18, CATHERINE STREET, STRAND.
1872.

TO

# MR. SERJEANT BALLANTINE,

JUSTLY STYLED THE

ABLEST ADVOCATE AND CROSS-EXAMINER OF THE ENGLISH BAR,

THIS SELECTION OF A CLASS OF CASES KNOWN

IN FRANCE AS

"DRAMES JUDICIAIRES,"

IS DEDICATED BY THE COMPILER,

H. S.

# CONTENTS.

# JUDICIAL DRAMAS.

## I.

### GHOSTS IN COURT.

WHETHER or not the defective ventilation of our courts of law be inimical to the subtle fluid of which phantoms are composed, or whether these sensitive essences, oppressed with the absurdities of forensic costume and manners, take fright at the first glimmer of a counsellor's wig, or at the titter that follows a counsellor's joke, there can be no question of the extreme difficulty that has always been experienced in bringing a spectre fairly to judicial book.

So long as the proceedings retain an extrajudicial character, no gentleman on the extensive roll of attorneys could devote his time and abilities more zealously to the getting up of a case than has your unfee'd film. Not content with fulfilling the office of detective, the indefatigable phantom has suggested needful testimony, indicated lines of prosecution, collected witnesses, and—all being ready—marched, so to speak, up to the very door of the judgment-hall. There, however, for one of the reasons above stated, or for some other, the spectre has invariably come to a stand. An objection to be sworn, in that impressive manner so familiar to the frequenters of English courts of justice, may have something to do with it. The prospect of a cross-examination by a sceptical person in horsehair, whose incredulity goes the length of doubting one's very existence, and whose questions, in any case, must look one's substance through and through, may be sufficiently alarming. Still, it is clear that such coquetting with the forms of legal procedure is, as Dogberry observes, most tolerable, and not to be endured. We need not, therefore, be surprised that a tacit understanding has been arrived at to eliminate the accusing shade altogether. If flesh and blood, that can speak well up to a jury, and stand bullying, cannot convict a man, shall a skulking shadow have that power? No. The ghost's word—appraised by the Prince of Denmark at " a thousand pound "—is now, in the eye of the law, literally not worth one dump.

Respect, however, for the fallen. It is one of the evil results of the " Spiritualism " which has spread like a rabies through society, that, in dealing with those wizards who are medium one day and conjuror the next, according to the amount of detection brought to bear on them, or to the tone of the opinion market, we are apt to acquire a habit of speaking with over-familiarity of things that lie beyond the hitherto ascertained limit of natural laws. This is surely a mistake. Nothing, in this educated age, astonishes one more than the extreme narrowness of that district which separates absolute scepticism from blind belief. So close are these neighbours, that, without risk of offending one or the other, the reasonable mind has scarcely space to stir. With the former, the mere act of inquiry seems to involve a sort of abandonment of principle; with the latter, the most superficial examination suffices.

Without in the least challenging the wisdom of that arrangement which has outlawed the ghost, it is singular to trace the manner in which, within the memory of this generation, what must be called, for fault of other phrase, supernatural interference, has, to all appearance, contributed to the ends of justice.

Thus, in the case of a notorious murder near Brighton, some thirty years ago, a dream, and a dream alone, led to the discovery of the crime, and of the victim's remains.

A curious instance of what, in Scotland, would have been termed second-sight, occurred, within the writer's recollection, in a midland county, and, though of course suppressed at the trial, was (an unusual circumstance) attested upon oath at the preceding inquest. A market-gardener, known, from his fine presence, as "Noble Eden," was murdered while at work in the fields at a long distance from his dwelling. His wife, ironing at a dresser by the kitchen window, saw him run swiftly past, pursued by another man, who brandished a stone hammer, as if threatening to strike. Aware that it was a spectral illusion, and impressed with an idea that some evil had befallen her husband, Mrs. Eden caused instant search to be made at the spot to which he had intended to proceed, when the body was discovered, cold and stiff—the murderous weapon, a stone hammer, lying beside him.

Another example of this species of warning attracted some attention in the "burking" times at Edinburgh—the voice of one of the victims, recognised under circumstances irreconcilable with any known law of nature, having led to the suspecting, and thence to the conviction, of the assassins.

A gentleman, lately living, used to relate that while resident near Fort George, N.B., the disappearance of an old woman, who, from her strict and sober habits, was employed by the whole neighbourhood as a messenger, created much excitement. Nothing could be discovered respecting her. The search, at the instance of her husband, was at length discontinued. One evening Mr. H. was sitting reading in his arbour, when the missing woman suddenly thrust her head through the leafy shield! There was a broad crimson streak round her neck, and, without her uttering a word, an impression seeméd to be conveyed to Mr. H.'s mind that she had been murdered, and that her body lay concealed, under stable refuse, in a distant byre. Search was made there, the corpse was found, and the husband was subsequently executed, on his own confession of the crime.

In the French courts, questions of ghost or no ghost—and, if the former, what might be the worth of the ghost's testimony—seem to have been permitted a wider range. Counsel has been freely heard on either part. In a case that, many years ago, stirred up the whole philosophy of the subject, so much curious matter was elicited as to make the record worth preserving.　It is an illustration of the familiar manner in which a not distant generation dealt with the subject.

Honoré Mirabel, a poor labourer on the estate of a family named Gay, near Marseilles, invoked the protection of the law under the following extraordinary circumstances :—

He declared that, while lying under an almond-tree, late one night, striving to sleep, he suddenly noticed a man of remarkable appearance standing, in the full moonlight, at the window of a neighbouring house.　Knowing the house to be unoccupied, he rose to question the intruder, when the latter disappeared. A ladder being at hand, Mirabel mounted to the window, and, on entering, found no one.　Struck with a feeling of terror, he descended the ladder with all speed, and had barely touched the ground, when a voice at his back accosted him :

"Pertuisan" (he was of Pertuis), "there is a large treasure buried close at hand.　Dig, and it is yours."

A small stone was dropped on the terrace, as if to mark the spot alluded to.

For reasons not explained, the favoured Mirabel shrank from pursuing the adventure alone, but communicated with a friend, one Bernard, a labourer in the employ of the farmeress Paret. This lady being admitted to their confidence, the three assembled next night at the place indicated by the spectre, and, after digging to a considerable depth, came upon a large parcel wrapped in many folds of linen. Struck with the pickaxe, it returned unmistakably the melodious sound of coin; but the filthy, and, as Paret suggested, plague-stricken appearance of the covering, checked their eager curiosity, until, having been conveyed home and well soaked in wine, the parcel was opened, and revealed to their delighted gaze more than a thousand large gold pieces, subsequently ascertained to be Portuguese.

It was remarkable, yet so it *was*, that Mirabel was allowed to retain the whole of the treasure. Perhaps his friends felt some scruple in interfering with the manifest intentions of the ghost. But Mirabel was not much the happier for it. He feared for the safety of his wealth—he feared for his own life. Moreover, the prevailing laws respecting "treasure-trove" were peculiarly explicit, and it was question-able how far the decision of the ghost might be held to override them.

In France, of treasure found in the highway, half

belonged to the king, half to the finder.  If in any other public place, half to the high-justiciary, half to the finder.  If discovered by magical arts, the whole to the king, with a penalty upon the finder.  If, when discovered, the treasure were concealed from the proprietor of the ground, the finder forfeited his share.  To these existing claims the phantom had made no allusion.  In his perplexity, honest Mirabel bethought him of another friend, one Auguier, a substantial tradesman of Marseilles.

The advice of this gentleman was, that the secret should be rigorously confined to those who already knew it, while he himself (Auguier) was prepared to devote himself, heart and soul, to his friend's best interests, lend him any cash he needed (so as to obviate the necessity of changing the foreign money), attend him whithersoever he went, and, in fine, become his perpetual solace, monitor, and guard.

To prevent the possibility of his motives being misinterpreted, the worthy Auguier took occasion to exhibit to his friend a casket, in which was visible much gold and silver coin, besides a jewel or two of some value.

The friendship thus happily inaugurated grew and strengthened, until Mirabel came to the prudent resolution of entrusting the whole treasure to the custody of his friend, and appointed a place and time for that purpose.

On the way to the rendezvous, Mirabel met with an acquaintance, Gaspard Deleuil, whom—Auguier being already in sight—Mirabel requested to wait for him at the side of a thicket; then, going forward, he handed to the trusty Auguier two sealed bags, one of them secured with a red ribbon, the other with a blue, and received in return an instrument conceived in the following satisfactory terms :—

" I acknowledge myself indebted to Honoré Mirabel twenty thousand livres, which I promise to pay on demand, acquitting him, moreover, of forty livres which he owes me.  Done at Marseilles, this seventh of September.

(Signed)          " LOUIS AUGUIER."

This little matter settled, Mirabel rejoined Deleuil, and next day departed for his native village.  After starring it there for a few weeks, the man of wealth revisited Marseilles, and, having passed a jovial evening with his friend and banker, Auguier, was on his way home, when, at a dark part of the road, he was set upon by a powerful ruffian, who dealt him several blows with some sharp weapon, flung him to the ground and escaped. Fortunately, the wounds proved superficial.

This incident begat a certain suspicion in the mind of Mirabel. As soon as he was able, he repaired to Marseilles, and demanded of Auguier the return of his money, or liquidation of the bond. His friend expressed his extreme surprise. What an extraordinary application was here! Money! What money? He indignantly denied the whole transaction. Mirabel must be mad.

To establish his sanity, and, at the same time, refresh the memory of his friend, Mirabel without further ceremony appealed to the law, and, in due course, the Lieutenant-Criminal, with his officer, made his appearance at the house of Auguier, to conduct the perquisition. Search being made on the premises, no money was found; but there were discovered two bags and a red ribbon, which were identified by Mirabel as those which he had delivered to his friend.

The account given by the latter differed, in some material particulars, from that of Mirabel. He had enjoyed, indeed, some casual acquaintance with that gentleman. They had dined together, once, at his

(Auguier's) house. He had accepted the hospitality of Mons. Mirabel, as often, at a tavern. He had advanced that gentleman a crown. Mirabel had spoken of a ghost and money, and had talked of placing the latter in his charge. At present, he had, however, limited his confidence to the deposit of two empty bags and a red ribbon. All the other allegations he indignantly denied.

Deeply impressed with the marvellous history, the Lieutenant-Criminal decided that the matter should be sifted to the bottom. The process continued.

Magdalene Paret deposed that Mirabel had called on her one day, looking pale and agitated, and declared that he had been holding converse with an apparition, which had revealed to him the situation of some buried treasure. She was present when the parcel, apparently containing money, was found; and she remembered Mirabel stating, subsequently, that he had placed it for safety in the hands of Auguier.

Gaspard Deleuil repeated the narrative told by Mirabel of the ghost and the gold, adding that he had met him on the seventh of September, near the Porte des Fainéants (Idlers' Gate), carrying two bags; that he saw him hand them over to a man who appeared to be waiting for him, and saw him receive in return a piece of paper; and that, on rejoining him, Mirabel stated that he had entrusted to Auguier some newly-found treasure, taking his acknowledgment for the same.

François Fournière, the third witness, confirmed the story of the spectre and the money, as related by Mirabel, who appeared deeply stricken by the extraordinary favour shown him in this supernatural visitation. On his pressing for a sight of the treasure, Mirabel took the witness to his chamber, and, removing some bricks from the chimney, displayed a large bag filled with gold coin. Having afterwards heard of Auguier's alleged dishonesty, the witness reproached him with it: when he became deadly pale, and entreated that the subject might be dropped.

Other witnesses deposed to the sudden intimacy, more noticeable on account of their difference of station, that had sprung up between Mirabel and Auguier, dating from the period of the discovery of the gold. Sundry experts bore testimony to the resemblance of the writing of the receipt, signed "Louis Auguier," to the autograph of the latter.

The ghost and Mirabel carried the day. In fact, it was a mere walk over the course. The Lieutenant-Criminal, entirely with them, decreed that Auguier should be arrested, and submitted to the "question."

Appeal, however, was made to the parliament of Aix, and the matter began to excite considerable notice. Persons were found to censure the ready credence given by the Lieutenant-Criminal to the story of the ghost, and, the case coming to hearing, an able advocate of the day buckled on his armour to do battle with the shade.

Is it credible (he asked) that a spirit should quit the repose of another world expressly to inform Mons. de Mirabel, a gentleman with whose existence it seems to have had no previous acquaintance, of the hiding-place of this treasure? How officious must be the nature of that ghost which should select, in a caprice, a man it did not personally know, to enrich him with a treasure, for the due enjoyment of which his social position made him so unfit? How slight must be the prescience of a spirit that could not foresee that Mirabel would be deprived of his treasure by the first knave he had the misfortune to trust! There could be no such spirit, be assured.

If there were no spectre, there was, according to all human probability, no gold; and, if no gold, no ground for the accusation of Auguier.

Descending to earthly reasoning, was it likely that Mirabel should entrust to Auguier a treasure of whose actual value he knew nothing, or that he should take in return a receipt he had not seen the giver write? How was it, pray, that the woman Paret and Gaspard Deleuil demanded no share in the treasure so discovered? Were these excellent persons superior to the common weaknesses of humanity—curiosity, and the lust of gain? The witness Paret certainly saw the discovery of a parcel; but the rest of her evidence was hearsay. The witness Deleuil saw the exchange of bags and paper; but all the rest—spectre included—was hearsay. And when the witness Fournière declared that Auguier, being taxed with robbery, turned deadly pale, Auguier frankly—nay, proudly—confessed it, stricken as that honourable burgher was with horror at a charge so foul and unexpected! The climax of injustice was surely reached when this respected, estimable, substantial merchant of France's proudest sea-mart, was, on the uncorroborated word of a ghost (for to this it must be traced), submitted to the torture. In criminal, even more than in civil cases, that which seems repugnant to probability is reputed false. Let a hundred witnesses testify to that which is contrary to nature and the light of reason, their evidence is worthless and vain. Take, as example, the famous tradition which gives an additional interest to the noble house of Lusignan, and say that certain persons swore that the fairy Melusina, who had the tail of a serpent, and bathed every Saturday in a marble cellar, had revealed a treasure to some weak idiot, who was immediately robbed of it by another. What would be thought of a judge who should, on such testimony, condemn the accused? Is it on such a fairy fable that Auguier, the just, the respected family-father, the loyal patriot, must be adjudged guilty? Never! Such justice might be found at Cathay, might prevail in the yet undiscovered islands of the Eastern Archipelago, but in France—no. There remained, in short, but one manifest duty to the court, namely, to acquit, with all honour, this much-abused man, and to render him such noble compensation as the injuries he had suffered deserved.

It was now, however, the phantom's innings. Turning on the court the night-side of nature, the spectre's advocate pointed out that the gist of Auguier's defence consisted of a narrow and senseless satire upon supernatural visitations, involving a most unauthorized assumption that such things did never occur. Was it intended to contradict holy writ? To deny a truth attested by Scripture, by the Fathers of the Church, by very wide experience and testimony, finally, by the Faculty of Theology of Paris? The speaker here adduced the appearance of the prophet Samuel at Endor (of which Le Brun remarked that it was, past question, a work commenced by the power of evil, but taken from his hand and completed by a stronger than he); that of the bodies of buried saints after our Lord's resurrection; and that of Saint Felix, who, according to Saint Augustine, appeared to the besieged inhabitants of Nola. But, say that any doubts could rationally exist, were they not completely set at rest by a recent decision of the Faculty of Theology? "Desiring," says this enlightened decree, "to satisfy pious scruples, we have, after a very careful consideration of the subject, resolved that the spirits of the departed may and do, by supernatural power and divine licence, reappear unto the living." And this opinion was in conformity with that pronounced at Sorbonne two centuries before.

However, it was not dogmatically affirmed that the spirit which had evinced this interest in Mirabel was the ghost of any departed person. It might have been a spirit, whether good or evil, of another kind. That such a spirit can assume the human form few will deny, when they recal that the apostles held that belief, mistaking their Lord, walking on the waves of Galilee, for such an one. The weight of probability, nevertheless, inclines to the side of this singular apparition being, as was first suggested, the spirit of one deceased—perhaps, a remote ancestor of Mirabel—perhaps, one who, in this life, sympathized with honest endeavour, and sought to endow the struggling toiling peasant with the means of rest and ease. And, with regard to this reappearance, a striking modern instance seemed pertinent to the question at issue. The Marquis de Rambouillet and the Sieur de Prècy, aged respectively twenty-five and thirty, were intimate friends. Speaking one day of the prospect of a future state of being, their conversation ended with a mutual compact that the first who died should reveal himself to the survivor. Three months afterwards the Marquis went to the war in Flanders, while De Prècy, sick with fever, remained in Paris. One night, the latter, while in bed, heard the curtains move, and, turning, recognised his friend, in buff-coat and riding-boots, standing by the bed. Starting up, he attempted to embrace the visitor, but the latter, evading him, drew apart, and, in a solemn tone, informed him that such greetings were no longer fitting, that he

had been slain the previous night in a skirmish, that
he had come to redeem his promise, and to announce
to his friend that all that had been spoken of a world
to come was most certainly true, and that it behoved
him (De Prècy) to amend his life without delay, as he
would himself be slain within a very brief period.
Finding his hearer still incredulous, the Marquis exhibited a deadly wound below the breast, and immediately disappeared.   The arrival of a post from
Flanders confirmed the vision.   The Marquis had been
slain in the manner mentioned.   De Prècy himself fell
in the civil war, then impending.

(The speaker here cited a number of kindred examples
belonging to the period, such as, in later days, have
found parallels in the well-known stories of Lord Tyrone
and Lady Betty Cobb, Lord Lyttelton and M. P. An-
drews, Prince Dolgorouki and Apraxin, the ex-queen of
Etruria and Chipanti, with a long list of similar cases,
and then addressed himself to the terrestrial facts.)

It was proved by Magdalene Paret that the treasure was actually found.   By the witness, Deleuil,
it was traced into the possession of Auguier.   By
other witnesses, it was shown that Auguier had made
use of many artifices to obtain the custody of the
gold, cultivating a romantic attachment for this

humble labourer, and seeking to inspire him with fears for his personal safety, so long as he retained possession of so large a sum. Upon the whole, unless it had been practicable to secure the attendance and oral testimony of the very phantom itself, the claim of Mirabel could hardly address itself more forcibly to the favourable judgment of the Court.

It may be that this little deficiency in the chain of evidence weighed more than was expected with the parliament of Aix. At all events, they demanded further proof; and the peasant, Bernard, was brought forward, and underwent a very rigid examination.

He stated that, on a certain day in May, Mirabel informed him that a ghost had revealed to him the existence of some secreted treasure. That, on the following morning, they proceeded together to the spot indicated by the apparition, but found no money. That he laughed at Mirabel, snapped his fingers at the story, and went away. That he nevertheless agreed to a further search—the witness, Magdalene Paret, being present—but again found nothing. That, subsequently, Mirabel declared he had discovered eighteen pieces of gold, then twelve, finally, thirty-five, but displayed none of them. That Mirabel had, however, sent by him twenty sols to a priest, to say masses for the soul of the departed, to whom he owed so much; and that he had spoken of handing over the treasure to Auguier, and taking the latter's receipt, which certainly seemed to be the same now produced, signed "Louis Auguier."

The matter was obscure and puzzling. There was, by this time, no question that this large sum of money had, somehow, come into the possession of Mirabel. He could not, by skill or labour, have realized the hundredth part of it. No one had been robbed, for the notoriety of the case would at once have produced the loser. If Mirabel had found it (and there were the witnesses who proved the discovery many feet below the surface, in an undisturbed corner of the terrace), who revealed the precious deposit to this poor simple clown? The scale was inclining, slowly and steadily, to the spectral side, when some new and startling evidence appeared.

Auguier proved that *subsequently* to the alleged delivery of the treasure into his hands, Mirabel had declared that it was still concealed in the ground, and had invited his two brothers-in-law from Pertuis to see it. Placing them at a little distance from the haunted spot, he made pretence of digging, but suddenly raising a white shirt, which he had attached to sticks placed crosswise, he rushed towards them, crying out, "The ghost! the ghost!" One of these unlucky persons died from the impressions engendered by this piece of pleasantry. The survivor delivered this testimony.

The case now began to look less favourable for the spectre. It was hardly probable that Mirabel should take so unwarrantable a liberty with an apparition in which he believed, as to represent him, and that for no explainable purpose, by an old white shirt! Was it barely possible that Mirabel was after all a humbug, and that the whole story was a pure fabrication, for the purpose of obtaining damages from the well-to-do Auguier?

It does not appear to what astute judicial intellect this not wholly impossible idea presented itself. At all events, a new process was decreed, the great object of which was to discover in the first instance how and whence came the money into Mirabel's possession.

Under the pressure of this inquiry, the witness Paret was at length brought to confess—first, that she had never actually beheld one coin belonging to the supposed treasure: secondly, that she did not credit one word of Mirabel's story: thirdly, that if she had already deposed otherwise, it was at the earnest entreaty of Mirabel himself.

Two experts were then examined as to the alleged reccipt.  These differed in opinion as to its being in the handwriting of Auguier; but a third being added to the consultation, all three finally agreed that it was a well-executed forgery.

This, after twenty mouths, three processes, and the examination of fifty-two witnesses, was fatal to the ghost.  He was put out of court.

The final decree acquitted Auguier, and condemned Mirabel to the galleys for life, he having been previously submitted to the question.  Under the torture, Mirabel confessed that one Etienne Barthélemy. a declared enemy of Auguier's, had devised the spectral fable, as a ground for the intended accusation, and, to substantiate the latter, had lent him (for exhibition) the sum of twenty thousand livres.  By an after process, Barthélemy was sentenced to the galleys for life, and the witnesses Deleuil and Fournière to be hung up by the armpits, in some public place, as false witnesses.

So far as records go, this singular case was the last in which, in French law-courts, the question of ghost or no  ghost was made the subject of legal argument and sworn testimony.

# II

# THE MYSTERY OF METZ.

THERE existed within the recollection of continental travellers of the present century, a large old cloudy daub covering certain square feet of the wall of one of the galleries of the Hotel de Ville, Frankfort, and, rather from its mystery than its merit, diverting many an eye from the monotonous assemblage of crowned ladies and gentlemen suspended in its neighbourhood. It exercised a fearful fascination. Issuing from the gloom of the picture might be distinguished strange symbols—red angry glints of fire, as from lamps half hidden; brandished weapons; and faces distorted with bigot-rage—while, barely visible in the centre, lay stretched upon a table a little naked child, bound upon crossed pieces of wood, and bleeding from innumerable, though apparently not mortal gashes. It was in this work that the excited fancy of the artist sought to commemorate one of those fearful atrocities affirmed by Baronius, the Chronicle of

Nuremberg, and other authorities, to have been prevalent among the Jews for ages, but more especially in the thirteenth century—the sacrifice of a Christian child, with all the attendant cruelties suggested by the suffering and death of the blessed Redeemer of mankind.

While, in justice to this extraordinary people—at once the most favoured and afflicted of the earth—it must be owned that some at least of these alleged crimes were nothing more than pretexts for oppression, yet the records of an age of ignorance and blind fanaticism furnish credible evidence that the origin of this new and hideous form of murder must rest with them.

Thus—selecting from the better authenticated cases—in 1220, a boy was murdered in Alsace; in 1225, a child was crucified at Norwich; and another, aged nine, at Lincoln, in 1255.

> O youngë Hugh of Lincoln! slain also
> With cursed Jewës, as 'tis notable,
> For it n' is but a little while ago,

says Chaucer, writing at the distance of little more than a century.

In 1236, several were killed at Fulda, the bodies being sent to Hagenau, to prevent identification.

Similar crimes occurred about the same period at Baden, Berne, and Munich. In 1287, the murder of the boy Werner (briefly referred to in Murray's " Handbook for Northern Germany," p. 279) created a wide and painful sensation. The circumstances not supplied in Murray, were as follows :—

Werner was a youth of fourteen, residing near Bacharach, and supporting himself by his own industry. One day, while working at Oberwesel, some Jews accosted him, requesting him to convey a quantity of mould into a cellar in the neighbourhood. This order happening to reach the ears of his landlady, she earnestly bade the boy beware, as the next day but one would be Good Friday, and he would assuredly be killed and eaten by his infidel employers! To this the lad simply replied, that he was in the hands of Providence. On the morrow, Thursday, he went to confession, and afterwards partook of the eucharist. Later in the day, the Jews repeated their directions, and enticing the poor boy into the cellar, fell upon and bound him. They then crammed a ball of lead into his mouth to stifle his cries, and tied him to a post head downward, hoping by these means to make him reject the wafer he had told them he had received. Unsuccessful in this, they proceeded to mangle him with scourges, after which they opened veins in different parts of his body, pressing them with pincers to promote the hæmorrhage. They then hung him up for three days, sometimes by the head, sometimes by the feet, till blood had entirely ceased to flow. The foul deed had, however, been witnessed by a servant of the house, a Christian, who, watching her opportunity, hastened to the magistrate, and conducted him at once to the scene of butchery. But the immense bribes offered by the Jews proved too much for his honesty; they were permitted to effect their escape in a boat, taking with them the body of the murdered boy, which, when clear of the town, they flung into the river. Legends affirm that, instead of floating down the stream, it breasted the torrent, swimming *up* towards Bacharach. The probability is that, having no weight wherewith to sink the body, the murderers drew it back into the boat, and subsequently concealed it in a little cave, covered with thorns and brambles, near Bacharach.

The picture heretofore alluded to has disappeared from the walls of the Römer of Frankfort; perhaps in consideration to the feelings of the Jewish community, which, of late years, has formed so large and

important a section of the population of that once free
city; perhaps because, like many another prejudice, it
had become at length completely obliterated. The
actual incident it was intended to illustrate has never
been very clearly set forth—the doubt resting between
two cases, the one in 1475, the other in 1669. Of
the former, scarcely any record beyond the date has
been retained; of the latter, some discursive notes,
thrown together by M. ——, parliamentary advocate,
furnish, when sifted, materials for the narrative that
follows :—

A little after noon, on the 25th of September, 1669,
Wilhelmina, wife of Gilles Lemoine the cartwright,
residing in Glatigny, went to a spring, distant some
few hundred yards from the village, to wash linen.
She was followed by her little son Didier, a pretty
rosy child, with fair long curls, aged about three. As
they went, the little boy stumbled and fell.

"Not hurt, not hurt, my mother!" shouted the
young hero, jealous of being assisted. "I am coming,
my mother. Go on!"

She did go on, never to hear her child's voice again.

Busied with her work, some minutes elapsed before
Madame Lemoine became aware that she was alone;
but then she hastily retraced her steps, calling sharply

as she went, for she fancied that the child had concealed himself, and she was at the moment in no mood for play.  Receiving no answer, she ran back to the house, and, unsuccessful there, hastened with her husband to the cottage of her father-in-law, which was close at hand.  No one there had seen the child, and now seriously alarmed lest he should have strayed into the adjacent wolf-haunted forest, the anxious parents assembled their friends, and, aided by the town-prefect in person, examined every inch of ground in the vicinity of the spring.  Their search in this direction proved vain; but a shout from one of the party who had reached the high-road leading to Metz, brought everybody to the spot, where, clearly traceable on the soft white dust, were seen the footprints of the little wanderer !

Soon, however, these tiny tracks were lost in the marks of wheels and hoofs, and again the searchers were at fault.

Suddenly there came up, riding from Metz, a horseman, wearing the livery of the Count de Vaudemont, who, to the question had he met a straying child, promptly answered that he had encountered, but a few minutes before, a huge black-bearded Jew, on a white horse, proceeding towards Metz, and carrying before him a little curly-headed boy, apparently between three and four years old. No sooner, he added, had the Jew caught sight of him than he had quitted the high-road, so as to preserve in passing the distance of a pistol-shot.

There could be no question that the child was Didier; and the unhappy parents hurrying on to Metz, inquired, at what was called the German Gate of the city, if such a person as they described had been seen to enter.

Yes. A turner named Regnault, living close to the gate, had observed him pass in.

At this moment, there came in through the gate an acquaintance of Lemoine, resident in the neighbouring village of Hex, who, on being informed of what had occurred, at once identified the Jew as one Raphael Levi of Boulay, whose face dwelt freshly enough in the speaker's recollection, inasmuch as, less than two hours since, Levi had passed him on the road to Metz, carrying *something* before him, covered with a cloak.

Where did he lodge, this Raphael Levi?

At the house of his cousin, Garçon, not a minute's walk from the gate.

To the eager demands of the Lemoines, Garçon's

servant persistently declared that her master was absent, and that nothing was known of any strange child.

The baffled inquirers were about reluctantly to withdraw, when a young Jewess, who had stopped in passing to listen to the debate, stepped forward, and, addressing the servant in German, warned her to afford them no information.

Now it happened that Lemoine understood German, and, with these ominous words, stole into his heart the conviction that his child had been kidnapped by the Jew, for purposes too horrible to contemplate. Already it might be too late to save the little innocent; but revenge at least was left, and to this Lemoine, secretly despairing of his child's life, devoted himself heart and soul. No time was lost in laying a formal complaint before the lieutenant-criminal of Metz; but before the suspected Jew could be apprehended, those of his people resident in the city wrote to him, earnestly advising him to appear and answer frankly to the charge preferred. Raphael Levi obeyed.

In the process which followed, Raphael Levi was described as aged fifty-six, born at Xelaincourt, of middle stature, black curling hair, very full black beard. A bold, determined man. Had travelled much in the Levant, in Italy, Spain, Holland;

whithersoever, in short, the affairs of his people summoned him. Of late years, resident at Boulay, in the duchy of Lorraine (six French leagues from Metz), where he exercised the functions of rabbi and chief of the synagogue.

On the day of the alleged abduction of the child Lemoine, he had quitted Boulay at seven in the morning, arriving three hours later at Metz, his errand being to purchase a ram's horn for the next day's Feast of Trumpets, and also wine, oil, and fish. These articles he delivered to his son, and despatching him homewards, followed himself an hour after noon. The village of Glatigny is about a league and a half from Metz, and lies some two hundred paces from the high road from Metz to Boulay. It has been mentioned that the child, in place of following his mother to the spring, had wandered into the road. The presumption was that Levi, finding him there alone, had caught him up on his horse, returned to Metz, delivered him into the keeping of others of his people, and finally retraced his way to Boulay to sleep. Eighteen witnesses were produced, five of whom testified to having observed, on the day mentioned in the process, a Jew answering the description of Levi enter by the German Gate. He rode a white horse, and carried before him, wrapped in his mantle, a child about three years of age, with long bright curls escaping from his little crimson cap. One only of the witnesses, however, Blaisette Thomas, spoke positively to the identity of the infant-carrying Jew, while the Vaudemont rider affirmed that the man he had encountered on the road exceeded the accused in height and size.

The Jews of Metz, who neglected nothing to secure the acquittal of Levi, now tendered proof that, on the day in question, he had been at three o'clock at Estangs, two leagues from Metz, and half a league from Glatigny, arriving at Boulay at four, accompanied by his son.

"Agreed," replied the judges; "that is very possible;" and thereupon decreed that the accused, Raphael Levi, should be *burned alive*—being previously subjected to the torture, ordinary and extraordinary, with the view of discovering what he had done with the child.

Appeal was instantly made to parliament.

Two days after the first decree had been pronounced —namely, on the 11th November—the jailer reported to the recorder that he had surprised Levi in the act of throwing out a letter to a servant of the prison;

and, on searching his cell, had found ten other letters, addressed at different times to the accused. These, the servant, Marguerite Houster, admitted having received at the gate from the prisoner's son. The letters were in Hebrew and in German, the Jews of Metz habitually using the latter tongue for conversation. Some delay occurred in discovering an interpreter for the Hebrew letters, but one was at last found in the person of a young man named Louis Anne, a shoemaker, formerly a Jew. He read his translations in the presence of the accused, who admitted their fidelity, with the exception of the letter taken from the servant, Houster.

The communication in question was addressed to the principal Jewish residents of Metz. It was read to them. They were united enough in condemning the interpretation of Louis Anne, but differed widely among themselves as to actual meanings—the accused himself repeatedly varying his rendering of the same passage. At length, in despair, the authorities summoned to their aid Monsieur Paul Duvalier, formerly a Jew, and an eminent physician of Metz, but since of Kaisersburg, in Alsace.

This gentleman made a careful translation, the correctness of which Levi acknowledged, objecting only to one word, " bound " (*lié*), in place of which he affirmed he had written " found " (*trouvé*), his object being, it was supposed, to induce an idea either that the child was yet alive, or, if dead, to conceal the kind of death to which it had been subjected.

As the terms of this epistle are curious enough, and as to its testimony the result of the trial was principally due, it is here given literally, after Duvalier's translation.

" Written by Raphael Levi, in his captivity, to the chief Jews of the Synagogue of Metz.

" DEAR DIRECTORS,—I languish to learn what the parliament hath pronounced, for the attorney of the king hath spoken, and I dwell in constant fear. Let me know, I pray you, the proceedings of the Court, and what the controller* doth before it.

" The jailer's servant told me that the Jew who brings my victuals said they bound (*lié*) the child. Ah, write to me concerning my witnesses—write me everything, so that I may for once receive a little comfort.

" That Homan † visited the prison to-day, and

---

* A person at Boulay, to whom he was in debt.

† Corruption of Haman. The most injurious epithet a Jew can apply.

said that he would upset all that justice had hitherto effected. Look, therefore, to the parliament. Invoke them, that I may be released from this wretchedness— debarred as I am from speaking to my dear wife and children—unable to reckon with the controller, my creditor. Ah! I am unhappy.

" I will die like a son of Israel, and glorify the name of God. All I ask is, that my daughter Blimelé, who is betrothed, be married, and that my wife and little ones be cared for.

" *I am plunged in this misery for the sake of the community. God will help me in it.*"

This letter bore no date, neither did any of the others, which contained little more than hints for the guidance of the prisoner when confronted with the witnesses. One of them, however, seems to have enclosed a piece of knotted straw, which the accused was earnestly exhorted to place under his tongue when called upon for his defence, pronouncing at the same time five Hebrew words, the purport of which neither he himself nor any of his interpreters could explain.

Another of the captured notes was acknowledged by the accused to be word for word as follows :—

" To Raphael Levi in his captivity.—In case, O

Raphael (the which Heaven forbid!) thou art submitted to the torture, thou wilt repeat thrice the following words: *Moi Juif, Juif moi, vive Juif, Juif vive, mort Juif, Juif mort.*"

Closely interrogated concerning these letters, especially the last, which was suspected to be a charm, Levi indignantly repudiated all dealings with sorcery, declaring that the above formula was nothing more than a prayer.

Still labouring to save their fellow, the Jews of Metz now had recourse to a stratagem, suggested, it may be, by the passage in Genesis xxxvii. 33: "An evil beast hath devoured him; Joseph is without doubt rent in pieces."

A report was industriously propagated that the child had been carried off by wolves, and liberal rewards, emanating from the Jews themselves, were offered to any person who might succeed in recovering a portion of the remains or attire of the infant, sufficient to establish his identity. Within a day or two of the announcement of the rewards, the child's little shirt was discovered, hanging on a bush at the distance of three feet from the ground, in a dense part of the wood, about a quarter of a league from Glatigny.

Nor was this all. A woman living at Katonfai, a little village not far from Glatigny, affirmed on oath that she one day encountered on the road three Jews of Metz, whose names she did not know. These men entered into conversation with her, appearing anxious to learn what was thought and said in the neighbourhood with respect to the missing child; and on her replying that, even if he had been devoured by beasts, some portions of his dress might yet be found, one of the strangers eagerly assented, remarking with significant emphasis, that the *head* at least might be forthcoming.

The observation seemed prophetic. Two days later —that is, on the 26th November, 1669—four swineherds, passing through the wood, came upon the head of a child, with the neck and part of the shoulder; two little frocks, one within the other; one woollen sock, and a little red bonnet; none of the articles of dress being either torn or discoloured with blood!

Thereupon the parliament directed a commissioner to repair to Glatigny, and report upon the discovery. In the presence of this officer, Lemoine at once identified his child's dress. As for the head, so much was it mangled and disfigured, that the little features were no longer recognisable by mortal eyes. The flesh, notwithstanding, was singularly firm and fresh, and the blood in the veins seemed scarcely dried. The swineherds described the manner in which the articles had been found, and one of them boldly affirmed that it was impossible the child had been mangled by beasts, since, not to mention that the clothes were whole and unstained, he had observed that, when a wolf attacked a sheep, or any other domestic animal, it invariably preyed upon the head first.

Two master-surgeons, after minute examination, gave it as their opinion that the child had lived and breathed much within the period (two months and a day) that had elapsed since his disappearance.

The accused, in refuting the testimony that sought .o fix his identity, returned to his *alibi*, and averring parenthetically that he had worn no mantle on the day of the supposed abduction, stated, as before, that he had arrived at his own dwelling at Boulay by four o'clock in the afternoon.

These two statements were contradicted, singularly enough, by two of his own witnesses, who asserted that, on the 25th September, he had passed them, as though coming from Metz, at about half an hour before sunset (this being about the equinox, would make it between half-past five and six); that he was mounted on a white horse, wore a mantle, was alone, and appeared so much agitated, that he permitted his horse to wander from the road, to which they, the witnesses, re-conducted him.

Certain neighbours of one Gideon Levi, a Jew, residing at Hex—one league from Glatigny, and three from Metz—deposed that, ever since the loss of the child, Jews of Metz were perpetually visiting Levi's house, sometimes in parties of three and four, even five and six, and this at all hours of the day and night. One swore to having seen Gideon Levi quit his house, and go into the wood, carrying on his back a *hotte* (scuttle); and another declared that Gideon had advised him to join in the search for the remains, and even indicated the direction in which they would probably be discovered. Upon this evidence, Gideon was apprehended and interrogated. He denied all knowledge of the crime; and admitted that, by the direction of the Jews of Metz, he had sent persons to search the wood, and promised a hundred crowns for the discovery of any trace of the young Lemoine.

Once only, during the protracted investigation, did the accused commit himself by inconsistent state-ments. He declared before the parliamentary com-mission, that he could not possibly have carried the

child upon his horse, the latter being already laden
with barrels of oil and wine, which he had purchased
at Metz—whereas, before the lieutenant-criminal, on
the 14th October, he stated that he had placed the
barrels on his *son's* horse, and sent him forward,
remarking that he himself, travelling more lightly,
would easily overtake him.

Upon the whole evidence, the Court decreed as
follows :—

"Annulled the former judgment. Declared the
accused, Raphael Levi, Jew, guilty of having, on the
25th September, 1869, upon or near the highway, near
Glatigny, stolen the body of the child of Gilles
Lemoine, aged three, whose head and neck have since
been found exposed in the adjacent wood. In reparation, condemned the said Raphael Levi to make the
*amende honorable* before the great door of the cathe-
dral church of Metz ; and, kneeling, in his shirt, a rope
about his neck, and a burning taper of three pounds
weight in his hand, to confess his crime, declare his
repentance, and ask pardon of God, the king, and
the law. This done, the said Raphael Levi should be
conveyed to the field of Seille, and there burned
alive, and his ashes scattered to the winds ; himself
having been first submitted to the question ordinary

and extraordinary, in order to discover in whose hands he deposited the child, and the manner of its death; the goods of the condemned to be confiscated; one thousand livres paid to the king, and one thousand five hundred to Gilles Lemoine, together with the expenses of the process.

" Ordered, further, that Gideon Levi be submitted to the question ordinary and extraordinary, to discover by whom the remains of the child Lemoine were placed in the wood: that Marguerite Houster, servant, be summoned before the council, and severely reprimanded for conveying letters to the said Raphael Levi; lastly, that Mayer Schaube, Jew, of Metz, be committed to prison, and his goods inventoried, with a view to more ample inquiry as to the place in which the child Lemoine was secreted. Done at Metz, in parliament, in the chamber De la Tournelle, January 16th, 1670."

Gideon Levi was subjected at once to the torture, but without obtaining from him any revelation; and as it was by that time late in the day, the execution of the sentence on Raphael Levi was postponed to the following morning. At eight o'clock, accordingly, the unhappy criminal was conducted to the torture-chamber. Casting one hasty glance around upon the terrible apparatus, he drew from his pocket a small volume in the Hebrew character, and proceeded to read from it certain words. But the jealous suspicion of Messieurs the Commissioners instantly took the alarm. These words might contain a spell similar to that contained in the formula he had been instructed to utter when submitted to the question. The book was taken away.

The sentence was then read, the condemned man evincing no emotion. When it was finished, he calmly observed that he had no complaint to make of his judges; but as for the witnesses, they had spoken falsely, and betrayed him to death. He warned the Commissioners that, should the agonies of the torture force any confession from his lips, he would revoke it within an hour. This declaration he repeated thrice.

The warning proved superfluous: so far from confessing anything, he never ceased, while consciousness lasted, to insist upon his innocence. It was remarked that during the severest moments of the torture—for example, while suspended in the air with heavy weights attached to his toes—the prisoner remained for a quarter of an hour in a kind of lethargy, apparently quite insensible to pain. Some of those present attributed this to the effect of the words they had imprudently permitted him to pronounce before the book was taken from him; "but," says the excellent advocate, gravely, "it is surely a simplicity on the part of any to believe that the speaking of certain syllables can be productive of such an effect!"

Torture having done its miserable worst, the criminal was conveyed to the cell for the condemned, and handed over for a time to two reverend persons— the Sieur d'Arras, curate of St. Marcel of Metz, and a Capuchin friar—who were awaiting him, with the benevolent purpose of exhorting him to embrace the Christian faith. The unhappy culprit, though acknowledging that he had not too deeply studied the mysteries of his own faith, still refused to substitute another, and turning away from his exhorters, seemed to await with impatience the closing scene.

Conducted at last towards the place of punishment, he tied round his left arm and forehead narrow strips of leather, with knots in the centre. One of the officers having demanded the meaning of this ceremony, Levi replied that in the knots were contained the commandments of his law, and that it was customary with his people, at the point of death to attach them thus to the head and arm. Still haunted with the idea of some concealed spell, the intelligent

Commissioners deprived the criminal of these symbols, and once more pressed him to acknowledge the abduction of the child, the place of its concealment, and the time and manner of its murder.

Raphael Levi returned thereupon to his first unqualified denial, asserting that he was perfectly innocent, and the witnesses forsworn. It was remarked that during the trial he had, nevertheless, made no exception to their testimony.

Still, the Church made one final effort to secure the convert. The curate and Capuchin pressed up to him, and were commencing a new exhortation, when the criminal, bound as he was, pushed them from him with his elbows, sternly desiring them to notice that he died as he had lived, a Jew; and that, dying in such a manner, his soul would assuredly be carried into Abraham's bosom, even adding that for the act imputed to him as a crime, he would not ask pardon of God himself! This last expression confirmed the then popular opinion that the Jews included the abstraction and murder of Christian children in the category of religious acts!

The courage and calmness of the condemned man, whatever their source, remained unabated to the end: Arrived at the pile he dressed himself unaided in the garment in which he was to suffer.  Attached to the stake, and pressed to the last moment on the one side to confess his crime, on the other to disavow his creed, the unhappy man continued to reply with as much courage as though he had not been standing on the verge of death.

At last, turning to the executioner, he begged him to put an end to the scene by strangling him with the rope that confined him to the stake.

And this was done.

# III.

## THE PRIEST-MAGICIAN.

IT is strange enough, yet unquestionably true, that the very severity of the laws enacted for the suppression of the imaginary crime of sorcery, tended greatly to its increase. By drawing attention to the practice, and dealing with it as with an actual offence, it became rooted in men's minds as a reality, and that once effected, no terrific penalties assigned to it by the law, sufficed to counterbalance the fearful fascination it was calculated to exercise over the weak and untaught mind. As "one fool makes many," so—in a more credulous age than ours—did one morbid imagination infect others with its wild and lurid impressions, and it is not too much to assert that every example of sorcery to which attention was compelled by a public execution, so far from acting as a deterrent, enticed fifty more self-deluded beings within the danger of the law.

A forcible instance of the ease with which this moral contagion is disseminated, is adduced by Malebranche:—A pastor, wearied with his Sabbath labours, his mind overwrought with the peculiar and exalted character of the subjects with which he has been called upon to deal, and his brain for the moment a little disturbed by the wine he has taken to recruit his exhausted frame, relates to his astonished family a species of temptation offered him, as he conceives, directly from the evil one. He narrates this supposed experience with the force and eloquence habitual to him, and with all the effect likely to be produced by such a communication proceeding from a husband, father, and spiritual guide. How is it possible that some degree of credence should not be accorded to the statement? The imagination of his hearers becomes heated. The idea, once so strange and fearful, grows familiar. The younger members of the family, when alone, renew the subject, and their immature reasoning faculties oppose no effectual barrier to the encroaching foe. They dream, and awake from sleep to compare the visions that have haunted them, in a manner to fortify their new belief, until their minds, thoroughly subjugated, accept, with the drunkard's fatal thirst, everything that associates itself with the accursed thing which is hurrying them to their fate. It was thus that sorcerers were made.

It was not until a more enlightened policy suggested the treating sorcerers as merely madmen, that the crime or practice began to subside. The parliament of Paris at length reversed the practice of preceding assemblies, and steadily refused to punish one accused of sorcery unless it involved some other crime. The effect of this wise disdain was first to awaken doubts as to the reality of the offence, then to make it ridiculous, finally, to all but abolish its existence, the death-blow being probably that royal decree which set at liberty every one at the time confined in the prisons of Rouen on accusations of the kind.

How far in earlier times the powers of evil were permitted to treat with man, may be still an open question. St. Augustine takes an affirmative view, but limits such intercourse to three especial ends— " ad probationem, ad pœnam, ad coronam "—to prove, to punish, and to reward. M. Nicole, in his " Instructions Théologiques," adopts this opinion, adding that the evil one has certainly power over the wicked, but that God sets bounds thereto ; while, with regard to good men, Satan has no power whatever, save only when God, for especial reasons, as in the case of Job, suffers him for a time to exercise it.

We cannot in effect deny the diabolical influence without seeming to challenge the truth of what we hold as the manual of truth—the holy Scriptures. It is probable too, that Pharaoh's magicians, the pythoness of Endor, and Simon Magus, were indeed sorcerers in the darkest sense of the word; but neither were such beings permitted to infect the troubled earth in any number, nor was their allotted time to be indefinitely prolonged. Holy writ instructs us that the kingdom of Satan is destroyed, and the great deceiver rendered powerless in those bonds which shall only be relaxed at the end of this being. The strong man armed has been vanquished by a stronger than he, and can harm and mislead us no more, save in accordance with our own mad will. He reigned until his conqueror came, may reign still, (we cannot say it is not so) where that redeeming conqueror has not been known; but he has neither right nor power over the followers of Christ. He cannot even tempt them without leave of God, nor harm them *then*, if they will but use the glorious weapons laid ready to their hand in the armoury of God. It is, in short, esteeming too highly of the prince of darkness, to credit him with the follies of later ages, as though they were instances of his unextinguished power.

With these remarks, too brief, perhaps, for a subject of such interest, but sufficient for our present purpose, we turn to the extraordinary history of the priest, Louis Gaufridy, which, at the commencement of the seventeenth century, engaged public attention to an unprecedented extent.

Momet Gaufridy, the father of Louis, resided at Beauveser, in Provence, his brother, Christophe, being curé of the adjacent village of Pourrières. In these two villages Louis dwelt, alternately with his father and uncle, until he attained the age of ten, when he permanently took up his residence with the latter.

At seven years old he met with a remarkable accident, falling headlong from a great height to the ground, without sustaining the least injury. The wiseacres of the neighbourhood insisted that the devil alone could have saved him from mortal hurt!

As he was intended for the church, his uncle, after some preliminary instruction, sent him to Arles. Here he remained four years, then went to Marseilles to study rhetoric, and subsequently returned to Arles, where he was ordained, without having graduated in theology, so slight, at that period, was the preparation required for the priesthood. He was forthwith appointed curate of the parish des Accoules, at Marseilles, and remained in that position six years, becoming a great favourite from his genial disposition, ready wit, and other social qualities which tend to popularity, if not always to the highest respect.

Six months before the death of his uncle Christophe, the latter sent to his nephew a manuscript in six folios, containing forty so-called spells or charms, in which were understood to be comprised all the mysteries of magic. So at least the old curé declared, and as he was a man of little learning, and, like most ignorant people, disposed to consider all things wonderful that they cannot understand, he recommended the work to his nephew as well deserving his perusal.

It seems that Louis was far from partaking his uncle's enthusiasm in the matter. After glancing hastily through the manuscript, he laid it aside, and forgot all about it for five years, when, seeking a lost volume of Cicero's Epistles for the use of a pupil, he came upon the fatal work which was destined to be his ruin. He read it now, read it carefully, then greedily. The strange characters seemed to glow and burn before his eyes, and as he reached the foot

of the page, each of which concluded with a cabalistic
refrain, a thrill of horrible delight urged him forward
to the perusal of the next.

It was at the climax of this feverish excitement,
which must have been closely allied to positive madness, that he believed the incident to have occurred
which cast such a lurid lustre over all his after-life.
The spirit of evil revealed himself in human form,
declaring at once his character and mission !

He was attired, related Gaufridy, as a private
gentleman, without sword, having all the bearing of
a person of condition, say, perhaps, a banker, or rich
merchant.. He had brown hair and beard, and his
face was very pale.

At first Gaufridy acknowledged that he felt considerable uneasiness, but reassured by the quiet and gentle-
manly manner of his visitor, his courage returned,
and he had the nerve to inquire with some composure,
what the object of this unexpected visit might be ?

"Say rather," was the answer, "what do you
require of *me ?*  I am ready to meet your wishes in
every particular."

Gaufridy hesitated.

"But what will you give me in return ?" continued
the stranger, with a business-like air that must

have been in harmony with his mercantile appearance.

"What do you demand?" asked Louis.

"Simply that you dedicate to *me* all your duties
and good works; nothing more," replied the other.

Gaufridy hesitated again. Something urged him
almost irresistibly to consent to what seemed so
simple and easy a proposition. But the thought that
among the required good works must be classed
those holy sacraments it was his function to administer, deterred him. He might imperil too many
souls. Might it not be a snare of the evil one to
secure more than he affected to be treating for?

Gaufridy boldly announced that he must reserve
the sacraments.

Contrary to his expectation Satan politely acceded,
and a kind of list or schedule being made out on the
spot, Gaufridy affixed his signature in blood drawn from
his arm.

This completed, he lost no time in testing the
value of the arrangement, and accordingly demanded
power to gratify the two dominant passions in his
mind—desire to be reputed wise, and to subjugate the
affections of every woman who happened to please his
eye. The prince of darkness readily assented, and

gave him, unasked, a formal document wherein it was explained that Gaufridy by merely breathing over a person of the other sex, would, if he pleased, inspire her with an irresistible passion.

All fell out as he had been taught to expect. The fame of his learning and sagacity spread far and wide. His breath displayed all the virtue he had hoped for to lead captive *others'* virtue. He saw, as he declared, the most beautiful women fall without a struggle into his net. According to his subsequent confession, it was not necessary actually to breathe upon his intended prey. If she were within hearing of his sigh, that was enough. It was the knell of her good fame.

Thanks to his newly-acquired reputation for learning, Louis Gaufridy became the intimate friend of the family of Mons. de Mandols de la Pallud, who had three lovely daughters, accomplished girls, of whom the youngest, Madeleine, had the misfortune to attract their guest. Gaufridy induced her to select him as her confessor, and his influence over the poor girl, (she was only twelve or thirteen when the acquaintance began,) shortly became unbounded.

The child fell into a state of melancholy, which caused her parents much anxiety; but the physicians declared her free from any definite ailment. At this period Gaufridy, walking with her one day in a sequestered garden, took the opportunity of impressing upon her that spiritual fathers have the power to dispose as they please of their spiritual children, and asked her consent to devote her—spiritually—to whomsoever he would. The girl consenting, Gaufridy presented her at once to his dark ally. Such an offering, so made, must, however, be regarded as merely complimentary, and there is reason to think that the giver himself considered it as little more.

Madeleine now expressed a desire to enter an Ursuline Convent, and was accordingly placed in a house of that order at Aix, where she fulfilled a sort of noviciate during three years, enjoying much greater tranquillity of mind—excepting on Wednesdays and Fridays, when she was revisited by her old melancholy in a painfully augmented form.

About this time (the end of her three years' residence in the convent), Gaufridy went to visit her, treated her with extreme tenderness, and engaged her to write to him, bidding her not to be surprised if, in spite of her satisfaction with existing arrangements, he should require her to return to her home, perhaps within a short time.

Not long after, she received a letter from him, in which he used these words :—

" I pray you to believe that, so great is the affection I bear you, I could desire that my heart were interwoven (*entrelassé*) and extinguished utterly in yours."

Here followed a design of two hearts transfixed and united by crossed arrows, and——

" Thus dearest friend, let it befal our mutual hearts."

Mademoiselle de Mandols dutifully presented this composition to the Superior, but the latter was able to see nothing but a mass of hieroglyphics, undecipherable without the key.

By this time Madeleine had begun to reciprocate the feelings so openly betrayed by her false guide ; and the necessity for change of air after an attack of fever, restoring her to her home, she was brought more closely within his malign influence. She did, however, make an effort to break loose, and entrenched herself in coldness and disdain.

One day Gaufridy offered her a fine peach, of which each ate half. It was (as he afterwards declared) a charm, and produced the effect intended, namely, to soften and attract her towards him, in which condition the unfortunate girl lavished upon him every mark of tenderness short of the sacrifice of honour.

He then gave her a nut, another and more powerful charm. This she subsequently threw into the fire; but it refused to burn, and after the lapse of a few minutes suddenly vanished. The effect, however, had been produced. The passion of the unhappy girl overcame every other feeling. The miscreant triumphed, and Madeleine fell.

After this her infatuation knew no limits. In her blind attachment to the man she followed him everywhere, even to the church, and it became difficult to disembarrass himself of her presence sufficiently to avert scandal.

Whatever might have been his real power of fascination, it is certain that Gaufridy but rarely availed himself of it with regard to others than Madeleine, at any rate to a culpable extent. It pleased his vanity to overcome the prude, and tame the coquette, but he seldom abused his opportunities. One of his victims was a woman named La Corbie, wife of François Perrin, a hotel proprietor of Marseilles. Having merely vindicated his power, Gaufridy ceased to cultivate this last acquaintance, but the lady was not to be got rid of so easily. She pursued him day and

night, like a restless phantom, neglecting her affairs,
and causing Gaufridy even more alarm than Madeleine, for La Corbie used no discretion at all, and
became a source of incessant torment both to herself
and to the object of her worship.

Two other women, named Bouchete and Pintade,
the latter a servant in his house, were victims of his
fatal fascination, but Madeleine was his real favourite.
For her he was content to run risks of which he
deemed none else worthy; and again and again
escaped, as if by miracle, from scandals which it
seemed impossible to avert.

For six years Gaufridy exercised with success, if not
without uneasiness, the power he believed himself to
have acquired.  But now the devil, that " liar from the
beginning," began to tire of keeping his word.  He
had covenanted to confer on Louis the reputation of
a wise and reverend man; and yet by some means a
dark, sinister rumour began to stir, attributing to the
young priest the most fearful practices, associated
with diabolic agency !

Whether the extravagancies of Mademoiselle de la
Mandols, La Corbie, and several others who had
fallen into his snare, became too pronounced for
further concealment, or what other circumstance

struck the key-note of the cry of reprobation about to burst forth, is not precisely known. But it was suddenly announced that Père Michaëlis, the inquisitor, had solemnly exorcised Mademoiselle de Mandols, whom he had found at the Sainte-Baume!

In his procès-verbal, the father adduced his reasons, *seriatim*, for holding the young lady as under diabolic dominion.

In the first place he observed, that although she had never learned Latin, and was unable even to read it, she replied freely in French to all his Latin questions. And the good father added that this by no means surprised him, inasmuch as the author of " Flagellum Dæmonum" had remarked, that possessed women do very rarely answer in the Latin tongue.

Secondly, he noticed that Mademoiselle de Mandols (who was then nineteen) had intervals of unpossession, during which her intelligence shone forth peculiarly bright and clear. Also that during a fortnight the fiend had occasionally administered charms, resembling lozenges of honey, to the girl, one of which he, the good father, succeeded in securing on its way to her mouth.

Thirdly, that during the process of exorcism she trembled so excessively that he was obliged, in regard for her life, to suspend the ceremony when half complete. That on placing one's hand on the head of the possessed, there was perceptible an extraordinary movement, as of an infinity of insects, which ceased in an instant on commanding the demon to retire.

Fourthly, on exhorting her to renounce the devil and all his works, the fiend immediately grasped her by the windpipe from within. She turned up the whites of her eyes, and became as one dead; but presently recovering, resumed the thread of her discourse. This energetic proceeding on the part of Lucifer convinced the excellent inquisitor that the fiend was driven to his last shift to prevent her renunciation of him.

Fifthly, she saw what was not actually before her eyes, viz., certain nuns passing from the dormitory into the chapel, naming them correctly one by one.

Sixthly, she spoke very minutely of the angelic orders, stating that the chief in each of the nine choirs had been involved in the angelic fall; that Lucifer had been the chief seraphim in the highest Hierarchy; that Beelzebub was the second to join Lucifer in his revolt, and is, next him, the most powerful of the fallen ones, having licence to come and go upon earth, while his leader is held captive, since the Redeemer's resurrection, in hell, albeit his legions yet retain their allegiance and obey his commands, unless over-ruled by God. She asserted that the third in power was the fiend "Leviathan," and added many other particulars concerning the diabolic kingdom, which filled many pages of the procès-verbal.

She affirmed that Saint Michael was the fourth angel created; he who resisted the revolted host under Lucifer, gave them battle, and defeated them.

Lastly, she named twenty-four evil spirits who pos-sessed her, repeating their names at various times with-out a mistake. She claimed to know the guardian-angel of every one on earth, and to what order they belonged, with other details, concerning the mass of which the good inquisitor intimated that they would, no doubt, be of the highest value and interest could they only be verified.

Asked why the devil entered into her in such angelic company, she replied that it was through the prevailing power of Lucifer, and with her own half-consent. She added that many of the Ursuline nuns had been delivered from the spells Gaufridy had cast upon them, and that *she* would be the last.

Asked why after certain prayers, certain evil spirits

at least, were not exorcised, one of them immediately
replied—

"If we be cast out how will the magician be detected?  God wills that we keep possession, because
it is His purpose to exterminate the whole band of
sorcerers, and we shall only depart when Louis
Gaufridy is either converted, dead, or delivered to
justice."

Father Michaëlis appended to this statement, that a
great tumult of voices of sorcerers of both sexes was
distinctly heard from beneath the church of St.
Baume, on the 9th January, 1610, at ten at night,
and that again, on the 20th, on a mountain near at
hand, was heard the same "charivari."  We do not
find this remarkable circumstance recorded in any
other history of the time.

The nomenclature—both angelic and diabolic—
supplied by Mademoiselle de Mandols, was absolutely
inexhaustible.  We can only mention a few appellations,
of which "Break-heart" and "Shut-lip," the two
familiar spirits attendant on Gaufridy, were most
frequently mentioned.  She stated that her good
angel was named "Fortitude," and that he had often
chastised the fiend who possessed her.  The guardian-
angels of others she severally described as "Clear-

Light," "Simplicity," "Vision of God," "Agility," &c., &c., and then proceeded to detail the doings of the famous "Witches' Sabbath," a ceremony which at that period commanded such general belief.

It was on a lonely mountain, near Marseilles, that Madeleine—borne safely and tenderly through the air by "Break-heart"—attended her first Sabbath of this kind.

She found a multitude of people, composed of all nations, already assembled, and noticed Gaufridy, in a seat of authority, receiving the homage of all as chief of the sorcerers and lieutenant of Lucifer. Beelzebub was enthroned at his side. The inferior sorcerers kissed the feet of this august pair, and committed a series of acts of impiety and filthiness, with which it is impossible to soil a modern page.

Gaufridy caused her to receive a mark on her head and bosom, and other parts more concealed. These marks would sometimes disappear, but invariably returned, and were considered to be indelible, even after conversion, as tokens that the bearer had at one time agreed to be a good and faithful servant of the devil. Certain jurists were disposed, however, to question the validity of such a bond, inasmuch as it was not, in legal knowledge, "synallagmatique"—

obligatory on both parties—the fiend never binding himself to be a good master during all his servant's life !

Summons to the Sabbath was given by means of a horn sounded by a diabolic herald, and audible (at least by sorcerers) in every part of the world at once.

By the side of the Prince was usually seated a Princess, whose countenance, glowing with a lurid radiance, shot terror throughout the sorcerer world; for though to the Prince, and indeed to all the wizard aristocracy, she appeared enchantingly fair—to the *oi polloi*, her black skin, flaming eyes, flat broad nose, and smoking volcanic mouth, rendered her an object of unspeakable alarm.

The chief business of these agreeable réunions seemed to be the planning schemes of evil, and feasting upon viands which had the peculiarity of never satisfying those who fed. Neither salt nor oil was permitted on the board, nor any knives, lest, by an unfortunate accident, two of these useful instruments happening to fall into a crucial form should spoil the mirth of the meeting! For the salt and oil, we know that salt is the symbol of wisdom, and oil an agent in the ceremonies of religion. It is to be presumed that salad, so dear to French palates, could never figure at these feasts.

Without tracing the subject with more minuteness, it is enough to say that in these alleged assemblies the Prince of Evil presented himself as the ape of Divinity, striving to reproduce in his Sabbaths all the chief ceremonies of the Church. The lights were of sulphur, and burned and spluttered with a fierce noise. The bell was a discordant horn. There was no music—a circumstance, wrote a French cynic, not unworthy the attention of those *dévots* who ascertain that he presides over the opera and theatre.

The feast concluded, carriages are called, and everybody, borne as he came, be it demon or owl, bat or broomstick, departs to his accustomed home.

Such were the matters gravely and sorrowfully reported by the excellent monk Michaëlis, and they were moreover embellished with so many curious particulars and marvellous incidents, that we cannot be astonished if his procès-verbal effectually awakened public attention, and therewith a persuasion, almost amounting to certain belief, that the possession of Mademoiselle de Mandols had been the work of the hitherto respected priest, Louis Gaufridy.

The parliament of Provence, resolving at once to sift the matter, appointed MM. Seguiran and Thoron, councillors, to the commission of inquiry.

Several witnesses offered themselves, and, first, Mons. Prota, a well-known notary, deposed that on searching Gaufridy's chamber, he had discovered neither book nor paper of a magical description ; but, on the contrary, every trace of Christian habits and opinions.  And this testimony was corroborated by Father Carenne, monk of L'Observance, and other credible witnesses.

The Sieur Berthe, provost of the Collegiate Church of St. Martin, described Gaufridy as "fort débonnaire "—an epithet which, connected as it is with an excellent French king, can scarcely be held applicable to a malignant wizard.

It became necessary to examine Madeleine herself, and being accordingly brought before Mons. Thoron on the 21st February, 1610, she communicated to him all that she knew; indeed a good deal more, for there was reason subsequently to believe that she had embroidered her narrative with so lavish a hand as to stifle what might have proved inconvenient truth under the load of ornament.

Assuming at first the demeanour of possession, she threw herself into strange postures, her fingers bent back into the form of a cross, but without apparent dislocation.  In this state she praised Gaufridy, declaring him a good man, worthy of divine honours, and that she had only accused him to work his ruin.

She then resumed her ordinary bearing, and, interrogated as to her connexion with Gaufridy, confessed the criminal nature of their intercourse, adding that she made this avowal by constraint of an impulse she found irresistible. But this uttered, she tried to snatch the examination paper from the clerk, affirming that all he had written was mere illusion—that it was Asmodeus, the demon of impurity, who had cast her into grotesque and immodest postures, and that Gaufridy had sent all those devils which tormented her.

The Sieur Garandeau, Grand Vicar of Aix, having placed a sacred relic to her lips, she refused to kiss it. She next recounted a conversation between Beelzebub and Gaufridy, in which the latter was recommended to have no fear of the law, but to reply to his judges in such terms as these :—

"I have been guilty of numerous offences against God, but in regard to witchcraft I am innocence itself, and this I will maintain even unto death."

"They will believe you," said the diabolic counsellor, "if you speak thus, and conclude that you

are wrongly condemned, and that your accuser is
mad."

She added that the fiend would effect Gaufridy's
release, if it were in his power.

Suddenly she fell into a state of violent convulsion.
Her limbs were contracted and distorted, her throat
appeared as if griped from within. She threw her arms
aloft, shrieking violently. " Who would have believed
that Madeleine would accuse Louis?" she gasped out.

Growing more confused, she declared that the
devils had inflicted on her these unspeakable torments,
because they knew that she was about to betray the
truth, and hoped to prevent it. When completely
restored, the girl proceeded to relate with perfect
clearness all the magical practices she maintained to
have learned from Gaufridy. While doing this the
convulsions occasionally returned, and when that
happened she praised and exonerated Gaufridy as
before, though it was noticed that her commendations
were accompanied by an ironical smile.

She declared that Gaufridy had become a wizard at
fourteen, and was at once promoted to the princedom.
That he had now celebrated all the Sabbaths (which
occurred only weekly) that his reign was therefore
drawing to a close, and that, should justice not over-

take his person, the devil would seize and appropriate him both body and soul.

"Here," remarked one of the examiners, "is a precious princedom! The man had but a bare subsistence."

"Pardon me," was the reply; "he had as much money as he desired. The devils had only to fish for it in the sea."

At this time Gaufridy had been actually apprehended, and was closely watched in his cell. Notwithstanding, Mademoiselle de Mandols affirmed that he was at liberty, and moving whither he pleased. A messenger being sent to learn the truth, it was found that the gaoler had permitted his prisoner for a few minutes, and under guard, the entire range of the prison grounds.

They now examined the girl's feet, which exhibited two bluish marks of unknown character, one of which was punctured with a pin without drawing blood, or producing the slightest pain.

This concluded the first interrogation.

The second meeting, February 24th, was attended by some higher dignitaries. Among the rest, Coriolis, president of the Court; MM. Julien de Percier, Raymond Meinier, and Jean Baptiste Chene, councillors ; and Margalet, councillor of the Exchequer Chamber.

Madeleine being asked by Thoron whether she herself, or the possessing spirit, would reply to the questions about to be put, replied with quiet respect that *she* would.

She then stated, in answer to queries, that she had passed a very troubled night, disturbed with visions, &c. ; but was better now, having confessed and communicated, and felt calm and tranquil in her mind.

She said that Gaufridy had made her sign eight deeds, and that she had resigned herself entirely to his control.

Addressing Thoron, she said—

" Our Lord has shown me great mercy. He inspired me to confess all to Father Michaëlis. I have confessed besides to Mons. du Vair, president, and to you also, Monsieur. I trust, therefore, that the Court will have compassion on my youth, remembering that I have been misled by a vile sorcerer, and that I shall be spared the punishment I deserve."

Encouraged with hopes of pardon, she regained her spirits, warmly thanked her judges, and confessed, further, that Gaufridy had marked her on the head, sides, &c. After this the convulsive fits returned more violently than before, the girl, or (as it was deemed) the possessing spirit, by her lips crying out incessantly, "*I burn! I burn!*"

Other examinations followed, but nothing of importance was elicited, and the Court now invited the Bishop of Marseilles to take part in the inquiry. The prelate immediately named Messire Pelicot, provost of the church of Aix, his vicar, and the processes, lay and clerical, continued simultaneously.

At Gaufridy's first examination he denied everything; but the testimony, by this time obtained, was fatal to his moral character; and the entire history of his libertinism, both as regarded Mademoiselle de Mandols and others, was laid open to the world.

On the 6th March, 1611, Father Michaëlis, in reply to questions from M. Thoron, declared that such knowledge as he had obtained of the disposition and doings of Mademoiselle de Mandols, having come to him under the seal of confession, he could communicate nothing without her consent.

M. Thoron represented to Madeleine that the welfare of religion and morals demanded this permission; and the girl, first stipulating for her own pardon, accorded it.

Two medical men, appointed by the Court, now

visited her, and made a voluminous report, of which we condense the portion most material.

They state that, being directed to visit and examine Madeleine de la Pallud, chiefly with reference to certain mysterious marks upon her person, and also to remarkable visitations to which she appeared to be subject, they attended at the prison, and found her on her knees at prayer. That they heard a loud exclamation to the effect that Beelzebub had arrived.

That, at the request of the Father Exorcist, they placed their hands upon the top and back of her head, and were sensible of an extraordinary agitation or boiling movement in the brain.

That the girl, having given a violent start and announced that Beelzebub had gone, it was observable that the aforesaid movement had entirely ceased.

That in a little while a voice announced that " Leviathan " had now arrived, when the agitation in the upper part of the head recommenced with increased intensity.

" Having," the report continued, "well and maturely considered this unusual case, we say that these movements do not proceed from the brain ; nor are they voluntary; nor producible by any known malady incident to the human frame. On our second visit we examined the patient's right foot, and observed upon the instep a greyish mark, as of an old scar. On puncturing this to the depth of one inch, the patient exhibited no sensation; nor did any effusion ensue.

" A mark on the left foot being punctured in like manner, and the needle having reached the depth of an inch and a quarter, the patient felt no pain; and only on the instrument being directed, experimentally, sideways, did she experience some slight sensation.

" Similar marks, with similar results, occurred on her left breast, and the patient then directed our attention to another, which we were told existed on the spinal cord, but which we failed to find. Marks, heretofore visible on other parts, had in like manner disappeared; and it was while we were expressing our astonishment at the circumstance, that the patient remarked, ' I would have concealed the others too, if God had suffered me.'

" All these strange marks belong to a hitherto unclassed category. We pronounce them to proceed from some extraordinary source, totally unconnected with any recognised condition of the human body.

" Signed, March, 1611, by MM. Fontaine and Grassy, physicians; MM. Meriadol and Bontems, surgeons."

Now came the important confrontation of the two unhappy subjects of this strange inquiry.

Mons. Thoron previously informed Madeleine that the fact of her proving able to repeat before Gaufridy the damning testimony she had given in his absence, would at once convince the Court that she was wholly delivered from diabolic influence. Strengthening food was given her, and the examination began; Gaufridy being for the moment kept apart.

To the general surprise and disgust of the "bench," Mademoiselle de Mandols at once declared that Gaufridy was innocent, that he had been her true friend, and that everything she had testified against him was illusory!

"That will not do for us," retorted the Court (in substance). "It is only her devil that speaks! Avaunt, Sathanas! Let her answer for herself."

"She shall *not* answer," retorted the spirit.

Madeleine moved her head restlessly about, as seeking Gaufridy, whom she declared she felt to be close at hand.

They asked her if she desired to see and to kiss him.

"Only," she replied, "to breathe a word of comfort in his ear."

Mass was now said; after which, becoming quite

calm, she retracted everything she had said in regard to Gaufridy.

They told her she lied.

She laughed.

Father Billet, an Augustine monk, now exorcised her; but she repeated the formula, and even anticipated the words.

She observed that the fiend tormented her in hope to drive her mad.

Suddenly, she became entirely dumb, and had violent convulsions.

Imagining that Gaufridy was the cause, and that he could not influence her in presence of the ecclesiastics, he was at length introduced. Madeleine gazed at him with a relieved expression; but, next moment, the convulsions recommenced, till she was completely exhausted, and the meeting was necessarily adjourned.

On reassembling, Thoron asked her if she had strength and courage to submit to the confrontation, to which she replied in the negative.

This, however, was held to be a pretext of the malignant spirit, and Gaufridy was brought forward; but Madeleine was allowed to sit where she could not see him.

Asked if he confessed the girl's charges against him, he replied "No; since she was possessed by an evil spirit, whose object was to ruin both." He indeed confessed the illicit intercourse; but denied everything else, and earnestly appealed to Madeleine to acknowledge that the whole charge of witchcraft was a delusion of the evil spirit who held her in possession.

But the girl was unshaken.

"You have confessed," she said, "the wrong you have done me. The loss of my honour was the result of the many secret and familiar discourses you held with me. Have you not set these terrible marks upon me? Are you not—you only—the cause of my being now in the power of this tormenting fiend? I have owned and made public my crime. May God inspire you to do the same!"

Gaufridy persisted that she still spoke under possession. But the president pointed out that she was now in a tranquil state—entirely herself.

She then related at great length the history of the various charms or spells laid on her by Gaufridy, when the sitting closed.

On the next occasion Gaufridy was confronted with various witnesses, when, after much hesitation, and with the air of one wearied out, he acknowledged that he had at one time resolved to renounce such magic arts as he had ever practised, and had even fixed a certain day for that final abjuration, when Lucifer himself appeared to him one evening under the form of a respectable burgess, and remarked:—

" You are doubting about this conversion of yours. If you resolve in favour of it, great misfortunes will overwhelm you, and I will be your ruin."

Gaufridy assured his agreeable visitor that he had no fear of these misfortunes; upon which the fiend departed, making a great disturbance.

Some days later, Gaufridy fell from top to bottom of the staircase at the Church des Accoules, and thought that the devil had tried to break his neck in this manner, but he received no hurt whatever.

Asked why, since he desired conversion, he had not applied to the Capuchin fathers, who had so frequently exhorted him thereto—he assured them that he was rendered proof against such wholesome inspirations by a certain unguent with which the fiend anointed his followers.

He went on to state that he had resolved at last to destroy his book of magic, and sought for it for that end, but the devil had taken the precaution to remove it from its usual position.  He (the devil) had previously warned him that, should he destroy the deeds, he would make a "tintamarre épouvantable," which Gaufridy felt it prudent to avoid.

From this he went on to describe the orgies of the diabolic Sabbath, and averred that the devil had a sort of clothes-store not far from Nice, from whence garments were supplied to all who frequented the assembly. Every one recounted the mischief he had contrived to do since the last meeting, and the presiding fiend administered correction to those who had done but little. The impious and filthy abominations which filled up the time at these feasts, as narrated by the unhappy visionary, will not bear detail.

A medical commission appointed to examine Gaufridy, discovered on his person similar marks, and with the like peculiarities to those on the body of the girl.

On a subsequent interrogation, Gaufridy recanted all his confessions, stating that they were made solely with the hope of escaping, by his frankness, a sentence of death. But it was now too late. On the 18th April, 1611, the Court pronounced the fatal judgment :—

" That Louis Gaufridy, priest, was convicted of

magic, sorcery, idolatry, and unchaste demeanour; of the seduction and subornation of Madeleine de la Pallud, Ursuline novice, and the delivering her to the possession of the power of evil. That having been examined medically (we condense the formal report) he was found to bear marks of a peculiar nature, callous, and producible only by the interposition of Satan. That he had carried on a long and familiar intercourse with the aforesaid Madeleine, including letters conveyed in characters which were visible to her only. That, under the cloak of her confessor and spiritual guide, he had charmed, suborned, and induced her to renounce God and his Church, and to present herself, body and soul, to Beelzebub. That he had, on various occasions enumerated, confessed to the practice of magic and sortilege, from the time of receiving a book of magic from his deceased uncle, Messire Christopher Gaufridy. That he had made use of this book during six years, invoking and conjuring spirits of evil, making pact and convention with them, for the purpose of winning to his will the said Madeleine and others, and in exchange therefor assigning and making over to the foul spirit all his good works and lawful aspirations by means of reciprocal schedules and instruments, whereof he induced the said Madeleine to take part. That he had presented himself at the Sabbath of fiends, where—(ceremonies described)—and adored and idolized the spirit of evil. For these causes," concluded the report, " we demand that the said Louis Gaufridy be declared convict, and being first degraded from his sacred orders by his diocesan, the Bishop of Marseilles, he should be condemned to make the ' amende honorable ' in public,. with head and feet bare, a rope about his neck, and holding in his hand a lighted torch, asking pardon of God, the king, and the law. Being then delivered over to the common executioner, he should be conducted through public ways to the place of execution, where, after being burned with hot irons in sundry parts of his body, he should be burned alive and quick upon a pile of wood purposely prepared, his ashes being subsequently scattered to the winds; and that previous to his execution he should be subjected to the question, ordinary and extraordinary, as much as he could bear, with the view of ascertaining his accomplices.

(Signed)　　　" RABASSE."

On the 23rd April, the Fathers Billet and Antoine Boletot reported that, at the conclusion of the

Easter festivals, Madeleine de Mandols had suddenly experienced severe pain in the region of the various marks on her person, and that Beelzebub had announced that, in testimony of her conversion, God had commanded "Fortitude" (her guardian-angel) to compel him (Beelzebub) to remove these marks, and restore the woman to her original state, which he had done.

To verify this important statement, the Court appointed a medical commission, who reported that the marks had indeed all but disappeared, and that the slight traces still perceptible were no longer insensible of pain.

"We say," concluded the medical sages, "that the revivification of these parts, hitherto without sensibility, is not producible by any power or faculty in the patient, nor by any art of medicine, and this is our decision. Signed, &c., &c."

On the 28th April, Gaufridy was interrogated on the sellette.

It was represented to him that the mercy of God was yet open to him, but that concealment of the truth might forfeit it. The exhortation was at first fruitless, but finally the unhappy man appeared to give way, and recapitulated at great length the whole history, both of his pretended magic, and the seduction of Madeleine and the rest.

The parliament of Provence then issued their final decree, in accordance with the sentence demanded.

In the torture-chamber Gaufridy displayed much firmness, or, as the examiners described it, obstinacy.

In vain he was told that since he had recognised at the witch-meetings Mademoiselle de Mandols, he might certainly recognise others.

To this he replied, that he knew her perfectly already. The rest were strangers to him, although he observed that several wore the habit of certain religious orders, which he refused to name.

No amount of torture sufficed to draw from him any other confession.

At length, amidst the execrations of an immense mob, the unhappy man—no longer priest—was conducted to the stake. He walked between two Capuchins, who did not spare to exhort and comfort him; but so great was his agitation, that, as they reported, the tokens of repentance he displayed were at best equivocal.

He had foretold that heavy misfortunes would attend his execution, and this was in a manner realized. The Sieur Desprade, who was betrothed to the daughter of the President of Brasle, was assassinated in the crowd by the Chevalier de Monteroux—a girl standing by being severely wounded in the momentary scuffle. The murderer escaped. Persons fell from the trees and were picked up dead, and an immense number of accidents of every kind undoubtedly attended the sinister ceremony.

"Such events," remarks a worthy writer of the time, "are fitting accompaniments of the death of a sorcerer—that pest of humanity."

But *was* Gaufridy a sorcerer? This very excusable question was mooted even while his own confession was ringing in men's ears. It was said that Mons. du Vair, premier president of the parliament, a most enlightened and every way distinguished man, avowed his disbelief. It seemed to him, and others like him, that Gaufridy, a man of corrupt heart and loose desires, practised in the deceit that had become necessary to cover his unchaste life, had, at length, succeeded in deceiving *himself*, and mistaken dreams for realities.

The force of imagination in melancholy minds makes visionaries : and that to such an extent, that the vision becomes at length the tyrant, the reason the slave. Malebranche merely divides them into two classes—visionaries of the imagination, and of the sense.

Gaufridy, it will have been seen, was unable to identify any attendant at the alleged witches' Sabbath, or to adduce a single fact of any kind in support of its reality. One of the most extraordinary features of these witch-trials was certainly the ready credulity of the judges, who never in any instance appear to have contemplated the possibility of any other solution than that suggested.

If Mademoiselle de Mandols flings herself into strange attitudes and contortions, it is no more than is done for a few shillings at any country-fair. If she replies in her own language, to questions in a tongue she is not presumed to know, must the devil, of necessity, have been her schoolmaster? As touching the callous marks on her person, how many people, never suspected of dealing with the powers of darkness, could show the same? And even in the days of these medical wiseacres, whose report we have given above, were there no chemical means by which a temporary insensibility to pain could be procured? What could be hoped for from the sagacity of judges who receive as evidence the assurance of several witnesses that they had reason (*what* reason?) to believe that a grey cat, which was often seen with Gaufridy, was a familiar spirit?

Many years after the execution of the reputed wizard, a case of alleged possession, in the person of Mademoiselle Thevenet de Corbeil, was brought by the Archbishop of Paris under the notice of the law. The facts reported to be ascertained were these :—

The young lady was lifted seven or eight feet from the ground, in a garden, without any visible support.

She raised her brother and his nurse three feet from the ground, also without support.

She was lifted when in bed three or four feet into the air, covered with the upper bedclothes, and preserving the same recumbent attitude.

She read in the mind of one of her attendants a particular resolution formed by her, and repeated the precise words of a prayer uttered by the same attendant, where it was impossible she could have been overheard.

Lastly, her convulsive fits were of such violence that, fragile and delicate as she was, strong men were unable to hold her.

Strange as were these circumstances, the testimony of the devil's complicity was not held conclusive, and the matter was allowed to drop.

Before concluding the subject, let us hear one word from Père Le Brun, who, in his Critical History of the practices of superstition, writes as follows :—

" A girl, who suffered from three distressing maladies—catalepsy, tetanus, and hypochondria—had wonderful visions, and was subject to violent movements, over which she had no control. In this state pins might be thrust into her arms, thighs, &c., without eliciting any sign of pain. Her whole frame became perfectly flexible, and in whatever position her limbs might be placed, no matter how unnatural, thus they remained till replaced by her attendants ; but, what was most singular, her body, from the waist upwards, was equally flexible, and as light as one of her arms in its normal state. She could be lifted a foot from the couch by one hand, and held thus, without difficulty, for minutes together."

This very interesting young person confessed, we find, to M. Argenson, lieutenant of police, that she had been indulging in trickery. Le Père Le Brun believed that she had been endeavouring to imitate the symptoms of catalepsy ; and, in fact, she had done little more than has been effected by many a clever charlatan.

It is strange that the feats of this class of performers did not awaken more suspicion in the minds of those who were called upon to examine the "wizards." The wonders wrought by a professed conjuror of the time, Madame Voisin, might have filled volumes. She told fortunes with great fidelity, having in her pay some intelligent domestic or humble friend in every important family. She sold an enchanted sword to a citizen for an enormous price. It was warranted to kill any one whom the bearer fought, without the latter sustaining any injury. For the buyer's better satisfaction she engaged a person in her confidence and pay to fix a quarrel on the former, and then suffer himself to be at once dis-armed by the miraculous weapon.

At last, however, the poor citizen receives a severe wound, and on remonstrating with the sorceress, learns that his antagonist, fortunately for himself, possesses an enchanted sword of greater power!

Madame Voisin had a magic basin by which she effected many wonders, as thus :—A gentleman having been robbed of a pair of pistols, went to ask her advice. Expecting this, she had caused to be prepared a representation of the thief's face (a fellow-servant having supplied all needful information), of the pistols, and of the place where they were stolen.

She desired her visitor to gaze steadfastly into a basin of water, when she causes to descend from above his head a sketch of the lost pistols. These are reflected for an instant in the water, and disappear. Again the picture descends. This time, it is the robber's face, with certain accessories, clearly indicating the locality of the theft. For this branch of art Madame Voisin entertained more than one accomplished artist!

A lady visited her, entreating to be told whether she would survive her husband.

"You shall know that by a sign," replied the sorceress. "The urn which stands among the porcelain on your cabinet will fall to-night while you sleep. If it break, your husband shall die first, if not, yourself."

As may be expected, the maid being in alliance with fate and Madame Voisin, the urn punctually falls, and is shivered to atoms.

Madame Voisin dealt in charmed cosmetics without limit. Madame Rachel could not have held the candle to her. She had a pomade which conferred perpetual beauty, brightening the eyes, reducing the lips, and, if necessary, the nose, and completely correcting nature's errors; while her spells for dealing with the hair, complexion, voice, &c., were as inexhaustible as, judging from the price willingly paid for them, they were effectual.

She did very striking things beside, such as causing a human body to fall piecemeal down the chimney, the parts reuniting, and appearing none the worse as a whole, a pleasantry in which we have seen the clown indulge with respect to his rival, harlequin. And she could furthermore produce thunder and lightning, which also we have seen done with more or less success on the boards!

One scurvy trick was played upon her by a still better conjuror, the Maréchal de Luxembourg. Nothing would satisfy him short of seeing the devil himself! Madame promised, and the fiend, surrounded with most alarming concomitants, duly made his appearance. But the Marshal, declining to be appalled, seized him by the throat, and would have passed his rapier through Satan's very body, had he not cried for mercy and confessed the fraud.

After all, those possessed of optical secrets are perhaps the most adroit conjurors. Light is a cheap material, and the stock-in-trade of a sorcerer as clever as Mr. Pepper may be very small indeed.

To guide the excited fancy is another and more

delicate proof of conjuring skill. With an illustration of this we bring the subject to a close.

Jean Faustus Cudlingen, the German philosopher, dining with some friends, who challenged him to teach them something remarkable, promised to show them anything they could agree upon.

It was in winter, and, by way of increasing the difficulty, he was invited to display to them a vine loaded with grapes, ripe and ready to be gathered. He promised, but upon condition that all should keep their places, and no one attempt to pluck the grapes without his leave, assuring them that neglect of *this* might be fatal to some of them.

This arranged, the host pushed the wine about among his excited and expectant guests, till, having reduced them to semi-intoxication, he, with a sudden and powerful effort of description, called up to their imaginations a splendid grape-loaded vine. One by one recognised the phantom, and at length strove to gather the fruit so temptingly pointed out to them. The desire intensified the fancy, as the fancy had awakened the desire, and the host prolonged this condition as long as he considered safe. Then, giving the word of release, the vine suddenly disappeared, while the guests found themselves, with knife in hand, grasping each other by the nose, and fully prepared to cut off an inch or two of those features by mistake for grapes, had not the host's inflexible command protected them.

Truly the mother of sorcery is simplicity.

## IV.

## AM I MYSELF?

IT was pleasantly remarked by a French gentleman,
of long descent but short means, that the anti-
quity of his house had at length exhausted its possessions.

Such, perhaps, was the position of the young Louis
de la Pivardière, Sieur de Bouchet, destined to be the
hero of a case which, towards the end of the seventeenth century, created an intense interest, and has
seldom found its parallel in the records of criminal
jurisprudence.

Louis de la Pivardière was the youngest of three
sons of a gentleman of noble lineage, but whose possessions at his death were scarcely sufficient to provide
his children with the means of an honourable subsistence.

In this position the young and handsome Louis had
the good fortune, as he thought it, to captivate the
affections of Madame de Chauvelin, widow of the

Sieur Menon de Billy, at that time about thirty-five, and the mother of five children by her first marriage. She had a moderate estate at Narbonne, producing a fair but not abundant income. Her beauty, which was but little impaired by time, and her refined and pleasing manners, rendered her a great favourite in the society in which she moved. Her marriage with Pivardière was celebrated at the close of 1687, and for two years all went well, their domestic felicity being only interrupted by passing fits of jealousy on the part of the young husband, which, however, had no other ground than his lady's devotion to general society.

In 1689 the Arrière-ban compelled the Sieur de Pivardière, as lord of Narbonne, to take his turn of service, and two years later he obtained a lieutenancy in the regiment of dragoons of St. Hermine.

By this time a certain coolness had been engendered between the pair, and the inevitable absence of Louis was endured by both with an amount of resignation hardly consistent with a real affection.

One of the most frequent and (to Madame de la Pivardière) most welcome visitors at the Château de Narbonne, was the reverend prior of the neighbouring Abbey of Miseray — a sequestered edifice nestling in the adjacent wood, and accommodating only some six or eight brethren at most. The prior, as domestic chaplain, attended to celebrate mass on Saturdays at the château.

It was not very long before sharp-eyed and many-tongued scandal began to comment upon the undeniable fact that the reverend gentleman's visits were becoming far more frequent than his spiritual duties seemed to demand. Louis was aware of the existence of such a rumour, but a certain dread of that mixture of censure and ridicule which attaches to a needlessly jealous husband, induced him to close eye and ear to the growing intimacy, and to merely absent himself more than ever from the scene of his annoyance.

While travelling from place to place on pretence of military duty, but in reality for solace of his mental trouble, Louis found himself one sweet summer evening wandering in the outskirts of Auxerre. Suddenly his attention was attracted by bursts of merriment proceeding from a group of young girls engaged in some youthful game beneath the trees. On one of them especially the young soldier's eyes were fixed with a curiosity and interest he himself could hardly understand. With blue eyes sparkling with mirthful excitement, and bright brown hair waving and glistening in the chequered light, Louis felt his heart irresistibly attracted towards the fairy figure, and without further ceremony set himself to making her closer acquaintance.

He very soon discovered that she was the daughter of a lately deceased innkeeper, named Pillard, a circumstance which gave him secret pleasure as increasing the facilities for, as he hoped, making this fair prize his own.

Without a moment's delay, the infatuated young man engaged an apartment in the little inn presided over by the widow Pillard, and entered heart and soul into the enterprise he had resolved upon. We need not pursue him step by step. That he speedily established himself in the good graces of the pretty rustic need not be a matter of surprise. Handsome, graceful, accomplished, and in earnest, Louis made short work of her affections. But here his progress was stayed. As good and pure in heart as she was fair in person, his young mistress refused all overtures unsanctified with the marriage rite, and would have dismissed her lover on the spot had he not, following out the impulse he had at first conceived, and determined through all obstacles to obtain his object, acceded to her conditions. .

He went through the ceremony accordingly under his family name of Bouchet, dropping that of la Pivardière, and taking every other precaution that suggested itself to him for the concealment of the mock marriage, as he had previously concealed from his victim the real one. This successfully effected, he took up his residence at the little inn, and, sacrificing pride to love, fulfilled the duties of host with a frank amenity that brought augmented custom to the house, and thus materially added to the comforts of the now happy family.

Within a twelvemonth the young wife, as she believed herself, being shortly to become a mother, it seemed needful to Louis that he should pay a brief visit to his abandoned home, and obtain, if possible, a supply of money.

Accordingly, making what excuse he might, he took horse for Narbonne, and arriving on the second day at the period of the evening meal, found a merry party assembled, and the reverend prior of Miseray dispensing the hospitalities of the château in its master's chair. At this sight, and the cold greeting he received from his wife, Louis' blood began to boil, but conscience whispered in his ear a quieting word. There was no scene; and Louis, taking occasion to mention that he must rejoin his regiment, if possible, on the morrow, found his lady so obligingly anxious that no financial impediment should arise, that he was enabled to take horse next morning with a lighter heart and heavier purse than he had brought with him.

Four years now elapsed without especial incident, save that Louis's young partner brought him four children, and that he himself paid an annual visit to Narbonne, from whence he derived what supplies he could towards the support of his establishment at Auxerre.· But a change was at hand.

Some of those who delight in communicating evil tidings found means to inform Madame de la Pivardière of her husband's pretended marriage, but without indicating name or place. She instantly adopted measures for verifying the statement, and had just obtained the required assurance, when her husband set out on his accustomed annual visit to the château.

It would appear that all Louis's old jealousy of the prior of Miseray had revived; for, halting at the village of Bourgdieu, seven leagues from Narbonne, he fell into conversation with a mason whom he knew, and remarked to him that it was his object to arrive late at the château, where he would probably meet with the prior, and would either take his life or lose his own.

No thought of his own infidelity seems to have softened the man's heart as he spurred homeward on his deadly errand. But perhaps he was of opinion with Lemaître that men, claiming for themselves virtues of the mind, exact from the other sex the less noble virtues of the body, maintaining, in fact, that man's honour is in no way allied with his chastity, while with woman honour and chastity are one and the same.

It was at sunset, on the fête of Notre Dame, August, 1697, that a splendid collation was taking place at Narbonne, at which many of the neighbouring gentry, who had attended the morning mass at the château, were present with their families.

To the astonishment of all, the master of the house strode suddenly into the room, and took his seat at the table. All the guests rose and offered their salutations. His wife alone retained her seat, her countenance so expressive of scorn and pent-up anger, that a lady present could not forbear some words of condolence.

"Is it thus," she murmured, "that a husband so long absent should be greeted in his own house?"

Louis overheard it.

"*Je ne suis que son mari—je ne suis pas son ami !*" ("I am only her husband—not her friend"), he answered bitterly.

The mirth of the feast departed with Louis's appearance. A consciousness of "something wrong" silenced everybody, and at the earliest moment good manners permitted, Louis and his resentful wife found themselves alone.

For a few minutes there reigned a gloomy silence—then, the lady—rising—offered to retire to her apartment. Her husband made a movement to attend her, and, being repulsed, at once demanded to know the reason of her contempt and anger.

"Go back to your new wife," was the indignant reply, "and ask *her* the reason !"

In vain Louis attempted to deny the wrong. She refused to credit—even to listen to—any defence, and heaping on him the bitterest reproaches, ended by declaring that, in a very brief space, he should be made bitterly to repent the injury he had done her. With these ominous words she withdrew, her husband retiring to a separate chamber prepared for him by her orders.

Warned, as it subsequently appeared, by one of the

maid servants that his life was not secure so long as he remained under that roof, Louis resolved to depart under cover of the night, and, taking with him his dog and gun, abandoned his horse (which had fallen lame the previous day), his cloak, and pistols—these being likely to encumber him too much in the fatiguing foot journey he proposed to make.

It was in evidence at the trial, that he passed through Bourgdieu, that he lodged on the 17th at Chateauroux, on the 18th at the hostelry de la Cloche at Issodun, and from thence set forward toward Auxerre, where he expected to arrive at dusk.

A few days later there started into life a sinister rumour. Louis de la Pivardière had, it was affirmed, been assassinated in his own house at Narbonne! How, when, or where the report originated, was never known. One thing was certain, that it grew and spread until nothing else was spoken of in the vicinity of the supposed murder, while all went on as usual in the château, and its mistress appeared in public with her accustomed grace and smiles, and a demeanour perfectly unruffled.

But one fine day there appeared at the gate of Narbonne the police-lieutenant of Chatillon, in attendance on the Procureur du Roi, and an inquiry followed.

Fifteen witnesses were examined. Some of whom, resident in the neighbourhood of the château, deposed to having heard a shot fired during the night of the supposed murder.

Madame de la Pivardière was thereupon ordered into custody. But the lady had fled. It was ascertained that she had removed from the château all that was most valuable and easy of transport, and taken refuge herself in the house of her friend, Madame d'Anneuil, pending the issue of the inquiry.

It was no convincing proof of guilt that she should have avoided the storm about to burst on her head. The innocent are often timid : she had reason, moreover, to believe that the lieutenant was no friend to the prior of Miseray, and ignorant as she was of her husband's place of concealment, she was unable to refute at once the calumny.

But the astounding circumstance was, that her two maids, Marguerite Mercier and Catherine Le Moine, being arrested, gave a precise and detailed narrative of the murder of the missing gentleman !

The former, Mercier, her mistress's godchild, and a great favourite, stated that Madame de la Pivardière, having got rid of all who might suspect her, introduced two male servants into her husband's chamber, by whose hands he was there and then put to death.

The second maid declared that she had been sent out of the way, and only returned when the murder was just accomplished.

The little Mdlle. Pivardière, aged nine, declared that in the middle of the night she had heard her father's voice exclaiming, " Ah, my God! have pity on me!"

A third servant, Jaquette Riflé, denied all knowledge of the assassination.

The first, Mercier, being ill and in danger of death, before receiving the last sacraments, confirmed her former deposition, and added that the prior of Miseray had assisted at the murder, and had dealt the last fatal blow!

There is perhaps nothing more inexplicable in criminal records, than the conduct of these two women, supposing that their testimony was false. They had no grudge against their mistress, who treated them with the kindest indulgence, and, in fact, had everything to lose—nothing to gain—by contributing to her ruin.

It was believed by some that a murder had really been committed, but upon the person of the servant of De la Pivardière, whom his master, under some feeling of distrust, had caused to occupy his bed, he himself escaping in the night, and that next day, on discovering her mistake, Madame de la Pivardière had, with the aid of the prior, buried the body of the murdered valet in the garden. This, it was suggested, accounted for the confidence of her denials, when charged with the murder of her husband. But there was no evidence of any kind to give reality to this hypothesis, and it was at least certain that M. de la Pivardière had brought no servant with him to the château.

The lieutenant now visited Narbonne, and instituted a close inquiry relative to some traces of blood found on the floor of M. de la Pivardière's apartment, but without result.

Meanwhile the lady had petitioned the " Chambre des Vacations" to cause a fresh process to be issued before another judge than he of Chatillon, and that search might be made for her missing but living husband. Her case was accordingly referred to the judge of Remorentin.

She herself pressed the search with the greatest

perseverance, and no long time elapsed before he was actually discovered in his humble home at Auxerre. When informed that he was sought for by his wife, the idea that he was to be arrested and tried for bigamy, presented itself at once to his mind. He took to flight. Overtaken at Flavigny, he, for the first time, learned the real state of affairs, and now his apprehensions on his own account were lost in anxiety for his wife.

He returned to Auxerre, and we may imagine the painful scene that ensued when he found himself compelled to avow his true position to the gentle loving woman who had believed herself his wife.

As for the latter, with a nobility of soul hardly to be expected under circumstances so trying, far from giving way to hatred against the man who had wronged her, and jealousy against the woman who was to take him from her, she did her best to comfort her mock-husband, and incite him to proceed, without the delay of an instant, to the succour of his legitimate wife.

De la Pivardière followed her generous counsel, and without an hour's delay executed a formal declaration before two notaries, confirming his own existence. He wrote to his wife and to his brother, and this done, started for Narbonne, where he found the château a scene of indescribable confusion, the perquisitions of the police, and the unauthorized intrusion of curious strangers, having reduced it to the condition of a house sacked by a mob.

Shocked at the disturbance of which he had been the unconscious cause, he proceeded forthwith to the judge of Remorentin, and demanded a formal and legal recognition; after which, accompanied by that official, he repaired to Luce, not far from Narbonne, where he was immediately recognised by at least a dozen people, the fact being admitted by the police who had the case in hand.

From Luce they proceeded to Jeumaloches, and, entering the church during divine service on St. Anthony's day, the appearance of the missing man so excited the assembly, that vespers were for some minutes suspended, every one gazing at him with distended eyes and quickened pulse, as though looking upon one really returned from the tomb.*  Later in the day more than two hundred witnesses, including

---

* Those who have read Charles Reade's powerful novel, "Griffith Gaunt," will be struck with the similarity of the leading incidents.

many persons of high consideration, testified on oath
to his identity, and subsequently his little daughter,
her nurse, the clergy and gentry of Miseray,
and numerous others, recognised the returned
man.

One would have thought that such a mass of evidence would have set the question at rest.  Far from
it.  The contest was only now beginning.  The law
appeared to consider that if the Sieur de la Pivardière
was not murdered and buried, he certainly *ought* to
have been, and declined to accept the contrary without much more satisfactory proof than that supplied
by the reappearance of the murdered individual among
his gratulating friends.

The Lieutenant of Chatillon at once bestirred himself, and, proceeding to Narbonne, ordered a strict
search to be made in the grounds and lake for the
body.  While thus engaged, the Sieur de la Pivardière himself joined the busy party, and laughingly
accosted the magistrate—

" Do not trouble yourselves, Messieurs," he said,
" to hunt at the bottom of any lake for what you may
find on the bank."

The lieutenant directed one scared look at the
speaker, then, springing on his horse, departed at full

gallop, amidst the cheers and laughter of De la Pivardière's friends.

To his friend, Monsieur Denyan, the advocate, the lieutenant apologized for his flight, on the ground that he really believed that he was looking on the spectre of the missing man.

" But why avoid it ?" asked Denyan, coolly. " A magistrate should be proof against such impulses. This—hem—phantom—came only to demand revenge, and to show you where to seek its mangled frame. Such a prodigy might perhaps surprise, but should not startle you. Instead of galloping away, my good sir, you should have drawn up a procès-verbal on the spot. The discovery of the shade of De la Pivardière beside the lake, was surely the most convincing proof of his decease !"

The Sieur, accompanied by the judge of Remorentin, now visited the prison, and presented himself to the two maid servants who had related his murder. To the surprise of every one, they positively denied his identity, pointing out the difference they professed to discover between their visitor and their master.

It was imagined that the Lieutenant of Chatillon had prompted this denial. He had kept the women up to this time in close confinement, without external communication, and he now protested strongly against the visit of the judge of Remorentin.

The Sieur now visited an Ursuline convent, and was recognised by his two sisters and the Lady Abbess. All his family unhesitatingly acknowledged him, and detained him among them for three weeks, during which period the Remorentin judge prepared a procès-verbal embodying these facts, and this being signed by De la Pivardière, it might be supposed that his difficulties were over. Not so. The tyranny of form prevailed still against reason and reality.

The irrepressible lieutenant resolved to continue his investigation of this murder of a living man. He managed to obtain from the Attorney-General an order of Court, staying the proceedings of the judge of Remorentin, and ordering a new and superior inquiry. The prior of Miseray was arrested, and placed—contrary to custom—in irons, pending the process. The Sieur de la Pivardière took part in the latter, as representing his wife, and in the first place demanded a safe-conduct for four months (protecting himself thus against process for the bigamy), and that the letters, &c., he had written since the date of his alleged assassination, might be compared with those preceding that date.

The pleadings were sufficiently curious, but would weary the patience of any reader, unless one were found who could take a professional interest in the intricacies of old French law.

De la Pivardière's counsel of course dwelt strongly upon the overwhelming evidence that established their client's identity; while, as regards the depositions of the two maids, their contradictions and retractations were pointed out with great perspicuity, and at inordinate length, seeing that the closing argument simply asserted that their testimony to the murder *must* be worthless, the victim having returned.

This rather reminds one of the French prefêt, who, being censured for not receiving a royal visitor with the customary salute, adduced a whole catalogue of reasons, ending with the not immaterial one, that there were neither cannon nor powder in the town !

The counsel concluded by attributing the trouble and calumny heaped upon Madame de la Pivardière to two great causes, an injurious cabal, and the mystery which her husband had, to hide his own misdoing, flung around his recent life.

After a plea of equal length from the opposite side, still adhering to the non-identity of De la Pivardière, the Court (July 23, 1698) issued a most verbose and elaborate decree, the substance whereof was to the effect that, further proceedings being judged necessary, the prisoners should be conveyed to Chartres, and M. de la Pivardière be placed in immediate arrest, with the view of setting the question of identity at rest for ever.

This decree, which puts the innocent, as it were, in the place of guilt, was not in effect prejudicial to his interests, since a judgment in his favour, without such previous inquiry, would have been void.

The presence of De la Pivardière was imperative, and since (having failed of his safe-conduct) he refused to appear, compulsion was necessary. Besides, his very absence favoured the imputation of imposture.

On the other hand, it must be borne in mind that at this time bigamy was a capital offence, and though the records of love can boast of many an example of men sacrificing their lives for their mistresses, those of marriage are almost barren of such instances.

In this difficulty help came from an unexpected quarter. De la Pivardière's noble second wife hastened to Versailles, and, aided by some persons about the king, petitioned the latter for the required protection for the husband who was about to abandon her.

Louis Quatorze was not the monarch to be wholly

insensible to beauty in grief! He raised the fair suppliant from her knees, with the gallant remark :

" Une fille, faite comme vous, meritait un meilleur sort."

And, having inquired into the particulars, granted an immediate safe-conduct for three months—in terms so ample that—as some one observed at the time— the Sieur de la Pivardière might, if so disposed, have gone through the whole gamut of crime, short of treason, without any one daring to interpose, until the period for which it was granted had expired. As things were, the protection was several times renewed.

Thus provided, the Sieur gave himself up, a voluntary prisoner, at Fort l'Evêque, Paris, September 1st, 1698.

The matter became at this time more than ever complicated by the death of the Lieutenant of Chatillon, whose heirs, from motives of respect to his memory, felt it their duty to continue the process he had originated.

Upon the second trial a large and distinguished bar appeared on either side, and gigantic efforts were made to increase the mystery—efforts so successful that it was not until the 14th June, 1701, that this extra-ordinary case came to an end.

The final judgment, after duly reciting the foregoing proceedings, decreed in favour of De la Pivardière, acquitting all those placed in arrest during the process, and condemning Marguerite Mercier (her fellow-servant, Le Moine, had died during the process) to make the public "amende honorable" in the usual form as a false witness, denying "in a loud and intelligible voice" her slanderous assertions, after which she was to be publicly whipped and branded with a fleur-de-lys on the right shoulder, thereafter to be banished, her goods being forfeited to the crown.

Whatever may have been the private wrong and suffering inflicted in this strange case, it was not without benefit to the commonwealth, many questions theretofore of great legal uncertainty having been definitively set at rest. A list of fifteen of such decisions were issued to the judges of the various courts, and became thenceforth indisputable law.

The Sieur De la Pivardière and his wife did not very long survive this event in their lives.

The Sieur, still cherishing his old jealousy, having only consulted his own honour and the safety of his wife in the recent proceeding, refused to return to his home. He, however, revisited the noble-hearted woman who had come to his rescue, only to bid her farewell. It would be difficult to realize the mingled love and grief of such a parting.

De la Pivardière subsequently obtained through his relation, the Duc de la Feuillade, a semi-military employ, in which he was killed while leading his brigade against a large band of " contrebandiers."

Nearly at the same time his lady was found dead in her bed from natural causes, at the château.

The prior of Miseray, who had long since ceased to visit at the latter place, died in high esteem, at a very advanced age.

It is pleasant to be able to state that the generous second wife was destined to see many days of peace and prosperity. She was twice married, lived for many years after the events above recorded, and enjoyed the well-deserved esteem of all who knew her, and were acquainted with the strange history in which she alone appears to advantage.

# V.

## ON YOUR OATH?

IS it not Lopez de Vega who remarks that Nature, wearied with her own variety, sometimes—for mere change—repeats herself with such marvellous fidelity as to defy the keenest critic to detect a difference? When the same assemblage of features is found accompanied with a similar expression, gait, and bearing, and when to these are superadded marks and tokens which might be supposed to be peculiar to the individual, the difficulty of distinguishing, especially if the mystery be increased by fraud, can astonish none.

Social history in all ages records these remarkable resemblances. Those moving in London society at the present moment may remember two accomplished sisters, whose most familiar associates would hesitate to depose suddenly, on oath, as to their identity. It has fallen to our own lot to encounter twin-brethren, whose intended wives were wont, at evening parties, to rely—for distinction—chiefly upon flowers worn by their betrothed in their button-holes!

The extraordinary trial which has of late engaged public attention, throwing everything else—save politics and racing—into the shade, has but one parallel in the annals of the law; and a comparison of the two cases may not be without interest, premising that what follows has no reference to the merits and issue of the recent trial, being intended merely to illustrate the singular obstacles that may sometimes arise in the way of a prompt settlement of a question of personal identity.

It is to M. Coras, advocate-general, subsequently a distinguished judge—and, it is melancholy to add, hanged in his crimson robes, with two colleagues, after the massacre of St. Bartholomew—that we are indebted for the most faithful report of the celebrated case of Martin Guerre. It is true that the learned writer, whose heart was in his profession, has enriched his narrative with remarks and researches of the highest value to the jurisconsult; but these we must of necessity omit, and confine ourselves sternly to the hard facts.

Martin Guerre was, at the mature age of eleven, married in January, 1539, to Mademoiselle Bertrande de Rols, of Artigues, of the same ripe years. The young lady was, according to M. Coras, as wise as she was fair; and belonged, like her elderly partner, to that class which La Fontaine describes as "half-burgess," that is, above the peasant and below the gentry. A certain provision was made for the wedded pair, and in the ninth year of their marriage a third member was added to the juvenile group, by the birth of a fine boy, who received the name of Sanxi.

But an envious cloud now gathered over the domestic sky. Naughty Martin was tempted to appropriate to his own use some wheat belonging to his father, and fearing the latter's displeasure, absented himself from home until the matter should blow over. Eight days were assigned—between Monsieur and Madame Guerre—as the probable period for this; but as many *years* actually did elapse before Martin was again seen, and during the whole of that time no token of his existence cheered his wife and child.

At length, one gloomy winter's evening, the way-worn traveller—if it were he—suddenly presented himself, and folding his Bertrande in his arms, and demanding his child, declared that he had returned a penitent man, resolved to atone by every office of affection and conjugal duty for the anxiety and distress he had occasioned.

Not the least question of the visitor's being indeed Martin Guerre seems to have occurred to anybody. His own four sisters, his uncle, and every member of his wife's family then at hand, acknowledged him without an instant's hesitation. And no wonder; for not only was the newly-arrived identical in form and feature with Guerre, but he showed himself familiar with circumstances which could be known only to the latter; and these were numerous and minute enough to suggest to Pasquier (in his " Researches") the idea that if this were not indeed Martin Guerre, he at least knew that gentleman better than the latter knew himself.

Pasquier adds : " The most wonderful feature in this wonderful story is, that this supposed husband never enjoyed an opportunity of intimate acquaintance with the man he undertook to personate."

But Coras, whose narrative we follow, and whose information must have been far superior to Pasquier's, contradicts this.

Madame Guerre, whose attachment to her lord had never wavered or diminished in his absence, received his representative with every token of the fondest affection; returning to her quiet wifely habits as before, and, in the period of three years during which they lived together, presenting the supposed Martin with two children, one of whom, however, died in infancy. In effect, according to our judicial historian, Jupiter himself did not more successfully personate absent Amphitryon than did the returned traveller Martin Guerre.

Whether or not the wife ever suspected that she was the victim of a daring imposture can never be ascertained. It was deemed impossible that some or other of those almost imperceptible yet positive differences, that must always exist between man and man, should not have at times awakened her suspicions. The probability is that they did so; and that her continued acquiescence in this singular connexion was the result, partly of personal liking for the man who enacted his *rôle* of husband with a tenderness and fidelity the original did not, and partly from a conviction that, impostor as he might be, her peace and respectability would be best consulted by keeping her own counsel and his. But this was not to be.

What circumstance prompted the first attempt to investigate the matter was not distinctly known. It was, however, at the pressing instances of Pierre

Guerre, an uncle of the missing man, and other connexions of the family, that Bertrande was at length
induced to invoke the vengeance of the law on her
pretended spouse. He was thereupon arrested, and
before the Court of Rieux Bertrande accused him of
having falsely and treacherously personated her
hnsband, Martin Guerre, and demanded that he
should be condemned to do penance in the usual
public form, should pay a fine to the king, and make
compensation to herself in the sum of ten thousand
livres.

The accused made an eloquent defence, maintaining stoutly his identity with Martin Guerre; and
complaining bitterly of the cruelty of his wife and
relatives, who, for interested purposes, had resolved
upon his ruin. He then explained the causes of his
prolonged absence, giving a minute and circumstantial
history of the seven or eight years, during which he
had served as a soldier, passing afterwards into the
service of the King of Spain. Consumed with the
longing desire once more to see his wife and son, he
had at length wandered back, browned and bearded,
to the village he had left a smooth-cheeked boy. But
his friends could recognise him yet. Yes, Pierre
Guerre, that very uncle who now sought his ruin,

was the first to load him with caresses, and only
changed in his demeanour when he—the accused—
requested an account of the moneys he had, as agent
for Martin Guerre, administered in his absence.  His
uncle had even attempted his life, and it was only
through the energetic interposition of his wife that
he had been protected from mortal injury.  He demanded to be confronted with his wife, persuaded as
he was that, being free from the cupidity that inspired
his persecutors, she would not conceal the truth;  he
required that she should be placed beyond the influence of subornation by his enemies;  and finally,
that the latter should be mulcted in heavy damages
for the wrong they had inflicted.

In the severe interrogatory to which he was subjected, he replied without hesitation and with unfailing accuracy to every question of family history :
naming the time and place of the birth of Martin
Guerre, his father, mother, brothers, and sisters, and
even more distant relations;  the day, month, and
year of his own marriage, the parties present, or
otherwise associated with the marriage, the dresses of
the guests, and a multitude of special incidents which
occurred on that and the preceding day.  He spoke
of Sanxi, his little son, and next proceeded to describe

his departure, journeyings, the cities he had visited in France and Spain, and the acquaintance he had made there; furnishing the names and addresses of those who could most readily confirm his narrative; and unquestionably leaving a very strong impression in his favour on the minds of his hearers.

The testimony of his wife Bertrande corroborated all the statements of the accused, so far as they came within her knowledge; but she positively denied his identity with her husband.

The court now ordered that an inquiry should be instituted into the conduct of Bertrande during the absence of her husband, and into the character and repute of the witnesses who so persistently pursued the accusation. The result was satisfactory.

On the resumption of the trial there were summoned no less than one hundred and fifty witnesses. Of these, *forty* declared on oath that the accused was unquestionably the long-missing Martin Guerre. They had been his intimate companions in his boyhood and youth, and their conviction was strengthened by the recollection of certain marks or scars, which time had not effaced.

On the other hand, a great body of witnesses as positively declared that the accused was *not* Guerre, but one Arnaud du Tilh, called "Pansette," with whom some, at least, among them had been acquainted from the cradle. The remaining witnesses, sixty in number, affirmed that so close was the resemblance they dared not pronounce an opinion.

The court now ordered that young Sanxi Guerre should be produced and compared with his alleged father. A formal report declared that there existed no resemblance; a second report averred that, on being compared with the sisters of Guerre, the boy's face exhibited an unmistakable likeness.

Greatly to the public surprise, the process resulted in the conviction of the accused. As Arnaud du Tilh, he was pronounced guilty of the alleged offence, and sentenced to decapitation. Appeal being made on his behalf to the parliament of Toulouse, the higher court decided that the matter had been insufficiently weighed, decreed a new trial, and ordered that Pierre Guerre and Bertrande should be successively confronted with the accused.

The confrontation, however, produced nothing, though it is recorded that the bearing of the accused, calm and confident, contrasted favourably with the downcast looks of his opponents.

Thirty new witnesses now appeared upon the scene.

Of these, ten declared him to be the true Martin Guerre, seven or eight decided in favour of Arnaud du Tilh, and the remainder refused definitely to give any opinion on the matter.

All this, remarks M. Coras, proved extremely perplexing to the judges, as well it might, and confirmed them in their impression of the precipitancy of the " court below."

On summing up the testimony, it resulted that forty-five witnesses declared the accused to be no Martin Guerre, but Arnaud du Tilh. Among these were several who had passed years in the latter's company, while the character of these deponents sufficed to place their evidence beyond suspicion.

The principal witness was maternal uncle of Du Tilh, one Carbon Bareau, who at once recognised his nephew, and seeing him in fetters, burst into tears at witnessing the disgrace he had brought upon the family. Other witnesses had been present when Arnaud du Tilh had executed certain deeds, &c., and these instruments were produced in corroboration.

All of them agreed in describing Martin Guerre as taller and darker than the accused, slender in body and limb, round-shouldered, with a high, divided chin, pendent lower lip, and squat (*camus*) nose, having the trace of an ulcer on one cheek, and a scar on the right eyebrow.  Now, Arnaud, the accused, was short and stout, having neither humpy shoulders nor squat nose.  It was singular enough, however, that both the marks referred to as indicative of Martin Guerre were perceptible in the face of Arnaud.

The shoemaker of Martin Guerre deposed that the dimensions of his foot exceeded by one quarter that of the accused.  Another witness alleged that Guerre was a skilful swordsman and wrestler.  The accused was a novice in either art.  Jean Espagnol, of Tonges, swore that the prisoner had revealed himself to him as Arnaud, but enjoining secresy, and declaring that Martin Guerre had made over to him the whole of his possessions.  Pelegrin de Liberos deposed that the accused had given him two hand-kerchiefs, to be delivered to Jean du Tilh, *his brother.*

Two other witnesses declared that a soldier from Rochefort, passing through Artigues, and hearing the accused called Martin Guerre, denounced him as an impostor; he himself having lately known the real Martin in Flanders, where he had lost a leg at the battle of St. Laurent, before St. Quentin.  It is indicative of the wife's good faith in the process, that she had, through great difficulties, obtained a legal verification of the soldier's testimony.

Finally, numerous persons declared that Arnaud du Tilh had from boyhood been a *mauvais sujet* of the worst description : a drunkard, a swearer, an atheist, and blasphemer ; a man, in short, " quoted and signed to do a deed of shame" such as that now imputed to him.

Such was the formidable case set up against the " claimant."   Let us now hear his answer.

Nearly forty credible witnesses asserted that he was actually Martin Guerre, whom the greater part had known from infancy.   Among these were his four sisters, with the husbands of two of the latter. Friends who had been present at his marriage with Bertrande de Rols confirmed their testimony ; and the housekeeper who, on the nuptial night, bore to the new-married pair the little collation, called in courtly circles *media noche,* among burgesses *réveillon,* positively identified the accused as the bridegroom.

A great number of the witnesses averred that Martin Guerre had two teeth in the left lower jaw broken, a drop of extravasated blood in the left eye, the nail of the left forefinger missing, and three warts on the left hand, one being on the little finger.   *All these peculiarities existed in the accused.*

It was moreover proved that the prisoner, on arriving at Artigues, recognised and saluted as old friends all those who had been intimate with Guerre; that in conversation with his wife he recalled to her memory incidents which could have been only known to herself and her husband; and it was stated, by way of illustration, that Madame Guerre having mentioned that she had preserved certain chests unopened, he desired her to fetch from one of them a pair of white pantaloons folded in taffeta. The garment was found as he had described.

With regard to the dissimilarity in appearance between the men, it was urged that a very considerable change must of necessity have occurred in Martin Guerre; nor was there anything remarkable in the slender stripling returning, after so long an absence, a stout and sturdy man; an alteration which, to the eye, would naturally diminish his stature.

The want of resemblance between Sanxi Guerre and the accused was pronounced to be of little value. How many sons might not be classed in the same category? The report of the soldier from Rochefort, being but hearsay, could not be accepted, the law expressly refusing credence to such testimony.

The indifferent character attributed to Arnaud du

Tilh could not affect the accused, who claimed to be another man, Martin Guerre; and it was at least in evidence that his course of life during the four years that had elapsed since his return had been without reproach.

Lastly, the marvellous accuracy with which the accused assumed and maintained the character he claimed, transcended, his supporters alleged, human ingenuity. His acquaintance with dates, incidents, conversations, &c. &c., in the actual life of Guerre, was as inexhaustible as it was shown, by irrefragable testimony, to be correct. M. Pasquier, who was strongly against the accused, finds himself driven to magic and sorcery for explanation of the phenomenon; an argument which, however plausible in *his* time, would be hardly acceptable at Westminster in *ours*.

Such was the conflict of reason and of evidence with which the judges of Toulouse were called upon to deal. All sources of information seemed to be now fairly exhausted. It was necessary to arrive at some conclusion; and the Court, according to M. Coras, were upon the very point of pronouncing the accused to be Martin Guerre, when there occurred an event so unexpected, so singularly timed, and so de-cisive, that the spectators may be excused for regarding it as a direct interposition of Heaven to overrule man's erring judgment, and avert a cruel wrong. The veritable husband — Martin Guerre — suddenly stumped into court, on the wooden leg described by the Rochefort witness, and claimed to be heard!

Arrested and interrogated, he denounced the impostor—whose history he gave in detail—and demanded to be confronted with him. It was done; and a singular scene ensued. The accused—Arnaud du Tilh—in his turn denounced the rival husband, boldly declaring that he was willing to be condemned if he did not on the spot convict the latter of fraud and machination.

Maintaining the same arrogant tone, he then proceeded to cross-examine the other as to certain domestic incidents which ought to be within his knowledge. The answers were delivered with hesitation; and the impostor—if such he were—certainly displayed a more intimate acquaintance with Martin Guerre's domestic history than did that gentleman himself.

On examining the peculiar marks deposed to by the witnesses on the part of Guerre, these were found duly existing in the newly arrived man, although less apparent than in the other.

The first claimant was now withdrawn, and the

second—he of the wooden leg—underwent a close interrogatory touching many domestic particulars which had not hitherto been submitted to either.

To these he replied with unfailing accuracy. But once more justice was at fault; for Martin Guerre the second, interrogated in his turn, replied with the like precision.

In despair the Court now directed that the four sisters, the two brothers-in-law, and uncle of Martin Guerre, the brothers of Arnaud du Tilh, and the chief witnesses who asserted the latter to be Guerre, should appear together, and decide, once for all, which was the real man.

All obeyed excepting the brothers of Du Tilh, whom the Court, with a consideration at that period somewhat rare, forbore to compel to give testimony which would probably affect the life of their relative.

The eldest sister of Guerre, who entered first, paused for an instant as if thunder-stricken; then, bursting into tears, fell on Martin's breast, and acknowledged him to be her brother. The rest followed suit; the witnesses hitherto most inflexibly against him passing one by one into the same view.

Last of all came Bertrande de Rols. No sooner

had her eyes lit upon Guerre than, weeping and
trembling, as M. Coras expressed it, "like a leaf in
the autumn breeze," she threw herself at his feet—
foot, rather—entreating pardon for having suffered
herself to be betrayed by artifice into so great a fault.
She laid part of the blame upon her sisters-in-law,
who had so readily accepted the imposture, but more
upon her own warm love for her absent husband, and
that eager longing for his actual return which had
contributed to the self-deceit.   She averred, that no
sooner had she become conscious of her error, than,
but for the dread of God's anger, she would have
concealed her grief and dishonour in the grave.   In
place of this she determined on revenge, and, as all
the world knew, had pursued to the death the de-
stroyer of her fame and peace.

The woman's natural manner, her beauty and her
tears, sensibly affected the whole auditory, save only
Martin Guerre himself.   That stern reasoner declined
to be moved by passionate words.

"Dry your tears, Madame," he said coldly.   "They
cannot and they ought not to move my pity.   The
example of my sisters and uncle can be no excuse for
*you*.   A wife must know her husband better than the
very closest connexions, and an error such as yours can

only be made by one wilfully blind. You —
you alone—are answerable for what has befallen
me."

The judges in vain attempted to soften the man's
bitterness.

"But I would willingly ask" (writes M. Pasquier,
discontentedly,) " whether this Monsieur Guerre, who
inveighs so bitterly against his wife, did not deserve
punishment as much as the other man, for having, by
his unprovoked desertion, been the primary cause of
her misdeed."

The records of this most extraordinary case do not
describe what was the demeanour of the convicted
impostor at the moment of discovery. He was, however, apparently one of those " resolved villains" who
defy the thunderbolt of vengeance until the very
moment it strikes them into nothing.

The Court decreed that Arnaud du Tilh, called
" Pansette," had been convicted of the several crimes
of imposture, falsehood, substitution of name and
person, adultery, rape, sacrilege, detention (*plagiat*),*
and larceny, and condemned him to do penance before

---

* Holding possession of a person who properly belongs to
another.

the church of Artigues, on his knees, in his shirt, with head and feet bare, a halter round his neck, and a burning taper in his hand, asking pardon of God and the king, Martin Guerre, and Bertrande de Rols his wife; that he should then be handed over to the common executioner, who should conduct him through the most public ways to the house of Martin Guerre, in front of which, upon a scaffold purposely prepared he should be executed by hanging, and his body burned. All his effects were forfeited to the crown. The decree bears date September 12th, 1560.

While under condemnation in the prison at Artigues, Arnaud made a full confession, declaring that the imposture had first suggested itself to him on his being mistaken by intimate friends of Martin Guerre for that individual himself. From them and others he had gleaned all necessary particulars of the past life and ways of the man he proposed to personate. He denied having had recourse to any magic more powerful than natural cunning and a retentive memory; but made no scruple of confessing to sundry other crimes, which had not come under the cognisance of the law.

His behaviour on the scaffold was penitent and becoming enough. It was found that he had left a

will, bequeathing all he possessed to his little daughter
Bertrande, and naming tutors and guardians in the
event of her mother's death. This instrument was
duly acted upon, the crown having ceded its
right to the confiscated property in favour of the
child.

# VI.

## HUMAN BLOODHOUNDS.

IT has been said that no man that ever lived is so devoid of the leaven of wickedness as, under certain circumstances, to be proof against the temptation to commit certain crimes, apparently foreign to his nature and inclination.

But for the minute official records from which the following narrative is derived, it would be almost impossible to believe that there existed in one family three such marvellous monsters as they who, in 1650, compassed the destruction of one of the most beautiful women of her time, as spotless in character as she was fair in aspect, the Marchioness de Gange.

The only daughter of the Sieur de Roussan d'Avignon, who died while she was yet a child, she was the presumptive heiress of the enormous wealth of her maternal grandfather, Joanis, Sieur de Nocheres. She was styled Mademoiselle de Châteaublanc, from one of the estates hereafter to be hers.

The girl's exquisite beauty, without the additional charm of her prospective wealth, would have suffced to assemble round her a crowd of admirers ; and when to the above advantages were added a sweetness and simplicity of character not always found in one so favoured by fortune, it cannot be wondered at that Mademoiselle de Châteaublanc was not left long to the enjoyment of single blessedness. She married at thirteen the Marquis de Castellane, grandson of the Duc de Villars, a gentleman brave, handsome, rich, and possessed of many courtly accomplishments.

The Marquis at once introduced his fair bride to the highest society, and she became, almost at a step, the brightest ornament of what was certainly the most brilliant Court of that period.

Louis the Fourteenth, then in his first youth, was the first to acknowledge the grace and loveliness of " la belle Provençale," as she was usually called, and the king's admiration naturally brought the whole Court to her footstool. His Majesty delighted in selecting her as his partner at the balls, and perpetually discovered some new charm in the fair Marquise. She was for a time the undisputed queen of beauty.

Her portrait, by Mignard, represents her of pearl-white complexion, touched with the most delicate rose, dark glossy hair, curling naturally, eyes as dark as the hair, but large, languishing, yet glistening like diamonds, rosebud mouth, with small perfect teeth, and an *ensemble* that recals the saying that human beauty is after all the most beautiful thing in nature.

Faultless in figure as in face, with hands and feet sculptors might have vainly sought among their most approved models, it might seem that in this lovely woman nature had for once resolved to make a master-piece. The picture by Mignard is more than corroborated in a work published at Rouen, in 1667, in which several pages are devoted to a description of her marvellous personal beauty.

In disposition sweet and genial, with a pure mind, and sound, if not brilliant intelligence, "la belle Provençale" appeared destined, if ever woman was, to pass the happiest of lives, admired, esteemed, beloved of all. Seldom, in this chequered life, has so fair a dawn been followed by so dark a noon.

She was at the height of her popularity when the Marquis, her husband, who commanded part of the French fleet in the Mediterranean, was lost, with his ship and others, on the coast of Sicily. She felt the shock deeply, and retiring for a time from society, resided with Madame d'Ampus, the aunt of her deceased husband, after which her affairs requiring her presence at Avignon, she placed herself in a convent there, and held intercourse only with her most intimate friends, and those connected with the management of her property.

Time, however, exercising its usual soothing influence, "la belle Provençale," more beautiful even than before, returned to the world, and from the crowd of suitors who eagerly presented themselves to compete for such a prize, selected the young and handsome Marquis de Gange. He was at this time about twenty, and was as a man little inferior in outward gifts to what his betrothed appeared as a woman.

In character they were literally as the poles asunder. The Marquis was proud, haughty, sullen, jealous, mistrustful; in effect, precisely the reverse of the amiable, noble-hearted woman, whose affections he had, unhappily for her, contrived to ensnare.

The world proclaimed it an admirable match, and such in truth it seemed. The Marchioness was at this time just twenty-two, the culmination as some have thought of youthful charms. La Bruyère once heard a wish expressed by a male friend that he could become a beautiful woman from eighteen to twenty-two, and then resume his sex!

Apparently the attachment of the young couple did not long survive the honeymoon. At all events they were quickly seen again in the vortex of society, and far more frequently apart than seemed consistent with mutual affection. The Marquis neglected his lovely wife, and though there were many quite prepared to impart what consolation their homage might, the lady never permitted the slightest approach to any tenderer feeling. It was enough for one of her admirers to betray the least symptom of an undue interest in her, to find himself at once relegated to the remotest rank of her acquaintance. Discreet, however, as she was, it availed nothing against her husband's causeless jealousy and suspicion, and these were kept alive and aggravated by the whispers of officious friends.

Ashamed of the ridicule that attaches to a jealous husband, and unable to give form and reality to what he suspected, young De Gange concealed his feelings as best he might from the world, and only suffered them to appear in his sullen and morose demeanour with his wife. Thus months, and even years, passed on, and brought no amelioration to their intercourse, until the Marquis's two brothers—a chevalier and an abbé— came on a visit to De Gange, and subsequently made it their permanent residence.

As these two persons were destined to play a great and fearful part in the tragedy that was to come, they merit some description. The elder, the Abbé, was a libertine and debauchée of the vilest stamp. To apply these terms to such as he—devoid of religion, heart, or feeling of any kind—is almost to wrong those men who, with half his guilt upon their souls, have been described in a similar manner. This miscreant churchman had adopted the sacred profession solely as a cloak for his misdeeds. Unhappily for his many victims, he was a man of the most fascinating manners, witty and accomplished, and skilled in acting to perfection any character in which it suited his present purpose to appear. "He was not a man," wrote an author of the time, "but a veritable devil—*rusé, artificieux, prenant toutes sortes de formes, même celle de l'honnête homme.*"

The Chevalier, on the other hand, was a poor weak creature, equally unprincipled but far less gifted—one of those, in fact, who seem born expressly to become the unresisting, unquestioning tools of men more actively vile. He was completely under the control of his brother, who, nevertheless, had the art to conceal the leading-strings wherewith he directed his puppet.

In a somewhat less degree the Abbé exercised ascendancy over his brother the Marquis, leading the latter to believe in his entire devotion to him and to his interests, and rendering himself so useful in a thousand ways, as gradually to obtain almost undisputed sway in his household and over his revenues; insomuch that De Gange at length sunk into a nominal master, leaving the wily churchman to do whatsoever he pleased.

It was hardly to be expected that a man of such ungovernable passions should be unmoved by the excessive beauty of the Marchioness de Gange. The Abbé was not only moved, but deeply smitten, and without an instant's unnecessary delay, began to weave the snares in which he hoped to entrap her. He laid himself out to please her to the uttermost, and, as a first step, laboured to effect a reconciliation between the ill-assorted pair; in which he succeeded to such an extent that the Marchioness, whose indifference towards her changed lord had been tending towards aversion, began to feel a renewal of her old affection, and certain brief months of happiness seemed to promise more auspicious days to come.

But the Abbé had no intention of denying himself the reward of his peacemaking, and his next move was to let his sister-in-law 'fully understand to whose influence she was indebted for the improved state of things, and who it was that could if he pleased undo the gracious work he had done.

Now the Marchioness, though pleased with the Abbé's wit and vivacity, had conceived almost from the first a strong personal dislike to the man, and it may be imagined how distasteful to her was the idea of being placed under an obligation of this description towards one who—something whispered her—was perfectly capable of abusing the hold it gave him.

Madame de Gange thanked him for his friendly service, but it was with a coldness that convinced him at once that no warmer fruit than gratitude could ever come to repay him for that service. Moreover, he now found her on her guard, and himself kept at such an unusual distance that he resolved to have an explanation with her on the first opportunity.

This speedily occurred. The Marchioness went on a visit to some friends in the country, and thither the Abbé, whose lively yet polished manners made him everywhere a welcome guest, at once followed her. Perhaps the passionate sentiment that possessed him lent unusual point and animation to his wit and conversation, for never had he been more agreeable—proving, indeed, the life and soul of the party.

One morning a hunting expedition being organized, the Abbé managed to attach himself to the beautiful Marchioness, as her squire, and thus quickly found the occasion he desired. Alone for a few minutes in an alley of the wood, and discarding, rather imprudently, that timidity which most frequently waits upon a genuine affection—he boldly declared his passion and implored for a return.

The Marchioness turned upon him a look that might have satisfied him without words how utterly he had mistaken the character with which he had to deal. Too much agitated and incensed to express the incredulity she felt, it was some moments before she could command herself sufficiently to reply. Then, in a cold and bitter tone she simply said—

"Monsieur l'Abbé, you seem to consider me a woman who is capable of receiving such a declaration in the light of a compliment. You are entirely mistaken. Now that you are warned, consider, sir, what I *ought* to say, and spare me the pain of uttering it."

The Abbé was too shrewd a man not to perceive that as regards any reciprocity of feeling the case was hopeless. But he had another arrow in his quiver, and he let it fly.

" Are you aware, Madame," he said, calmly, " that your happiness is absolutely in my hands? That I can at pleasure render you the most miserable woman upon earth? I can, be assured, undo all that I have done for you—nor can anything that you may say or do prevail against my power. Your husband will believe nothing you can say to my discredit. You are—I repeat—utterly helpless. Why then should we be enemies, rather than the dearest friends and allies? Give me but the regard I covet, and your life shall be henceforth serene and joyful as the most exacting spirit can desire."

The Marchioness turned and looked him full in the face so steadily that, libertine as he was, he almost cowered under the dark fire of her splendid eyes.

" If, sir," she answered, " you have learned to love me, learn also to respect me. Know that, were I certain to undergo the most cruel suffering ever laid upon humanity, I would not seek to avert it at the cost of honour. More than that, learn that if I were capable of so great a crime and weakness as that to which you would tempt me, *you*, Monsieur l'Abbé, are the last man on earth who would be likely to inspire me with the feeling it implies."

With these words she turned her horse's head and joined the rest of the party.

That evening the Abbé discovered that he had pressing business at Avignon.

Baffled, but not discouraged, he now directed all his efforts to the increasing of his influence over his brother; and, far from depreciating the Marchioness to him, lost no opportunity of congratulating his brother on the possession of a wife as good as she was fair. For a time, therefore, the poor lady retained her late found happiness. She abstained from any marked avoidance of the Abbé, but at the same time took sedulous care never to be for an instant alone with him.

The Chevalier—fool as he was—had not, on his part, escaped the influence of her attractions, and his manners being gentle, he found himself not un-welcome to her as a companion, and even flattered himself that he might in due time succeed in rendering himself yet more agreeable. Of course the jealous and penetrating Abbé detected his hopes at their very birth; and, perceiving that his brother was encouraged while *he* was repulsed, was at first half-disposed to believe that the Marchioness in some measure returned the sentiment. He accordingly set a watch upon the pair, but nothing rewarded these disinterested efforts. Still the species of rivalship which existed between the Chevalier and himself disturbed and irritated him. He resolved to have an understanding with the other, and accordingly observed to him, in his curt decisive way—a style that never failed with the weak Chevalier—

"Hark ye, brother; we both love yonder woman—both pursue her. But only one can succeed. I do not wish to cross your way. Do your best to win her! I will stand aloof—for we are too nearly allied to enter into a competition of such a sort. Only mark this—when you have tried *and failed* (and take your own time for the essay), then frankly retire, and allow *me* the opportunity of judging whether I can succeed better."

The Chevalier was not a little moved at this unexpected manifestation of brotherly regard, and—not to be outdone in generosity—offered some faint resistance. But the magnanimous Abbé was firm.

"No, no," said he; "not a word. I shall see, with sincere satisfaction, that good fortune attends you. I am master of myself. I can exercise a certain control over my most ardent desires ; and I assure you, I prefer my brother's friendship to the love of any woman."

The touching little contest ended with a tearful embrace.

The wooing of the love-sick Chevalier was not more fortunate than that of Roderigo.  On the contrary, no sooner did Madame de Gange perceive the drift of his attentions, than she at once placed him at an equal distance with the Abbé.  The Chevalier affected patience and humility—but the lady, determined that there should be no mistake, gave him such unquestionable proofs of her disdain, that he finally abandoned the pursuit, and announcing to his self-denying brother that the coast was clear, declared his intention of overcoming his fatal passion.  The Abbé highly commended this manly resolution.

The tactics of the latter now underwent a change. Hitherto policy suggested that he should act the peacemaker between husband and wife; but this having led to no profitable result, he now resolved to try the opposite course.  And this required some tact and management, for the Marquis was not a man to be hoodwinked like the Chevalier, and though submissive to the Abbé's stronger will, was far from being its slave.

It cost the tempter no small pains to bring his brother into the belief that the Marchioness's acquaintance with a young nobleman who was frequently in her company had in it something dangerous to his honour.   He did, however, succeed ; and now began a miserable time of jealousy, sullenness, even, it was rumoured, of personal outrage, in the encouragement of which the miscreant Abbé found ample revenge for the mortification of his defeat.   Although fully aware of the malign influence at work against her, the unhappy lady made no attempt to explain to her husband its nature and cause, being too sensible of the little weight any such representation was likely to carry.

At the height of this misery it occurred to the Abbé to make one more bold effort to conquer the fair fortress he had reduced to such cruel straits.

Having—not without difficulty—contrived to surprise her alone, he bluntly accosted her.

" *Eh, bien*, Madame ! are you and I destined to be always enemies ?   Why—*why* will you compel me to make war where I would fain bring peace ?   How easily might you at once win back your husband, and secure *me* for your friend !   Instead of that, you force me, against my heart and will, to disturb your peace,

10—2

while at the same time you repulse and persecute one whose only fault has been the loving you too much.”

Madame de Gange gazed haughtily at him, then turning away, left him without a word.

Just at this period, the death of the Sieur de Nochères, whose great wealth descended to the Marchioness, compelled the family to visit the Château de Gange, seventeen leagues from Montpellier, and nineteen from Avignon. It was a lonely residence, and the Marchioness experienced an inexplicable repugnance to the visit.

Her gloom and uneasiness had perhaps been augmented by an incident of a suspicious nature that had recently occurred at Avignon. After having partaken of some cream-ice, she had become extremely ill—several others, who had done the like, being similarly affected. Through the use of emetics, all escaped without serious illness ; but the ice, on analysis, proved to have been impregnated with a strong mineral poison. The circumstance recalled to her memory that a person in Paris, who professed to draw horoscopes, had warned her that fate had decreed that she should die a violent and unexpected death.

The affair of the poisoned ice made considerable noise at Avignon, but no regular inquiry followed, and the Marchioness, who should have regarded it as a warning, was the first to banish it from her mind. Then followed the death of the Sieur de Nochères, and the increase of fortune accruing to her had the effect of rendering her husband more considerate. The Abbé treated her with quiet respect, while the Chevalier, according to wont, simply followed his brother's lead.

It was proposed to pass the autumn at Gange; and the Marchioness, oppressed with the strange presentiment before alluded to, determined first to execute a will. In this instrument she made her mother heir, with power to assign the inheritance, at her discretion, either to her little son, aged six, or her daughter, then nearly five.

She kept the will secret, but made a formal declaration before the magistrates at Avignon and other witnesses, that should she die and be found to have made a will of more recent date, she thereby formally disavowed the latter instrument, expressing in the most distinct and emphatic manner words could convey, her desire that the will just executed should alone be regarded as authentic.

She distributed money to different religious bodies for masses for her soul, lest she should die without the sacraments of the church, and did this with a sorrowful earnestness that betrayed her secret apprehensions.

In taking leave of her friends, her manner was that of one about to be led forth to certain death, and moved every one to tears. History is full of such presentiments, and it would sometimes seem that the forewarning—like the snake's eye—exercises a fatal fascination, and paralyses the efforts of the victim to escape the danger.

Arrived at Gange, she was received by Madame de Gange, her mother-in-law, with every demonstration of tenderness. This lady, who usually resided at Montpellier, but was now on a visit to her son, possessed many excellent qualities, and the party thus assembled at the gloomy old château enjoyed their sojourn far more than some of them, at least, expected. The three brothers behaved to the Marchioness with studied respect—her husband with marked affection—while the Abbé and Chevalier, carefully abstaining from all such advances as had justly offended the Marchioness, did their utmost to promote the general good humour and hilarity.

Madame de Gange was entirely deceived by this unlooked-for calm. She began to believe that happy days were yet in store for her. But her gentle, trustful nature was no match for the dark and traitorous spirits with whom she had to deal.

After a few pleasant weeks, old Madame de Gange returned to Montpellier. The Marquis immediately afterwards left for Avignon, but before his departure there was too much reason to believe that he took his full share in planning the hellish tragedy thereafter to be enacted.

Left thus alone with her two most cruel foes, the Marchioness's fears might have returned, but for the consummate art with which the Abbé—and under his tutelage, the Chevalier—continued to disguise their bitter hatred under every form of respectful, yet not obtrusive politeness.

When at length the crafty Abbé saw that his arts had succeeded, and that his sister-in-law's confidence had returned, he one day availed himself of an opportunity to turn the conversation on the will executed by her, the substance of which had it appears been made known—and to warn her that, so long as such a document existed, she could not expect that there could be any permanent good understanding with her husband. He expressed his fear that she still cherished a hostile feeling towards the Marquis, who, nevertheless, now anxiously desired a perfect reconciliation; and he dwelt strongly upon the necessity for removing such an obstacle as the will was likely to prove. If this were done he offered to guarantee that everything and every one should henceforth be entirely subject to her wishes—that, in fact, she should reign absolutely in the hearts of all.

So eloquently did he plead, that the Marchioness—ever inclining to the gentle and generous side—actually revoked her will, and executed another in favour of her husband.

The Abbé probably believed that there was no necessity for cancelling the declaration she had made before the magistrates. At all events, he took no pains to procure that step. He had reason to suppose that his aims had thus far completely prospered; and the monster now quietly prepared for the consummation of the frightful crime that had been resolved upon. By what arguments he induced his less inhuman brother, the Chevalier, to aid in the intended murder, was never known. The result, in any case, was to secure his full co-operation, and they now only waited for a favourable moment.

It so happened that, on the 17th May, 1667, the

Marchioness, feeling indisposed, sent to her apothecary for a draught such as she was in the habit of taking. It was sent; but, perceiving something unusual in the colour or smell, she laid it aside, preferring to use instead something from her own medicine-chest. There was no doubt that the draught from the apothecary had been intercepted and poisoned by the Abbé.

The inquiries of the latter gentleman and his brother on the following morning after the health of their sister-in-law were most affectionate, and it must have been with at least as much surprise as pleasure that they learned that her ladyship appeared to have derived much benefit from the medicament she had swallowed on the previous day!

Suspecting *her* suspicions, they decided to adopt more prompt and certain measures.

The Marchioness, who—according to custom, occasionally received visitors in her bedroom—one day assembled an unusually numerous party. She had never appeared more beautiful, nor in gayer mood; while the Abbé and Chevalier, brooding over their infernal scheme, contributed little or nothing to the wit and mirth of the circle. Rallied good-humouredly by their hostess on their unwonted distraction, the two murderers forced themselves to take sufficient part in the conversation to satisfy her. More they found impossible.

A collation being presently served, the Marchioness not only did the honours with her accustomed grace, but set the example of eating heartily. It was late before the party broke up, when the Abbé attended the guests to their carriages, while the Chevalier remained alone with the intended victim. Seated at the foot of her bed, wrapt in gloomy reverie, the man's sinister look at length began to arouse the Marchioness's fears. She concealed them, however, and continued to rally him, trying in vain to divine the secret of his demeanour.

Quickly and fearfully was she enlightened. A heavy determined step advanced along the corridor. The door was rudely opened, and the Abbé re-appeared, an altered man. In one hand he held a pistol, in the other a glass of some dark thick liquid. His eyes gleamed as might a tiger's about to bound upon its prey ; and so terrible was his aspect, that the unhappy woman, as she gazed upon him, felt her hair rise upon her head ! Closing the door behind him, he approached the bed, then, pausing for a minute, fixed his glowing eyes upon her as if he intended by this mute pantomime to announce to her his cruel purpose, and freeze his victim with horror before accomplishing it.

Meanwhile, the Chevalier, whose face wore a similar expression, drew his sword and ranged himself beside his brother. At first the unhappy lady had imagined the latter only meant to protect her, but his vengeful looks quickly dispelled this illusion.

At length the chief assassin broke the terrible silence. Speaking in a calm and low, yet determined, voice, he addressed her :—

"Madame, you must die. Choose one of the three alternatives I offer you—sword, pistol, or poison. No delay. Make your selection."

"*Die!*" gasped the unfortunate woman; "and wherefore? Of what crime have I been guilty? You decree my death—and you inflict it—but why? How can I have deserved so cruel a fate at your hands?"

No answer being returned to her agonized remonstrance, she turned to the Chevalier.

"What have I done to *you*, my dear brother, that you should be as cruel and inexorable as *he?* Surely *you* cannot have the heart to take my life! Have you forgotten the many proofs of friendship and esteem I have given you?" (She had again and again supplied him with money, and but two days before had given him a note for five hundred livres.) "If I have given you any offence, will nothing appease you but my blood?"

Far from softening the man's heart, her piteous appeals only seemed to confirm his murderous purpose. With brutal roughness he bade her accept her inevitable fate.

"*C'en est fait* (it is settled). Take your choice, Madame—or we will choose for you," was his only reply; and again the threefold means of death were set before her.

Seeing, then, that her death was resolved upon, the Marchioness—with one glance of bitter reproach, and one silent prayer to the Almighty witness of that scene of murder—took from the Abbé's hand the poisoned draught, while the Chevalier on one side, and his brother on the other, held their weapons to her breast. In swallowing the deadly liquid some drops fell upon her neck, blackening the white skin with their corrosive power.

So determined were her murderers to do their work effectually, that, observing some sediment remaining in the glass, the Chevalier collected it with a spoon, and bringing it to the brim of the goblet, offered it once more to the victim's quivering lips. She received it in her mouth, but with much presence of mind retained it there, and affecting to sink fainting on her pillow, rejected and concealed it among the folds of her *robe de chambre*.

"In heaven's name," she gasped out, "since you have taken my life, do not also destroy my soul! Send for a confessor, and let me at least expire as a Christian should!"

The two wretches withdrew, closing the door behind them, and went in search of the chaplain—a man entirely devoted to their interests—whom they despatched to the chamber of the unhappy woman.

No sooner was she alone, than the hope and desire of life aroused her to a desperate effort. Leaping to her feet, she threw over her a loose robe that lay near, and rushing to the window, which looked, from a height of twenty-two feet, upon a paved courtyard, she prepared to cast herself below.

Her dress caught, and she would inevitably have fallen head-foremost on the stones had not the chaplain arrived at the critical moment, and, catching her robe, so changed the position of her body, that, though she fell, she alighted on her feet with little harm beyond a severe shock. The miscreant priest, seeing her on the point of escaping, caught up a heavy pitcher of water, and dashed the vessel down upon her, in hopes of fracturing her skull. It fell, however, several inches distant, and once more her life was preserved. So far safe, she now grasped her long hair, and forcing it down her own throat, induced by the irritation so caused a violent sickness, which relieved her of much of the deadly drug she had been compelled to swallow.

It was essential now to complete her escape. But all the doors opening from the court were locked, and even that leading to the stables defied her efforts to open it. Suddenly an ostler made his appearance. She uttered a cry of joy.

"Save me, good friend!" she cried; "they have given me poison! Open, open, for mercy's sake, and let me find succour!"

The man, affected, supported her carefully on his arm, and conducting her through the stables, placed her in the care of some women whom he summoned to her aid.

While this was passing, the miscreant chaplain had hastened to warn his employers of their victim's flight. They followed instantly, telling all whom they met that the Marchioness had had an access of madness—an assertion to which her wild and troubled looks, bare feet, and dishevelled hair, gave strong confirmation. Ultimately her murderers overtook her, some four hundred yards from the château, near to the residence of the Sieur de Prats, where she had hoped to find efficient protection.

The Chevalier, forcing her within the gate, gave the explanation already mentioned, while the Abbé, pistol in hand, kept guard at the gate, declaring that he would kill the first who offered to interpose, the family of the sufferer not choosing that she should be seen while in her delirium. It was hoped through this delay that the poison might have time to work its full effect.

Monsieur de Prats happened to be absent, but his lady was entertaining a party of friends, one of whom, the daughter of the curé of the place, managed to convey to her, unseen by the Chevalier, a restorative draught, which somewhat allayed the thirst and fever the poison was beginning to excite. Another gave her a glass of water; but this the Chevalier dashed from her lips, declaring that there must be no interference with the " patient," with whom he alone knew how to deal, and begging that every one would leave the room.

Alone with her executioner, the unhappy woman, throwing herself on her knees, made one more effort to move his pity : she entreated him to spare what remained of her life, promising in the most solemn terms never to denounce the crime that had been intended against her, but to interpret it to the world in any manner he chose to suggest.

Her agonized entreaties, her beauty, and her sufferings, had no effect upon the monster she addressed; on the contrary, they seemed only to infuriate him more.  He drew his sword, and using it as a dagger, stabbed the unfortunate suppliant twice in her bosom.  Uttering a shriek, she sprang to her feet, and had just gained the door, when the assassin, overtaking her, dealt her five more wounds, with the last stroke breaking the weapon, the point of which remained in her shoulder.

Leaving her writhing on the ground, the wretch hurried away in search of his brother, whom he found still at his post beside the door.

" *Retirons-nous, Abbé! l'affaire est faite!*" he exclaimed.  But the other was not yet wholly satisfied, and they lingered to see what would follow on the alarm.

The guests and servants had meanwhile found the

unhappy Marchioness, bathed in blood and insensible, but still living, and, throwing up the windows, they cried aloud for surgical aid.

At this the Abbé, resolved to silence the victim at once and for ever, rushed back to the chamber, and like one who scarcely knew the desperate act he was committing, placed his pistol to her heart; but his arm was seized by Mdlle. Brunelle, and the ball passed harmlessly through the window.

The Abbé dealt the brave girl a stunning blow with his clenched fist; then, striking at the Marchioness with the pistol-butt, tried to dash out her brains. But now the women, with a combined rush, flung themselves upon him, and with pushes and furious blows, forced him from the room.

This done, one among them who knew something of surgery, extracted the point of the broken sword, and stanched the various wounds, the sufferer meanwhile displaying marvellous fortitude, and desiring the operator to apply her knee to her back in order to disengage the sword-point more readily. It seemed as if the Chevalier in his fury and confusion had failed to inflict any mortal injury.

While this was passing, the assassins, availing

themselves of the advancing night, effected their escape to Auberas, another of the Marquis's estates, about a league from the château.

In this retreat they decided to remain for the present, bitterly reproaching themselves for having done their work so imperfectly, as, not only to have failed of taking their victim's life, but to have exposed themselves to the most imminent danger.

In the meantime the authorities of De Gange had taken cognizance of the horrible affair, and, as a first precaution, surrounded the house with an efficient guard. The news spread in every direction, and from all sides the nobility and gentry of the neighbourhood hastened to offer their sympathy and kind offices to the rescued woman. The Barons de Semenez and Sinestons came among the first; and the Baron de Tressan, grand provost, started at once on the track of the murderers. But he was too late. They had escaped by sea from Pataval. We shall pursue their subsequent fortunes in an after page.

The best medical assistance France could supply being obtained from Montpellier, the Marchioness appeared to be regaining strength. Her husband, who was at Avignon, and had no doubt expected that his wife's destruction would be effected by the dumb agency of poison, expressed the most becoming indignation against her intended assassins, vowing that he himself would willingly be their executioner could no other be found. With all his rage and anxiety, it was notwithstanding noticeable that the Marquis deferred his departure for Gange, until the evening after the day on which he received the afflicting tidings. It was equally remarkable that, though he met and conversed with several intimate friends before leaving Avignon, he never once mentioned to them what had befallen!

Arrived at the château, he was received by his suffering wife with all the demonstrations of tenderness due to the most affectionate of husbands. She only uttered some gentle reproaches for having left her so long without his loving protection. Such a reception was perhaps the bitterest punishment he could have suffered. But the Marquis possessed great self-control, and gave no outward indication of compunction, seeming only to consider the physical condition of the patient, and to contribute as far as in him lay to her restoration. Observing this solicitude, the kind-hearted lady regretted even the tender reproof she had ventured upon, and besought him to forgive it, and regard those too hasty words as wrung from her rather by the pain she was enduring than from any feeling of resentment.

Encouraged by this gentleness, the Marquis ventured to moot the subject of the declaration confirming her will, which she had made at Avignon. For it appears that the vice-legate had refused the Marquis's request to register the later will made at Gange, until the declaration concerning the former had been annulled.

This, however, she firmly refused. And this imprudent step of her husband, so far from forwarding his views, gave strength and consistency to the suspicions she had already, in spite of herself, conceived respecting him.

Madame de Gange now earnestly begged to be transported to Montpellier, for the advantage of being nearer the most eminent physicians; but such was her state of prostration that her medical attendants at Gange positively refused to allow the attempt to be made.

On the day succeeding the Marquis's arrival, the Marchioness's mother, Madame de Rossan, arrived at the château with a party of friends. Nothing could exceed her astonishment at finding her son-in-law, not only at his wife's bedside, but evidently on the most affectionate footing with her. She was fully per-suaded of the man's perfidy and cruelty, but proof was wanting; and such was the disturbance his presence excited in her mind that she found it impossible to re-main, and after a stay of only three days, took her leave.

The poor patient now desired to partake of the last sacraments of the Church ; but what were her surprise and alarm when she recognised in the priest who prepared to administer the holy rite the person who had sought to arrest her flight! Fearing that he might even attempt to poison her by means of the sacred wafer, she insisted that he should partake of it with her, and this was done.

From this moment she occupied her moments of relief in imparting to her little son those sentiments of piety and faith in which she herself had found such consolation, and which, coming from lips about to close for ever, would, she hoped, be more deeply impressed upon his mind.

The parliament of Toulouse now appointed Mons. de Catalan, Seigneur de Masquères, their commis-sioner to interrogate the dying lady. Dismissing every one from the chamber, this gentleman sought to obtain from her the full history of what had occurred, and with some difficulty succeeded.

The Marchioness stated that she had visited Gange with strange reluctance, and that the misery she had undergone in that fatal house struck her, even in remembrance, with a mortal terror. She entreated to be at once removed from it, and the commissioner promised that her wishes should be complied with.

It was, however, too late. That night her pain increased. She became delirious, then sank into stupor; and next morning, May 5th, surrounded by her weeping attendants, passed quietly away.

Thus, in the very prime of beauty, and in all respects a model of womanly excellence, died, the victim of two dastard assassins, the fairest woman of her time.

Without an hour's delay, M. de Catalan issued his warrant for the arrest of the Marquis, who was still in the neighbourhood. The latter declared that he had intended to pursue to the death the murderers of his beloved wife. He was conveyed to the prison at Montpellier; and, arriving at night, found the city illuminated that he might be better seen, while the populace, lining the streets, pursued him with hooting and imprecations, till the gaol-doors shut him from their sight.

The women of Montpellier seemed to regard the

murder of the Marchioness as an injury to the entire sex, and went into mourning as for one of royal blood.

A *post-mortem* examination showed that the unhappy lady had not succumbed to her wounds, but to the deadly effects of the poison, which had destroyed the coats of the stomach, and even blackened her brain! That her constitution should have resisted for nineteen days such cruel injuries, caused the greatest astonishment. It was said that she had never, in her brightest and happiest time, appeared half so lovely as in those last days of agony.

Her mother, Madame de Rossan, took possession of all the property, in accordance with the will executed at Avignon, and now devoted herself entirely to the duty of bringing to justice the murderers of her child.

She published a " mémoire " or petition, setting forth, with much legal ability, the reasons which existed for regarding the Marquis as an accomplice in the crime. This document, much too long for insertion, was replied to by the Marquis in another " mémoire," which, though brief, provoked considerable discussion among the magistrates conducting the process. It is true that, although no human being entertained the slightest doubt of his guilt, there was a certain lack of actual proof; and on this the Marquis dwelt with all the earnestness of a man who feels that his life hangs upon a thread.

In the end the Court adopted that middle course which is the last resort of bewildered human judgment, and decreed as follows :—

" That the Abbé and Chevalier de Gange, for the crimes proved in the process, should be broken alive on the wheel. That the Marquis de Gange should be degraded from nobility, his goods forfeited to the crown, and his person condemned to perpetual exile. And that the priest Perrette should be stripped of his clerical habit, and be sent to the galleys for life."

The last-named wretch died in his fetters before reaching Toulouse.

Great dissatisfaction was felt and expressed at the comparatively lenient sentence passed upon the guilty husband. But a short time, however, was to elapse before he was summoned to a higher judgment.

The Marquis and the Chevalier escaped to Venice, and offering their swords to that Republic, were sent to the relief of Candia, at that time in the twenty-second year of its siege by the Turks. Here, in a few weeks, the Chevalier was killed by the explosion of a bomb, and three days later the Marquis, while fighting with valour, in a sally from the town, was slain by the springing of a mine under the party he commanded, a death too glorious for men so soiled with crime. Readers may remember the remark of Maréchal de Villars, who when informed that Maréchal de Berwick had been slain by a cannon-ball before Philipsbourg quietly replied—

"Monsieur de Berwick was always in luck!"

The fate of the miscreant Abbé was of a different kind. He had escaped to Holland, and repaired to Vianne, a district near Utrecht, under the rule of the Count de la Lippe. Having changed his name and embraced the Protestant faith, he was introduced to the Count by a friend, as a French gentleman of rank and merit, and was received with all the distinction such a character deserved.

The Count was highly pleased with his new acquaintance, and recognising in him a person of refined manners and excellent understanding, confided to him the education of his eldest son, then nine or ten years of age.

By his care of this youth the latter grew up to be an estimable and accomplished man, and the Abbé received numerous marks of gratitude and regard from the Count and Countess and all their household. But he was far from being at peace. The stings of a guilty conscience were never blunted, and he groaned inwardly under a vague perpetual fear. It was very soon to be realized.

Some French political refugees, who desired to take up their residence at Vianne, and build dwellings there, demanded a formal permission from the chief legal authority of the place. That gentleman referred them to the Count himself, hinting at the same time that it would do their cause no harm were they to engage in their interests a certain Monsieur de la Martellière, in whom the Count reposed the highest confidence. This was the Abbé, who had adopted that name.

The wily churchman, however, fearing that he might be recognised by one or other of the new comers, dissuaded the Count from granting their request.

By this time his influence with the latter had so greatly increased that he scarcely took any measure of importance without consulting the Abbé. In the midst of this seeming prosperity a change occurred. The Abbé had the misfortune to become attached to an amiable young lady, a cousin of the Countess, and sought her hand. But the Countess inflexibly opposed the union. In vain they sought to overcome her objections.

" The Sieur de la Martellière," she replied, " seems a very worthy man. We owe him much, and readily acknowledge his high desert. But he is a kind of Melchisedec! We know nothing of his origin. His manners are courtly, and it is impossible to believe him to be of obscure birth. Still we do not choose to risk a mésalliance. When he leaves us, we shall present him with an acknowledgment proportioned to his great services; but the honour of our house compels us to refuse his present claim."

The young lady saw that remonstrance was in vain. She did not, however, abandon her resolution to marry the Abbé; but confined herself for the present to reporting to him the conversation that had passed.

The Abbé pondered deeply upon the course he should pursue, and finally adopted the most extraordinary, and manifestly the worst for his own interests, he could possibly have selected.

He had come to the conclusion that by frankly revealing his lineage, he would overcome the difficulty started by the Countess, and that in gratitude for his service to the family he would be able to command forgiveness of his horrible crime.

He demanded an audience of the Countess.

Alone with her in the cabinet he cast himself at her

feet, asking pardon for recalling to her recollection his faithful services, and entreating to know by what fault of his he had now the misfortune to find her opposing his dearest wishes.

"Monsieur," returned the Countess, "my lord and I are deeply sensible of all we owe you. But be just to yourself. Confine yourself, I beg, to demands such as we may concede. You shall have no reason to doubt our gratitude; but cease, I pray you, from urging an alliance to which we cannot consent. We are ignorant of your parentage, and the mystery with which you have thought fit to surround it, leaves room to believe that it may be the reverse of noble."

"Madame," said the Abbé, resolutely, "if I could make myself known to your highness without incurring your resentment, you would at least own that on the score of birth no obstacles exist to my desire." He paused a moment.

"Speak, sir," said the Countess, encouragingly.

"Know then, Madame, that you see before you that unhappy Abbé de Gange, whose crime has made his name as familiar as it is infamous."

The Countess started, and recoiled as from a venomous reptile.

"But, Madame," he continued hastily, "I have

deeply and bitterly repented of that horrible deed; and my conduct and teaching during the many years I have been honoured with your confidence may prove to your highness the sincerity of that repentance. Let me implore——"

"Begone, man!" exclaimed the Countess, her eyes flashing, and her finger, with which she pointed to the door, trembling with passion. "Leave me this instant. *You* that monster? That atrocious coward and murderer, the Abbé de Gange? Your hateful name soils every lip that utters it. Great heaven! that we should have confided to such a human fiend the training of our child! Begone, I say, and without a word!" He went.

Even more indignant than his lady, the Count de la Lippe was with great difficulty restrained from at once giving up the refugee assassin to the laws. As it was, the man was commanded to quit the country without an hour's delay.

Repairing to Amsterdam he obtained a subsistence by teaching languages, being occasionally assisted secretly by his former pupil, to whom at least he had been an excellent preceptor.

The young lady to whom he had paid his addresses subsequently followed him to Amsterdam, where they were married, and resided in much comfort for several years, considerably enriched by a fortune that, in a short time, devolved upon the lady.

Ultimately the Abbé, whose later life had been without a stain, died in good repute, and not a little regretted by the friends among whom he had moved.

To one of the most trusted of them the unhappy man confessed that his life had been troubled by constant visions of his victim, as she appeared in the cruel moment at which he offered her a choice of death. At these times he suffered from an indescribable horror. It was, he declared, impossible to conceive such a " syndérèse."*

The daughter of the murdered Marchioness married the Marquis de Perrard, aged seventy-two, who had once vainly wooed her grandmother !

The young Marquis de Gange entered the army, and distinguished himself on many occasions, proving himself, in every characteristic except bravery, the reverse of his unfortunate sire.

---

* A word, without synonym in English, signifying an impression of remorse and horror combined.

# VII.

## "IT WILL OUT."

STUDENTS of classic literature may remember that when the Emperor Caracalla invited Papinianus to justify the fratricide of which he, Caracalla, had been guilty, that polite jurisconsult replied that the murder of one's brother was an act more easy to commit than to excuse.

Some time before this, Papinianus' conscience had like to have been put to a still severer test. Caracalla had accompanied his father, Severus, to Britain; and, riding one day in his train, under the control of a frightful impulse, drew his sword to assassinate him. A cry from some one induced the intended victim to turn his head. At his look, Caracalla's weapon stole back to its sheath. That evening Severus summoned his son to his chamber; Papinianus and Castor stood beside him, and on the table lay a naked sword.

"If, my son, you desire my life," said the old Roman, sternly, "take it now, and here—not in the light of day and before mankind.　If you want courage for such a deed, here stand two men whom I, their emperor, have commanded to obey you."

What mild censure would have emanated from the worthy Papinianus had the offer been accepted, can only be matter of conjecture.　Caracalla, as we know, turned out so excellent a son, that when at length Severus died the natural death of age, he put to death the entire medical staff, whose exertions had failed to prolong his parent's days.

Solon and Romulus, whose criminal codes embraced every imaginable delinquency, assigned no unusual penalty to parent-murder — in a noble pretence of doubt that so foul a crime could stain the annals of humanity.　Unhappily, as ages rolled on, it became apparent that the malignity of human passions re-cognised no such limit; whereupon said Cicero (*pro Roscio Amerino*), "Since there is no law so sacred that man's audacity shall not violate it, those whom nature cannot restrain must be deterred by terror-striking punishment."

The Roman law ordained that such a criminal be enclosed in a leathern sack, together with a dog, a cock, a viper, and an ape (the first to signify the parricide more brute than man; the second as type of a wild libidinous nature; the third in allusion to the pain which was believed to accompany its nativity; the last because its half-human features destroyed the sole remaining distinction), and with these companions flung into the nearest river.

In later times, the law of almost every nation has annexed to the usual penalties of murder some circumstance of obloquy calculated to mark its detestation of this horrible form of turpitude.

In this country an exceptional punishment—burning alive—was, as in the case of husband-murder, sometimes applied.

At York, in 1705, Mary Coole was convicted of parricide. In her defence she boldly asserted that her crime was no worse than that of the Parliament of England, who had destroyed the king their father; or of the queen, who had permitted hers to die in exile. She was deprived of her tongue and hand, and condemned to the stake.

In France, much later, this crime—even the intention of it—was punished by cutting off the hand; after which the culprit was broken alive on the wheel, his body burned, and the ashes scattered to the winds. And such was the inevitable penalty at the period when the following remarkable case was added to the black archives of French crime.

The 16th of October, 1712, a fête-day in the little town of St. Barnabé near Marseilles, was, moreover, a day of reconciliation in the family of the Sieur de Salis, a retired officer of distinction, inhabiting a handsome villa just beyond the town.

This gentleman's family consisted of seven children—viz., two daughters (professed nuns) and five sons: Antoine (a lieutenant in the navy), Jean-Baptiste, François-Guillaume, Etienne-Gayetan (in the army), and Louis-César, a lad of thirteen.

M. de Salis, at forty, had married a woman twenty-two years his junior—very beautiful, but of a violent, implacable temper. Their married life had consequently been one series of bitter quarrels and hollow reconciliations. In all these, Madame de Salis had never lost sight of one especial object — that of weakening the bonds of duty and affection between the children and their father, and attaching the former exclusively to herself; an aim in which, as will be seen, she had been but too successful.

On the day above mentioned, M. de Salis had been induced to forgive his second son, Jean-Baptiste, a grave dereliction of duty, in having married, without consent, the pretty penniless daughter of M. Senelon, curate of the parish.

The reconciliation was, however, complete ; and the old gentleman had insisted upon his son's remaining to dinner, though engaged to partake of that meal with his father-in-law.

The dinner had passed off with unwonted good humour and cordiality, and Madame de Salis had withdrawn to her own apartment, when François-Guillaume, intending to go to the fête, applied to his father for some money for the purpose. Now it was one of the mother's plans for maintaining her ascendancy with the children, to be herself their purse-bearer. Her husband, therefore, unprepared for his son's request, and having indeed but little to spare, tendered him a coin of such modest value that the latter conceived himself insulted.

This may seem a trifling cause for anger. In point of fact it was but the breaking forth of that hidden fire which had never ceased to smoulder in the hearts of all the sons against their unhappy father.

The latter becoming irritated in his turn, words rose higher and higher ; others (especially the newly-pardoned Jean-Baptiste) joined in the quarrel ; and finally, Madame de Salis, rushing in, and taking the part of her sons, increased their fury tenfold.  At length François-Guillaume, not content with vituperating his father, in his maniacal rage drew his sword.

At this last outrage M. de Salis started from his seat, and summoning a Turkish servant — one Hassan Ali—bade him saddle a horse, loudly declaring his intention to proceed straight to Marseilles and lodge a formal complaint against his unnatural children.

Not reflecting that the parent who threatens most loudly is often the slowest to execute, and completely blinded by passion, Madame de Salis exhorted her sons to oppose their father's exit, assuring them that, should he do as he had threatened, their ruin was inevitable.

The old gentleman persisting, a desperate struggle commenced, the maddened woman actually dragging him back by the hair of his head, while the sons secured his arms and legs.  Thus overpowered, he was flung to the ground, and, in falling, received on the forehead a wound so severe as almost to render him unconscious.  Rallying a little, the unhappy father appealed in touching terms to his cowardly assailants.

“ What have I done to you boys, that you treat me as though I were your deadly enemy ? If you have ceased to obey and honour me as a father, at least remember that we are still united in a common humanity. Look at these grey hairs ! Will my own children be my murderers ?”

Finding his remonstrances produce no effect, M. de Salis now uttered a loud, lamentable cry ; and it was probably in attempting to stifle this that Jean-Baptiste grasped him so tightly by the throat as to reduce him to complete insensibility. In fact, whether or not he died at this instant was never fully known. What is certain is, that the guilty band felt they had now gone too far to recede ; and, with clutching, convulsive hands, and—it was said—the sword of François-Guillaume, made their horrible work complete.

During the frightful scene, the younger son, Louis-César, had crouched weeping in a corner, longing, but not daring, to succour his father. For a similar reason, the Turkish servant had remained inactive. The only other domestic, Susanne Borelli, was absent at the fête.

No sooner was the parricide consummated than dismay succeeded. The actors in this tragedy, disordered, breathless, flecked with blood, stood gazing in each other's white faces, as though they wist not what next to do. The bright autumn sun streamed in full upon the recumbent figure of their victim. They almost recoiled before the mute inquisitor; but, as yet, there was no voice of vengeance. "Patient, because eternal," says Tertullian.

The instinct of self-preservation soon aroused them to action; and she whose influence had brought about the deed, was the first to regain sufficient self-command to take measures for averting its consequences. Aware that the chief danger lay in the chance of some one of the party, in the first horror of what had passed, involuntarily betraying himself and the rest, she assumed a calmness she was far from feeling, and affected to treat the matter in the light of a mere misadventure.

She had the firmness to search her husband's pockets, and take his keys and money. Of the latter, she gave a portion to François-Guillaume, desiring him to go, as he had proposed, to the fête; but to return early, and help in " putting things to rights."

She ordered Jean-Baptiste and Hassan Ali to convey the body to a chamber on the top floor, and bring the key to her.

Her next step was a bold one. She sent Louis-César to the curate, M. Senelon, requesting his attendance ; and, on his arrival, quietly informed him that his son-in-law Jean-Baptiste and François-Guillaume had killed their father.

Madame de Salis had judged M. Senelon aright. Horror-stricken as he was, he could not bring himself to denounce the husband of his child. Compelled therefore to aid the concealment of that atrocious crime, he suggested that the body should be placed in bed, and that it should be given out that M. de Salis had died of apoplexy.

On learning, however, that the marks of violence were too apparent for this explanation, the curate proposed that the body should be let fall from an upper window into the garden, dressed as it was, and with the finger still retaining the ring of a bird-cage which usually hung outside, and in striving to reach which it might be surmised that M. de Salis had over-balanced himself and fallen. Having, as it were, forced himself to give this advice, the curate turned to withdraw; but pausing on the threshold, spoke a parting word—

" Though I have consented—against my conscience and my duty—to aid in the present concealment of this unnatural and horrible deed, be sure that no human craft or caution will secure your permanent safety. Prepare yourselves, by your future lives, for the inevitable judgment, even of man. Preserve your secret with what fidelity you may, mark my warning— *it will out!*”

Now was seen a curious feature of humanity. Jean-Baptiste, who had been foremost in the murderous assault, trembled from head to foot at the very thought of the fresh indignity he was called on to inflict upon the senseless corpse. He at first positively refused to lay a finger on the body; and it required all his mother’s influence to overcome his repugnance. As it was, he was seized with a deadly sickness in the act; and the dishonoured frame that fell prone among the crushed flowers was hardly more livid and corpse-like than he who dropped it there. As for Madame de Salis, who had by this time regained all her natural self-possession, she neglected nothing that might further the deceit. She threw her husband’s hat into the garden; and then going down to her hen-house, killed some fowls, and sprinkled the blood about the prostrate body.

In a few minutes shrieks and cries warned the neighbours that something had happened at the house of De

Salis ; and these, rushing in, found the family in the act of lifting up the body from the earth. It was placed upon the nearest couch, amidst tears and plaints; and every means for restoring animation resorted to with well-acted assiduity. These exhausted, Madame de Salis gave herself up to the wildest grief, tearing her hair, and exhibiting every token of despair; the rest, each according to his several gift, imitating as best they might.

A magistrate now arrived, and, attended by two surgeons, examined the body. Not the slightest suspicion of foul play visited their minds. The medical men reported that M. de Salis had died from injuries received in an accidental fall; and the bereaved family were quickly left to the free indulgence of their sorrow.

This satisfactory proceeding removed a great source of anxiety. The whole party, excepting the young Louis-César, assembled at supper with renewed courage, the mother assuring them that, were they but true to themselves, their future life would be far happier and more peaceful than hitherto.

Matters did go on for some months with a tranquillity hitherto foreign enough to that unhappy home, when a little cloud made its appearance above their horizon.  M. de Salis had possessed but slender means beyond the provision he received from Government.  The family soon began to feel the pressure of poverty; and, finding their resources all but exhausted, the sons—with the exception of Antoine, already provided for—wrote a joint letter to their uncle, the Count de Salis, describing in touching terms their destitute position, and entreating his influence to ameliorate it.  In answer to their application, the Count conferred on the family a pension of six hundred livres a year.

In this interval, certain suspicions having arisen in the minds of the two absent sons, Antoine the sailor and Etienne-Gayetan the soldier, these two arranged a joint visit to their home; and, taking their youngest brother apart, subjected the lad to so close and searching an examination, that he ended by divulging the horrible secret, and describing minutely the tragedy of which he had been a witness.  Then followed a family consultation, in which fresh pledges for the concealment of the secret were exchanged; and these would probably have been observed, had not the allowance granted by the Count proved a source of fatal division.  Madame de Salis insisted that this money should be paid over to her, as most competent to use it for the general benefit. To this her sons, who had ceased to treat her with their wonted deference, demurred; and the party separated, Madame de Salis repairing to Aix, Guillaume-François and Etienne-Gayetan remaining at St. Barnabé, Jean-Baptiste and Louis-César taking up their residence at Marseilles.

It was not without opposition from Jean-Baptiste that Etienne-Gayetan took possession of the paternal mansion, &c. The latter's object, however, had not been a selfish one. He was a good economist, and believed himself capable of developing the resources of the little property for the advantage of all. An angry correspondence followed between the brothers, and arrived at such a point that Etienne-Gayetan was induced to remind his elder, that not only the latter's fortunes, but his life, were at the mercy of the man he vilified. Jean-Baptiste was of violent and headstrong disposition. The threat only enraged him the more. Whether he was transported beyond himself, or whether he secretly believed that his brother would never take the step at which he darkly hinted, at all events he replied with disdain and defiance. Thereupon Etienne-Gayetan seized his pen, and, with pulses still throbbing, wrote to an old comrade of his father's—the Marquis de Montolieu—a precise detail of the frightful transaction.

Scarcely had the Marquis read and reflected on this startling communication, when a visitor was announced—Louis-César. What precisely passed at this interview never appeared. It ended, however, in the lad's dismissal, carrying with him the letter, and a verbal caution to Jean-Baptiste, which the Marquis probably believed would suffice to induce the accused either to stand forward and clear himself, or to rid the country of his presence.

Jean-Baptiste resolved to attempt the former. In great alarm he wrote hastily to the Marquis, and with much ingenuity and no small eloquence, cast the whole guilt of the murder upon his mother and his brother Guillaume-François. Here were already two traitors to the guilty compact. Another quickly succeeded.

Madame de Salis, made aware of the quarrels among her sons and the threats of Etienne-Gayetan, became extremely uneasy. She lost sleep and appetite. Her mind perpetually recalled the scene of murder, with sensations of horror and dread such as had not accompanied the act itself. A consciousness of impending vengeance associated itself with every idea that crossed her mind, with every habitual movement of the day, with every nightly vision. At length, in despair of other means of saving herself, she wrote to the Count de Salis, her brother-in-law, revealing the bloody deed in all its atrocity, but laying it to the charge of Jean-Baptiste alone.

The horror with which her correspondent received this information may be conceived. It was some time before he could collect himself sufficiently to make any reply. When he did so, it was conceived in the following terms :—

" I forward to you, my dear sister, a letter which has been addressed to me under your seal. It is probably from some enemy who has copied your handwriting so skilfully that one might almost swear it was your own. Destroy it forthwith, and be careful to give no grounds for attacks of such a character from any one whomsoever. I shall write to my brother's old friend, the Marquis de Montolieu, recommending my nephews to his care, in the hope that he may be able to reconcile their differences, and recall them to their filial duty."

Meanwhile the letter of Jean-Baptiste to M. de Montolieu had thrown the latter into the greatest consternation. Of the murder he entertained not the slightest doubt.   The question which perpetually suggested itself to his conscience was, whether, or for how long, he should suffer the actors in a crime of such atrocity to pollute society with their presence. After much consideration, he resolved to confide the matter to an intimate friend, the Marquis de Cavoy; and accordingly, to him he transmitted the whole fatal history, intimating at the same time his determination to isolate the guilty family from society.

The Marquis de Cavoy immediately communicated with the Count de Salis, proposing to use their united influence to obtain a decree of banishment.   But to this the Count objected that his object—that of keeping the matter quiet—would be defeated, as the King would infallibly inquire the grounds of the application for the *lettre de cachet*, and on learning them, would, with equal certainty, deliver the criminals into the hands of justice.   He promised, however, to write a soothing letter to M. de Montolieu, and also to restore peace in the divided family.

Up to this moment, it will be seen, the prudence and sagacity of·the Count de Salis had averted the danger that had been caused by the imprudence of Madame de Salis and her sons.   But divine justice had decreed the revelation of the crime, and brought about this result in an unexpected manner.

The Count de Salis, before permitting his friend the Marquis de Cavoy to depart, had exacted from him a promise to destroy the letter of M. de Montolieu, which he had left in his cabinet. On returning home, the Marquis, mindful of his promise, took out the letter and placed it in his pocket, intending to burn it in a brasier in the hall. As he entered that apartment, a servant announced a messenger from the minister of justice, M. de Pontchartrain, who desired to see him instantly on a political matter of importance, on which they had already several times conferred.

De Cavoy hastened to the minister's residence, and a discussion, which drove the business of the morning entirely from his mind, ended in M. de Pontchartrain requesting his friend to leave with him all the papers connected with the subject of their consultation, and to visit him again on the following day.

An hour later, as the statesman still sat in meditation, the documents before him, a strange expression in one of them chanced to catch his eye—*" atrocious murder."* He took up the paper, and read it from beginning to end. It was the letter of the Marquis de Montolieu !

It at once occurred to the astute minister that his friend had purposely chosen this manner of bringing the affair to his knowledge, with the view of avoiding the painful duty of coming forward as actual informer. In any case, however, M. de Pontchartrain felt that there was but one course open to him ; and this he at once adopted. Going straight to the palace, he laid the matter before the King. The latter, struck with horror, directed that the parties should be immediately arrested, and that M. Lebret, president of Provence, and M. Lagarde, procureur-general, should take measures for bringing them to condign punishment.

Early on the succeeding day M. de Cavoy, having discovered the loss of his letter, made his appearance in some disorder at the minister's house, and desired leave to examine the documents he had left. M. de Pontchartrain at once informed him of what had been done, mentioning at the same time the impression he had conceived that such a proceeding would be in accordance with his visitor's wishes, since it was not to be supposed that he (the latter) would knowingly cast a veil over so horrible a crime. M. de Cavoy retired without reply.

It so happened that M. Lagarde was supping at the house of M. le Bret when the missive conveying the king's commands was delivered to the latter. Both these gentlemen had been personally acquainted with M. de Salis and. his family; both were alike thunderstruck at the startling intelligence.

M. Lagarde avowed his entire disbelief. That Madame de Salis was possessed of a warm temper had been pretty generally known; but that this lady, and her orderly and seemingly dutiful children, should have been guilty of such a diabolical crime, appeared positively incredible.

His host agreed with him. It was now eight months since this supposed murder. The magistrates had attended at the time; the surgeons had made their report. Such charges were not unprecedented, as the work of secret slanderers who had a grudge against some unfortunate family.

But on M. Lagarde's arriving at his own house, he found a communication awaiting him from M. de Pontchartrain, in which the crime, with all its details, was fully set forth. He was enjoined to lose not a moment in securing the murderers; and accordingly issued the necessary directions, in pursuance of which lieutenant of police Bonnet, with an escort of archers, proceeded to St. Barnabé, and, quietly surrounding the house, arrested the two sons, Guillaume-François and Etienne-Gayetan, in their beds.

Finding that Jean-Baptiste and Louis-César were still at Marseilles, Bonnet induced his prisoners to write to their brothers, proposing a general family council, for the arrangement of their affairs; and that they should, for that purpose, come on the morrow to St. Barnabé.

Bonnet himself, attended by three archers in disguise, was the bearer of this missive, and, on reaching the residence of the brothers, met Jean-Baptiste in the act of going out. The latter perused the note with an air of doubt and perplexity; and, after a minute's hesitation, returned a verbal answer, to the effect that if his brothers desired a conference, they had better come to *him* at Marseilles. Thereupon Bonnet placed both brothers in the custody of his archers.

But a few hours elapsed before the indefatigable lieutenant made his appearance in the apartment of Madame de Salis, at the house of her friend, M. Aillaud, of Aix. On learning his errand, the unhappy woman fell into a paroxysm of grief and terror. She clung to a pillar, crying out that she would not quit the house without a promise that she should have an interview with the procureur-general. The latter was appealed to, and acceded to her wish; but the interview, at which several persons were present, led, as might be expected, to no result beneficial to the prisoner; and she was then lodged in the prison at Marseilles, within whose gloomy walls she encountered her four sons.

The King now reiterated his commands that the process should be commenced without a day's delay. But in the brief interval that necessarily ensued, no care had been taken to separate the accused from each other. In consequence they had concerted a line of defence which threatened, at the first interrogation, if adhered to, to defeat the ends of justice.

The first important witness was the Turk, Hassan Ali, who deposed that the death of his master was occasioned by a fall from the window while feeding a pet bullfinch.

This dreaded witness having thus delivered himself, a zealous friend of the accused hastened to smuggle him away into a place of concealment. Something, however, in the man's demeanour had awakened suspicion in the mind of the experienced procureur-general. He sharply censured the lieutenant for not having included this witness among his prisoners.

The lieutenant replied that, the minister of justice having limited his instructions to the arrest of the mother and sons—while aware of the presence at the death-scene of Hassan Ali—he, Bonnet, had naturally concluded that there was a certain object in thus leaving the man at liberty. The matter was quickly settled through the imprudence of the Turk himself, who, venturing from his retreat, was re-arrested, and lodged in gaol.

In the meantime the second witness, Susanne Borelli, had undergone examination, but had revealed nothing of importance. It was manifestly on Hassan Ali that the prosecution would be compelled to rely. To extort the truth from him all legal means were speedily put in action. He passed through two protracted interrogatories without approaching a jot nearer to the truth. It was then resolved to place him in a dungeon, upon bread-and-water; and the effect of this system was soon apparent.

Hassan Ali purchased an improved state of things by denouncing Guillaume-François as the parricide, and faintly implicating Jean-Baptiste. These two were consequently placed in separate cells. But here the matter seemed to rest. So long as both were silent, the testimony of Hassan Ali was innocuous.

Five months elapsed, when the Turk suddenly requested leave to amend his former statement; and now exonerated Madame de Salis and Guillaume-François, declaring that Jean-Baptiste alone was guilty.

In addition to this testimony, other parties came forward to declare that Madame de Salis had expressed her intention to practise upon her husband with some slow poison, that should at least confine him to his bed, and thus leave her the sole direction of the household.

This was confirmed by Jean-Baptiste, who acknowledged that his mother had on several occasions sent him to purchase the drugs—which, however, the chemist had refused to furnish.

Finding the tide set so strongly against her—and inspired, above all, with resentment against Jean-Baptiste—Madame de Salis now resolved to take her turn at confession, and accordingly denounced the former as the sole assassin. She declared that her only reason for reserve had been a natural reluctance to betray her son to the scaffold; but that since

Hassan Ali had evidently been tampered with on his behalf, and been prevailed on to inculpate herself and Guillaume-François, she now resolved to declare the truth.

Invited to reconcile this statement with her letter to M. de Montolieu, she denied the inferences attempted to be drawn from the latter—and (for M. de Montolieu had died in the interval) this point was abandoned.

The mother and son were now confronted. The latter uttered no reproach; he listened in silence to her deposition; then addressed her, in a low, quiet tone, as follows—

" Can you in your conscience, mother, persist in a statement that casts upon *me*—the least guilty—the whole burden of such a crime ? Was it not Guillaume-François who drew his sword upon my father ? Did not you yourself, at the first commencement of the quarrel, rush from your apartment, seize our victim by the hair, and, when he was flung to the ground, assist in trying to strangle him ? Was it not Guillaume-François who struck him on the temple with the sword, while I in vain strove to stanch the flowing blood ?"

His mother hung her head without reply; and

now the other two brothers, Guillaume-François and Louis-César (the guilty and the innocent), added their testimony, the general effect of which was to exonerate their mother, and to lay the crime on Jean-Baptiste.

The process, which had lasted nearly twelve months, at length terminated with the following decree :—

" Jean-Baptiste—guilty of murder and parricide—condemned to have both hands cut off; his arms, legs, thighs, and body to be bruised and broken ; afterwards to be fixed upon the wheel, there to linger so long as God shall please ; after which, his body to be burned and scattered to the winds. A fine of ten livres to the king.

" Guillaume-François, the same, sparing one hand.

" Louis-César—guilty of not interposing — condemned to be present at the execution of his brothers; then to perpetual banishment.

" Madame de Salis—for aiding in the murder—sentenced to decapitation.

" Hassan Ali—for failing to assist his master—to stand for two hours in the pillory.

" Etienne-Gayetan and Susanne Borelli, acquitted."

An appeal having been subsequently made against the sentence, the whole of the prisoners were conveyed to Aix, where the mother was lodged in a chamber of the Conciergerie, and the brothers Jean-Baptiste and Guillaume-François in separate cells.

The case had by this time created an extraordinary sensation; and when at length the judgment on appeal was delivered, the greatest anxiety was evinced by all ranks to obtain a place of hearing. The imposing hall of the Palais de Justice was crowded with persons of the highest distinction, not a few of whom were connected by family ties with the accused. The decree confirmed, with some slight modifications, the former sentence.

It was expected that Madame de Salis would have fallen into a transport of passion and despair; on the contrary, she bowed her head submissively, only murmuring—

" *On ne me rend pas justice* " ("They do not do me justice ").

Justice, that is, to her crime; for it appeared that her conscience was now fully awakened, and that she desired only to make what atonement was possible to God and man.

The condemned persons met in an adjoining apartment.   They were to see each other but once again—on the scaffold.   At six o'clock they were to die.

Jean-Baptiste, holding up his heavy chains with both hands, knelt at his mother's feet, and entreated pardon for the testimony he had been compelled to give.

Madame de Salis knelt likewise, embraced her son, and assured him of her complete forgiveness.   Then, addressing her children generally—

"They are about," she said, "to separate these mortal frames; but our souls, let us humbly trust, shall be reunited in heaven.   Thank we God, who has brought us to this just and merciful condemnation.   Think no more of the life we quit, but of that to which we hasten; and follow me, my children.   *I* led you to this guilt; *I* will precede you to its punishment."

Then followed a brief dialogue between Jean-Baptiste and François-Guillaume.   The latter had preserved a somewhat sullen demeanour, and was disposed to deny his full participation in the murder.

"You will forgive me, brother," said the elder, "for having confessed the truth?"

"You have not always kept to the truth."

" You are right as to the first interrogatory, but not the latter," was the reply; "and you yourself, François, have done as much."

" Well, that is true ; and I—I wish——"

And François, melting, threw himself into his brother's arms.

" For my part," continued the latter, " I never truly believed that Heaven would suffer such an act to go unpunished.  I never passed the place of execution at Aix without repeating to myself, ' *There* I must end my life; it is but a question of days.'  There is but one thing that troubles me : the punishment is not equal to the crime.  They will but burn my corpse.  They should rather give my body living to the flame."

A Capuchin informed the speaker that he would not be left to linger on the wheel.  They would accord him the pardon-stroke.

" Still further mitigation!" exclaimed the prisoner. " Do they think I cannot bear all that my guilt deserves?  I ought to linger, not for one, but many days—ay, many weeks.  They should tear from me each day some fragment of this guilty frame.  It is my desire to breathe my last sigh in the midst of the worst pangs justice can inflict."

The wretched family engaged separately in devotional exercises for the intervening hours. At six o'clock the executioners entered the prison. Madame de Salis was the first to appear. She shed tears, but was otherwise calm and self-possessed. She frequently pressed her lips to the crucifix she carried, murmuring—

" Mother of grace, Mother of mercy, defend us from the assaults of the enemy of souls."

François-Guillaume followed. He stretched out his arms to the assistants—

" Bind these impious hands," he said, " stained with a parent's blood. They should not only be bound, but burned in a slow fire."

Madame de Salis then knelt before the altar, and uttered a prayer that touched the hearts of all :—

" My God, I offer Thee my spirit, my heart, my soul, my body; my spirit, because it dwells only upon Thee ; my heart, because it loves but Thee ; my soul, because it pants for Thy presence; my body, that it may be offered in fitting expiation for my crime. I offer Thee this head, about to fall ; and would that I had ten thousand, that I might give them all !"

The condemned exchanged a last embrace, and the procession was then formed; the two sons being placed together in one cart, their mother following, supported by the Turk, Hassan Ali, in another. An immense multitude lined the way; and although a strong body of archers escorted the procession, it had frequently to halt while room was made to pass.

Arrived opposite the church of St. Sauveur, the carts drew up before the door, in order that the usual *amende honorable* might be made. But the criminals were not required to descend. The reverend director of the Capuchins performed this humble function in their name, entreating pardon of God, the king, and the law.

The cart which bore the two brothers being the first to reach the scaffold, they were assisted to mount the steps; and the crowd, ever awake to the minutest circumstances that mark these solemn moments, did not fail to note, as a coincidence, perhaps intended by divine justice, that Guillaume-François, who had been the first to commence the fatal quarrel, was the first to set foot on the platform.

Seeing her sons ascending before her, Madame de Salis became much agitated, declaring that the authorities had broken faith with her, having promised that she should be the first to die.

Her confessor assured her it was merely a proceeding rendered necessary by the relative position of the vehicles, and pointed out to her the executioner, hastening to assist her to ascend. In another minute she was standing on the scaffold, with a serene, contented look; and, turning to the people, besought, in low humble tones, their prayers for herself and her children.

Turning to the executioner, she said, "My friend, I do not fear death; but lest, in its agony, my woman's nature should prove too weak, I pray you not to put me to any needless pain."

The executioner took off a black scarf she had hitherto worn on her head, and tied it over her eyes. She then moved in the direction of the block, and, feeling for it, knelt, and laid her head quietly down. The headsman approached his broad blade close to the slender white neck—raised it aloft—struck. The head dropped forward; but though the victim was dead, it needed the application of a knife to complete the decapitation. Head and body were placed together in a coffin, and Guillaume-François was the next summoned.

He had heard the fatal blow, although from intervening objects he had not been able to witness it, and was told that all was over. He desired to see the body. The confessor, fearing the sight would unman him, objected; but the young man persisting, he was conducted to the side of the coffin. With one deep sigh he turned away, and strode to the block, laying his right hand upon it.

" This," he said, " is my first expiation—this impious hand. Take it quickly."

The executioner struck, but so unskilfully, that the blow was not wholly effectual; and in the sudden anguish the young man uttered a loud cry. A second blow divided the quivering muscles; then Guillaume-François laid down his head. The same want of skill caused the headsman again to fail in doing his office at one blow; for though he struck with such force that the criminal was slain and the block itself overturned, it needed a second stroke to make the work complete.

Jean-Baptiste came forward with firm step and unchanged mien. The block had been removed, and a huge and heavy cross substituted. To this, his upper garments having been removed, the prisoner was now firmly bound; this done his hands were struck off, one after the other ; then the brawny headsman, seizing a ponderous iron bar, broke in succession his legs and thighs, and finally dealt him three several blows, on the stomach, chest, and throat. This last was the “ pardon-stroke,” instantly mortal.

Thus came this murder “ out.”

# VIII.

## THE TRAGEDY D'ANGLADE.

IT was in the year 1687, a period more than commonly fruitful in extraordinary crimes and social incidents of a strange, sinister character, that a splendid mansion in the Rue Royale at Paris numbered among its tenants François Comte de Montgomery and his lady, who occupied the basement and first floor, and the Sieur and Madame d'Anglade, who rented the second and third floor apartments.

The Count Montgomery was a man of wealth, keeping up an expensive establishment, and moving in the first circles of society. Mons. d'Anglade, whose means were comparatively small, was seen less frequently in the haunts of fashion, but had many friends in distinguished position, and reckoned among them his neighbours the Montgomerys.

These latter, proposing to visit their country residence at Villehousin, invited the D'Anglades to bear them company. The invitation was at first accepted, but subsequently declined, and the trivial nature of the excuse put forward was afterwards dwelt upon with great insistance in the process that was to follow.

The Count and Countess left Paris on Monday evening, September 22nd, 1687, intending to return on the succeeding Thursday. They were followed by François Gagnard, the priest Manceau, their steward, and other domestics; and the only remaining members of the household were a lady's-maid of the Countess, named Formenie, a little footboy, and four girls employed in embroidery work.

 The Montgomerys returned one day sooner than they had intended. Their reason was a singular one. On sitting down to dinner the Count had noticed a drop of blood upon his napkin, and another on his plate, the origin of which was not discoverable. The circumstance, trivial as it was, disturbed his rather superstitious mind, and, oppressed with some presentiment of evil, he at once resolved to return to Paris.

The steward, page, and valet, returned a few hours after their master.

On the same day the Sieur d'Anglade, who had been supping with the lady of President Robert, returned home at eleven o'clock, accompanied by the Abbés De Fleury and De Villars. As he entered, the Count and Countess were still at supper, and Mons. d'Anglade, pausing to pay his compliments, was presently joined by his wife, who joined in the lively conversation which followed.

The next morning, early, the Count Montgomery waited upon the Lieutenant-Criminal of Châtelet, and announced that during his recent absence a chest or coffer had been forced open, and that there had been abstracted from it thirteen bags containing 1000 livres each in silver, 11,500 livres in gold pieces of two pistoles, 100 new louis d'or, and a pearl necklace worth 4000 livres.

The lieutenant, procureur, and a commissioner, immediately proceeding to the house, made an examination which led them at once to the conclusion that the robbery could only have been effected by some one familiar with the house, and a general inquiry was resolved upon.

Mons. d'Anglade was the first to demand that his apartments should be searched, and himself conducted the lieutenant into every room in his occupation. Coffers, cabinets, drawers, &c., were opened and searched; beds were taken to pieces, pillows and mattresses pierced and sounded, but nothing suspicious was discovered, and the searchers next mounted to the garrets, Madame d'Anglade excusing herself from accompanying them further on the ground of fatigue.

In the first room, concealed in an old chest full of ragged linen, was found a rouleau of seventy louis d'or, wrapped in a genealogical paper which the Count identified as belonging to him. He declared that these pieces formed part of the hundred stolen from him, identifying them by the dates of 1686 and 1687, and now, without further ceremony, charged the d'Anglades with being concerned in the robbery, and demanded that they should be submitted to a separate interrogation. This was done, and a certain hesitation in their answers, hardly to be wondered at under the circumstances, increased the suspicions of their guilt.

Unfortunately, it so happened that Madame d'Anglade drew attention to the fact of the door of the servant's bedroom having been found unlocked, observing that this circumstance implicated the valet, and that if search were made, something might probably be found there. Search *was* made, and in a recess were found five bags containing each 1000 livres, with another, in which there wanted 219 livres of a similar sum.

" Acknowledge," said the Count, turning exultingly

to his wife, " the value of my presentiment.  Had we returned only on the day we intended, this plunder would have been removed."

No other part of the rooms occupied by the Count was searched—a remarkable omission, seeing that the recent discovery bore suspiciously upon his own domestics.  He indeed offered to be answerable for the latter; but what can be thought of the impartiality of the magistrate, who, on the discovery of the louis, turning to d'Anglade, coolly remarked—

" Monsieur, if *you* did not commit this robbery, it was *I*."

The unfortunate d'Anglades were forthwith placed in arrest, and conducted—the husband to the Châtelet, the wife to Fort L'Evêque, where they were confined in close cells, in complete isolation from the outer world.

Two days later, the process was opened.  They found themselves accused of burglary.

An important witness appeared in the person of the Count's sister, who deposed that she had seen d'Anglade near the door of the Count's valet, both before and after his master's arrival.

Another witness affirmed that d'Anglade was an habitual gambler; and a third deposed to having resided with him in a house from which some silver plate had been stolen, and never traced. Many circumstances as trivial and irrelevant as those already stated were heaped together, and it was deemed necessary to apprehend the valet and coachman of d'Anglade, and his wife's maid. The coachman was, however, set at liberty.

On the 25th October, 1687, the Grand Council stayed the process, on the ground that it charged to the accused the crime of burglary with violence, while in fact it had been effected without injury to the locks by the medium of false keys.

D'Anglade appealed against the conduct of the former process by the Lieutenant-Criminal, but the decision was adverse to him, and the case being returned to the judgment of the lieutenant, d'Anglade was placed at the further disadvantage of pleading before a magistrate whose impartiality he had arraigned.

He was soon to feel the effects of this. On the 19th January, 1688, the judge ordered that he should be submitted to the question, ordinary and extraordinary.

D'Anglade appealed to parliament.

The latter decreed that he should undergo the question as intended, but "*manentibus indiciis*"—*i.e.*, corroborative proofs still required—and the non-confession of the accused not freeing him from the charge.

Thus the unfortunate D'Anglade, although he underwent the torture without admitting a syllable of the accusation, was condemned on the strength of the testimony already obtained.

On the 16th February the following sentence was pronounced.

D'Anglade was condemned to the galleys for nine years.. His wife was banished for the same space of time. The two were fined 20 livres to the crown, 3000 livres " civil reparation," and 25,673 livres restitution to the Count Montgomery, besides the pearl necklace, or, in default of it, 4000 livres. From the sum total were to be deducted the monies recovered by the searchers, and those found on the person of the prisoner when apprehended. All costs and expenses were likewise defrayed by the accused.

D'Anglade, whose health was but feeble, appeared completely overcome and prostrated by this fatal result. Nevertheless, he was removed from the judgment-chamber only to be cast into a dark and miserable dungeon in the Castle of Montgomery, languishing in that confinement without air, comfort, or companionship, until he was conducted forth to the Château de la Tourville, and riveted to the dreaded galley-slave's chain.

In this miserable condition the man's better nature supported him; and the religious feelings that in happier times had never lost their influence, now, like friends, faithful at need, came to his aid and held him up under a weight of misery that few indeed could have supported. Not a word of revenge or hatred passed his lips. Imprisonment, the torture, the shame became indifferent to him, as he permitted his thoughts to rest on One who had suffered more, and the chain grew light to him as he gazed in thought on Him who bore the cross.

He declared that he heartily forgave those who had been instrumental in his ruin; and when, as was supposed, near his end, declared, in receiving the holy sacraments, that he was innocent of the crime imputed to him. This declaration he committed to writing.

Contrary to all expectations, the unhappy man recovered, and prepared to undergo the sentence passed upon him. It was said that the Count de Montgomery not only took measures to ensure his departure with his fellow-prisoners before he had sufficiently recovered, but even took post by the road-side in order that he might feast his eyes upon his suffering victim. The latter, too weak to travel on foot, was lifted by two men into a cart, and, at the close of the day's journey, laid on some straw in a barn or stable.

Arrived at Marseilles, he was conducted to the convicts' hospital, and it was at once evident that he would never leave it again alive. In effect, but a short time elapsed before this unhappy victim of mistaken justice yielded up his breath, maintaining to the last that deep religious sentiment that had been his stay, and commending to the care of the all-just, all-merciful Father his unfortunate wife and child. He died on the 4th March, four months after his arrival at Marseilles.

In the meantime his unfortunate wife had been undergoing cruel sufferings. Seized with painful illness, the result of the shock occasioned by their misfortune, she was reduced to the brink of the grave, and in the wretched dungeon to which she was consigned had scarcely any attendance save that of her little daughter—then about five—who, with a care and judgment beyond her years, tenderly administered to the wants of her distressed parent.

It was some time before she was allowed even the comfort of spiritual aid; but a priest was at length admitted to her; and now the poor woman, supported, like her husband, by strong religious hopes, began to resign herself with greater calmness to the fate that had overtaken her.

Her little nurse now fell ill. Her disorder was accompanied with cold perspirations, yet the poor mother was allowed neither linen nor fire. In spite of the cold of an exceptionally rigorous winter, their only source of warmth was a little pan of coals, which when exhausted was never refilled. Only at the end of five months were they removed to a better cell—which indeed had a tolerable window, but the latter being always kept closed, it was with difficulty the prisoners escaped suffocation from the fumes of their charcoal fire. But now a change was at hand.

Within a short time of the sad death of Mons. d'Anglade, certain anonymous letters were addressed to more than one person in official position, in which the writer stated that, being on the point of entering a monastery and wishing to disburden his conscience of a heavy secret, he desired to make known that the Sieur d'Anglade was completely innocent of the theft for which he had been condemned; that the real authors of the crime were one Vincent Belestre, son of a tanner at Mans, and the priest François Gagnard, almoner of the Count de Montgomery ; and that a woman named De la Comble had it in her power to throw much light on the transaction.

One of these letters was addressed to the Lieutenant-Criminal, who placed it in the hands of the exempt Dèsgrais.

Another was directed to the Countess de Montgomery, who, however, kept it secret.

A gentleman named Loysillon received a third, and this proved of much value in the process that was to follow.

The friends of the Montgomerys, however, declared these communications to be an artifice of Madame d'Anglade, the object of which was to shift from her husband the obloquy of the crime.

Measures were, however, taken by the authorities to ascertain the character and doings of Belestre and Gagnard, with the following result.

Vincent Belestre had, it appeared, while yet a mere youth, been concerned in a murder which compelled him to fly from home and friends, and assume a false name. He enlisted in the army, but in consequence of a fray, in which a sergeant of his regiment was killed, as was supposed by his hand, he deserted and became a vagabond—living by mendicancy and roguery, until, becoming acquainted with François Gagnard, his fortunes underwent a sudden change. He was known to be in the possession of large sums in gold and silver coin, wore laced clothes, and actually purchased an estate near Mans, worth from nine to ten thousand livres.

With respect to Gagnard, that worthy was ascertained to have been born in humble life, the son of a turnkey of the prison at Mans; that, having forfeited the bail he had given to answer some offence, he had fled to Paris, and there subsisted on the masses he performed at Saint-Esprit, until he entered the household of the Count de Montgomery as almoner. While in this position, he had always seemed in poverty; but on quitting it, launched into every kind of extravagance, indulging himself in the greatest luxuries, and entertaining a mistress, to whom this ornament of the priesthood appeared to deny nothing.

Upon this disclosure, the two rascals were at once apprehended; or, to speak more correctly, transferred to other custody, both being, singularly enough, in confinement on other charges—Gagnard for having been present at a recent murder, Belestre for having swindled a person from the country of five hundred livres.

The woman De la Comble made her appearance and gave most damnatory testimony as to the two accused. She was confirmed by two or three other witnesses, and yet something might still have been wanting in the chain of evidence had not the imprudence of the prisoner Belestre unexpectedly supplied it.

A witness was produced to whom some persons unknown had communicated circumstances connected with the robbery. To him Belestre petulantly remarked that he spoke under the prompting of certain persons of doubtful character—viz., one Giraut, the Abbé de Fontpeire, La Roque, and La Fonds.

From this observation the magistrates drew the inference that the parties named had been accomplices in the crime. The whole were apprehended, and the truth was at length completely revealed.

Following the advice of her guardian and representative, the child, Constance Guillemot d'Anglade, now applied to the Courts, claiming that the two accused should be declared guilty of the robbery of the Count de Montgomery, and the innocence of her father and mother be placed on public record.

It was urged that the Count had in his charge declared that the doors of his apartments had been found locked as he had left them, and must consequently have been opened with false keys. It was now proved that Belestre had manufactured such, and had purchased others at La Valée de Misere; that he had exhibited a key to one of the witnesses, pointing at the same time to a bag of money, with the remark :—

"This should be a key of gold, for it has opened my way to all you see there."

The witness having asked him to explain, Belestre stated that he had taken an impression in wax of the proper key, and fabricated the false one. In fact, this extremely candid practitioner was shown to have owned to several indifferent persons that his favourite method of becoming rich was by the use of such instruments, one of which he habitually carried about him, calling it " la gaillarde dorée."

Since the robbery, Belestre was proved to have shown to a witness one hundred louis in a bag. The latter, believing that this was part of the Count's money, listened at the keyhole of the door of a room in which Belestre and Gagnard were dining, and overheard a little dialogue.

"Eat, drink, my friend," said Belestre; "let us be jolly now Monsieur le Marquis is at the galleys."

"Nevertheless, I'm sorry for him," replied the other, with a sigh. "He was a good fellow enough, and did me many a good turn."

"Bon — bon!" exclaimed Belestre, ironically. "How can you pity a man whose ruin makes our fortune?"

They were interrupted at this point by the woman De la Comble, who brought them wine. After she had left, they expressed much uneasiness lest their talk had been overheard.

This eavesdropping witness was in fact the Abbé de Fontpeire, and the author of the anonymous letters.

The woman De la Comble, *alias* Cartaud, in whom Belestre had great confidence, deposed that he had shown her great quantities of gold and silver, besides a fine pearl necklace, at a period just subsequent to the robbery. Upon being asked where he got them, he replied, "at play."

She further stated that he had previously told her he was about to make a "coup" in company with Gagnard, who would keep everything quiet, and that a signal was to be made to him by throwing a pebble at the window. She added that, being afterwards at the Luxembourg with Belestre, the latter had sent her away, saying that some gentlemen were coming to make a division of what they had obtained, and, on retiring, she encountered Gagnard, who betrayed much embarrassment.

Interrogated as to this partition, Belestre said that he had, with Gagnard, a partnership at play. But Gagnard, questioned separately, denied that any such partnership existed.

De la Comble further deposed that Belestre had shown her a hundred louis in a leathern belt, and having reproached him with the wrong done to those from whom he had stolen it, he replied that such people were not deserving of pity, since they still possessed enough. All goods were in common. There was only the difference in the manner of taking them.

The contract for the purchase of the property recently bought by Belestre for between seven and eight thousand livres, was produced.

Many other witnesses confirmed in minor points the above testimony. It was a singular fact in connexion with this case, that during the process against the two unfortunate D'Anglades, the entire body of

Paris thieves were cognizant of the circumstance that Belestre and Gagnard were the real culprits. It was freely talked of among them, and was known even at Mans.

Gagnard, when called on for his defence, declared that he had been in the country at the time of the robbery, but had sent the keys to Belestre to enable him to forge the imitations, and had subsequently shared in the proceeds of the crime.

Belestre accounted for being in possession of so much money by stating that he had accumulated it by keeping a canteen at Courtrai, and that he had won at play of a freebooter two thousand livres. This story on investigation proved groundless.

A kind of biography of the two prisoners being about this time made public—evidently spurious, and attributed by some to the Count de Montgomery—a counter-biography was published by Mdme. d'Anglade, containing some curious details.

Pierre Vincent, it stated, was the son of a tanner at Mans. He enlisted in the regiment of Normandie, became sergeant, receiving the surname of Belestre; and being concerned in the cowardly murder of a poor tradesman at Mans, was condemned to the galleys in 1676. This was his first crime. On his release he became a robber in good earnest, and his skill and resolution soon placed him in the very first rank of the aristocracy of crime. Many of his exploits were set forth at length in the memoir, and he was shown to have passed under many different names—"Beaulieu," "La Grange," "Des Touches," "Belair," &c.

The memoir traces the history of Gagnard in like manner, and then proceeds to describe minutely the mode in which the robbery of the Count de Montgomery must have been effected.

Towards the month of December, 1690, Belestre sought out one La Combe, formerly a soldier in his regiment, and inquired of him the means of obtaining insertion of a short notice in the *Gazette d' Hollande.* La Combe, pleased to render a service to his old sergeant, introduced the latter to one Ribon, who, on payment of a crown, inserted in the journal a paper given him by Belestre, to the effect that—" There have been lately executed at Orleans two criminals, one of whom, at the last moment, confessed that he had committed the robbery at the house of the Count de Montgomery, for which the late Marquis d'Anglade was condemned to the galleys."

This paper seemed to be regarded by Belestre as a kind of passport, if not pardon, and he never stirred

without it.  It was found upon him when apprehended.

Nothing was now wanting to the conviction of
these miscreants, and their condemnation speedily
followed.

Belestre first underwent the question, but confessed
nothing.

Gagnard was less determined.  He admitted the
robbery, and added that had the magistrates who
conducted the first inquiry interrogated *him*, he was
in such confusion and perplexity that the truth would
have at once escaped him.

The innocence of the d'Anglades being thus at
length established, the parliament granted letters of
revision to that effect.

The daughter now put forward a claim for damages
against the Count, and on this point greater difficulties arose.  The process was continued for many
months, and a vast amount of legal knowledge was
brought to bear on the subject, the question turning,
substantially, on the degree of justification that might
be pleaded by the Count on the ground of circumstances certainly suspicious, though subsequently explained.

At length the Court delivered its final decree.

It discharged the memory of the d'Anglades, husband and wife, from all complicity in the alleged crime, and declared their imprisonment and the confiscation of their goods unjust and injurious. It ordered the erasure from the records of all mention of their process, and condemned the Count de Montgomery to restore certain sums calculated on the base of money seized, the sale of effects, the loss of interest, &c., and amounting in all to nearly 30,000 livres.

This decree, dated 17th June, 1693, terminated this remarkable case.

# IX.

## THE FRENCH MACHEATH.

BREATHES there the student of French annals of
the past century that would not blush crimson
in confessing that he had never heard of Cartouche?

What Cæsar was among warriors, such was the
great, the unequalled Cartouche among the most
illustrious miscreants whose names have come down
to us invested with that slightly lurid halo belonging
to superb guilt, and also with a considerable amount
of factitious lustre that never was theirs at all.
There is, it would appear, something in the character
of distinguished men of this class which dazzles and
bewilders, inducing every successive biographer to
add some bright but unauthentic touch, until at length
nothing is left of the great original save an indistinct
outline and a name.

Such a portrait was presented to the public some
twenty years ago in the three volumes entitled
" L'Histoire de la Vie et du Procès de Cartouche,"

wherein the hero is represented as an accomplished
gentleman of the bandit tribe — half belonging to
melodrama, half to opera-comique, rich in costume,
curious in arms, swelling with high and generous
sentiments, but with false ideas of honour, and maddened with ambition to achieve, at whatever cost,
renown.

He was, in reality, nothing of the kind.

The true Cartouche was, in fact, one of the most
remarkable types presented by the Parisian lower
world at the beginning of the last century. His
existence, which would at any other period have been
an impossibility, is now a fact of history, perhaps
about as well worth studying as those immortalities
of more exalted French circles, so complacently read
of in these latter days by those who have the fortune
to inhale a purer moral atmosphere.

The circumstance that such a man, established with
his band in the very heart of Paris, creating, so to
speak, a state within a state, and, not by a stroke of
genius but the mere force of circumstances, laying
under contribution high and low by means of a force
better organized for attack than that which society
commanded for defence—such a fact is not only in
itself noteworthy, but it tends to the explanation

of other points in history not easy to comprehend.

It is this which has imparted to the name of the French Macheath its lasting popularity. More than one distinguished robber, even of his own time, surpassed Cartouche in originality, in audacity, or in intelligence—Mandrin, for example; but the universal renown of Cartouche is centred permanently in the theatre of his deeds—his immortal name remains indissolubly associated with that of the queenly capital of France.

And whence shall we draw sound materials for a brief biography of this great thief?

Delessarts, in his " Procès Célèbres," has sketched some certain adventures of this hero of the gallows, but owns, with his usual candour, that they savour somewhat too strongly of romance.

St. Edme, with less honesty, copies legend after legend, ending with selections from that very untrustworthy book, "L'Histoire de la Bastille."

Similar fictions are retailed in the two great judiciary journals, and also in an article by M. Horace Raisson in the *Gazette des Tribunaux.*

The only authentic sources available to us are the parliamentary registers, and four scrolls, deposited with the archives, containing the interrogatories, confrontations, and *procès-verbaux* of the execution of several hundred malefactors between the years 1721 and 1725.

Here we discover the first part of the process against Cartouche. But alas! we must not exult too greatly. In all the 734 cases, one only is devoted to Cartouche himself. In the others, his name is either omitted, or appears mixed up indirectly with robbers of the most desperate class. There is nothing, we say with sorrow, in this large mass of evidence, &c., which reveals to us Cartouche the organizer, the soul and spirit of crime, the unclassed Cæsar—let us say, the impetuous Alexander of the streets.

Poets are not to be taken "au pied de la lettre," else might we quote Ragot de Grandval (father of a celebrated actor of that name), who somewhat misused his unquestioned gift in the concoction of "Le Vice puni," or "Cartouche," curiously illustrated by Bonnart, commencing—

> "Je chante les combats, et ce fameux voleur,
>     Qui, par sa vigilance et sa rare valeur,
>     Fit trembler tout Paris," &c. &c.

A little work by a Jesuit father, Patouillet, styled 'Apologie de Cartouche," or "Le Scélérat sans reproche," appears to have been little more than the groundwork for a theological controversy.

Such are the scanty materials with which to construct our biography; and yet they may suffice, the legal records supplying the naked, brutal facts, Barbier and the gazettes the reports and tone of feeling of the day, Grandval and Le Grand tradition, manners, and costume.

It is beyond doubt that Cartouche was born at Paris in October, 1693, and was named Louis Dominique. His birthplace was on the confines of that thickly-populated, essentially Parisian quarter, La Courtille, which comprised that portion of the town lying between the Poissonnière gate and the front of the Bastile.

According to the best authorities, Cartouche *père* was a respectable wine-seller, who had amassed by steady industry a very handsome fortune. Anxious to provide for his son a higher position in the social scale, he sent him early to the college of Clermont, where, in all probability, he found a fellow-pupil in Voltaire. At this establishment, tradition states the young hero displayed those dawnings of genius in the pilfering line, destined to ripen into the perfection of theft in its highest aspects.

It was hardly to be expected that a mind of such a stamp would long submit itself to the restraints of discipline and study, and accordingly we next light upon him in the company of a band of gipsies; who, charmed with his monkey-like agility and mischievous pranks, adopted him a child of the gang, and in-doctrinated him in many little matters which proved to him of essential service in his subsequent career.

His gipsy friends formed the most sanguine antici-pations as to his future; and well they might. The boy was a real prodigy. Bold and crafty, inventive, nimble as an ape, pliant as an acrobat; with an un-conquerable love of wandering, of pleasure, and of idleness, together with a remarkable ability to endure, when necessary, privation and fatigue. Such were some of the qualities that met in this celebrated man.

His residence with these excellent people might have lasted about three years, when one fine day the parliament of Rouen issued an abrupt decree, com-manding all gipsies to quit the province immediately— or sooner.

The Bohemian band obeyed with the usual alacrity. But in their haste, Cartouche, who for the moment was lying ill in a neighbouring hut, was left behind;

and on his recovery found himself alone and friendless in the streets of Rouen, without a red cent in his pocket.

As if Providence decreed him one chance more, who should fall in with him than a well-to-do and warmhearted uncle, who not only regarnished both his stomach and his pocket, but replaced him safely in the paternal home, where, if no fatted calf celebrated his reappearance, he was at least received with indulgence, and his sins—by this time not a few—remitted.

Many a comparatively trifling snare may be the cause of man's final fall. Monotony slew Cartouche. So long as the complete novelty of a calm and regular life retained its charm, all went well; but when the rising at five, the thick soup at breakfast, always smoking at the same hour on the same table—the same duties—the same talk—began to pale, then Cartouche remembered with regretful sighs his "august abodes" in tent and hedge, and fretted, like the caged eagle, to be free.

To do him justice, he struggled for a while with this desire; and even sought solace in the education of his brothers and sisters—that is to say, in the language and useful arts he had acquired among his gipsy friends. Under his able tuition the young people became proficients in slang, and the words *cagou*, solitary thief; *coësre*, master beggar; *coquillard*, thief in pilgrim's dress; *courteau de boutanche*, servant who hires himself with the purpose of robbery; *détacheur de bouchon*, cutpurse; *franc mitou*, shammer of sickness; *bubin*, curious variety of the last-named, showing fictitious bites of a savage dog, and alarming into charity people who dare not drive him away; *narquois*, mendicant soldier; *polisson*, vagabond so scantily clad as to excite disgust and pity; and finally, *orphelin*, antithesis of "cagou," or gregarious robber. These and many such phrases frequently struck surprise and some half-defined uneasiness into the souls of the Cartouches *père et mère*.

From meditating on his lost liberty to making efforts to regain it, was a short step for our young hero. Circumstances precipitated this. He had formed a connexion with a young laundress of the neighbourhood, to whom, in the gushing fondness of his heart, he offered such rich repasts at the first restaurateur's of La Courtille, that his father, made aware of these luxurious doings, followed and detected him—ascertaining, moreover, enough of his general habits to be certain that he was already fairly launched in a career of unblushing crime.

Without an hour's delay, the father proceeded straight to that "providence of families," the lieutenant-general of police, from whom he readily obtained an order for the transmission of his son to the House of Correction at St. Lazare.

It was too late. The young gentleman had disappeared, marching off with arms and baggage, and (no doubt in absence of mind) his father's money-box !

A brief period was now spent in general practice at church, or in crowded assemblies where money promised to be plentiful; and Cartouche had little left to learn in the walk he had chosen, when a singular incident occurred.

He had been attending a charity sermon, the results of which had certainly been more profitable to his individual self than to the object proposed, when he was suddenly collared, and a determined voice demanded "his money or his life !"

Cartouche preferred to retain both, and made such effectual resistance that his assailant gave back.

"Gently, gently, my young game-chick !" said the latter, with a burst of coarse laughter. "Not so hot. You have beak and claws, and that's just what I like. Shake hands, my lad !"

. Cartouche still remained on the defensive.

"Come, come!" resumed the other, impatiently; "be easy, man! *Que diable!* People of *our* sort ought to understand each other at a glance. Hark ye—I was in the church too; but instead of working for myself, I watched *you! Peste!*—what a hand!—what quickness of eye!—what softness of execution! Tears came into my eyes as I followed your supple movements, and the success that attended them. Here— take this" (giving him a red silk purse stuffed with gold), "that's only a bit of my morning's work. I'd ask you to drink with me, but something better invites us. Come back to the Jacobins. A rich old German is hanging about the confessional, awaiting his turn. Now you shall see, *mon jeune coq*, whether or no I am worthy to work at your side."

Two minutes later the German's purse was transferred to the pocket of the speaker.

M. Gaguis—such was this gentleman's favourite name—inhabited a sordid den in an alley of the *Tripot-de-Bertault*, whose close and stuffy atmosphere and poverty-stricken aspect were in some measure redeemed by the presence of two charming young ladies—Fanchon and Michon—of whom the former was the wife (waiving the ceremony) of M. Gaguis;

the latter her sister, waiting for an eligible opportunity to settle—like her elder.

Now, Cartouche was at this period about seventeen, and if not handsome, far from unpleasant in his exterior.  Grandval sums him up in three lines as—

> "... à la fleur de son âge,
> Brun, sec, maigre, petit, mais grand pour le courage ;
> Entreprenant, hardi, robuste, alerte, adroit."

Introduced to the ladies by his admiring friend, he received from Fanchon a motherly kiss, from Michon a coquettish glance, from the effects of which the visitor had hardly recovered when he was invited to partake of the banquet—rabbit in onions—which had been prepared by the fair hands of the latter maiden.

An immense jug of Auxerre wine accompanied the viands, and there being but two glasses in store, Cartouche and Michon drank together, and found the Auxerre wine unusually palatable.

Dinner over and the jug emptied,

"*Ah-ça,* my young comrade," remarked Gaguis, "you see how we rub on—never melancholy—never idle !  What do you think of domestic life ?  Hang solitude !  You know the proverb :—

> ' Quand les bœufs vont deux à deux—
>  Le labourage n'en va que mieux.'

> (' When the beasts plough two and two—
>  Labour's the lighter, and sooner through.')

I had a partner lately, but owing to some words with *la pousse* (the peace-officers) he has been offered a lodging at the expense of *Mons. le comte de la carrache* (the gaoler). I offer you his place."

" *Tope* " (agreed), said Cartouche, glancing at Michon. And the bargain was made.

The marriage (morganatic) of the younger pair was celebrated on the spot, at, so to speak, the altar of nature, and with the simple ceremonial of the introduction of a fresh jug of wine, in which the *partie carrée* drank success to the united household.

The little family circle thus decorously arranged, the gentlemen went steadily to work, and, as may be conjectured, considerable profits accrued from their combined energies. But alas! the most sunny life has its occasional clouds.

The Cartouche honeymoon had not waned when Fanchon—the staid and matronly Fanchon—began to betray so pronounced a partiality for her new connexion as to excite the ire and jealousy of her true proprietor. A general row ensued. The two gentlemen henceforth worked on separate beats; and this circumstance—indirectly, indeed—contributed to the complete disruption of their heretofore happy home.

Gaguis, troubled by these domestic broils, and doing his work, as it were, mechanically, and without due caution, was seen by the police in the act of stripping a citizen of his laced cloak. Chase was given, and our friend, by skilful doubles, had all but shaken off his pursuers. But one quick eye had detected him darting into the alley of refuge. The house was searched. M. Gaguis was apprehended, and transmitted to Marseilles, while the ladies were lodged in safe custody elsewhere. Cartouche, who was absent, returned, to find the whole of his adopted family in the law's paternal embrace.

Our hero was not a man to succumb entirely to such a blow. Work—sheer, uncompromising work—was his panacea. But change, even in this, was needful to him. He took to dice and cards. Haunting the better hells, he used the skill acquired among the gipsies to such purpose that suspicions were awakened, and, at length, M. Cartouche, detected in the act, was kicked into the street, and debarred for ever from *that* branch of industry.

Tradition affirms that his next *début* was in the

character of a police spy. This, however, is apocryphal, and it is possible to malign even such a man as he. It is certain that he very quickly appeared as a recruiting-sergeant; and that he had acquired ideas of discipline and subordination is manifest, as will be shown by his manner of dealing with the skilled and desperate band we find somewhat later rallied round their accomplished general in Paris. Nay, it was his aim to impart to this force an organization and system approximating as closely as possible to the military, appointing lieutenants, sub-lieutenants, sergeants, watch, rallying and pass-words, &c. &c.

This completed, the campaign opened with night skirmishing. Thus, some three or four of the band would pounce upon an unwary citizen, whom a blow on the head from a loaded bludgeon reduced to temporary silence. When the victim regained sufficient consciousness to give an alarm, the troop was at safe distance, arranging the next affair.

Le Grand has given a dramatic picture of the scene that wound up the night's depredations, from which, however, it is evident he has eliminated much that is revolting to feeling and taste. His report establishes the sometimes disputed fact that the bandit force divided the capital among them in regular districts:—

*Car.*—Now, gentlemen, what success to-night? Who had charge of the Pont Neuf?

*La Ramée.*—My captain, it was the wide-awake one, assisted by Merciless and your humble slave.

*Car.*—The proceeds?

*La R.*—Four rapiers; two gold-knobbed canes.

*Car.*—Have I not told you I don't care about silver swords? What rubbish is this! I have half a mind to make you return them.

*La R.*—The hilts are good, and they cost us nothing.

*Car.*—Well, well—*passons.* Who was on duty at St. Denis?

*Harpin.*—No-quarter, l'Estoccade, and I.

*Car.*—What have you *pincé* (grabbed)?

*Harp.*—Some linen and muslin.

*Car.*—Humph! Poor coarse stuff! Well, who transacted business in the Rue des Noyers?

*Bel-Humeur*—La Fantaisie, Fond-et-Cale, and I.

*Car.*—What have you picked up?

*Bel Hu.*—A couple of marquises, who had supped at Cheret's.

*Car.*—And got——?

*Bel-Hu.*—Their coats, swords, and hats.

*Car.*—Nothing else? Do you mean to say they had not watches?

*Bel-Hu.*—Certainly; but they had been treating some lorettes.

*Car.*—I see. To-morrow, you will rob these damsels. No poaching on my manors. Who was on guard in the Rue Fromenteau?

*La Pince.*—The Earless, Debrideux, and I.

*Car.*—Whom did you fall in with?

*La Pince*—An abbé in a scarlet cloak.

*Car.*—Any cash?

*La P.*—Not a sous. He had in his pocket only a fan and a patch-box.

*Car.*—The guard at the Faubourg St. Germain?

*La Branche.*—Burn-Beard, Crackjaw, and I.

*Car.*—Profit?

*La B.*—We can't tell yet. A Gascon gave us a world of trouble. And after all, the rascal had not a sous in his purse! There was a pocket-book, indeed; but that contained only genealogies, assignations, and tailors' bills. Fact, mon capitaine. Believe me, we are men of honour.

*Car.*—I begin to doubt it, I promise you! Come, come, gentlemen, rob, pillage, swindle whomsoever you please; but, hang it! no nonsense among ourselves.

That age, the period of Cartouche, was the age of nicknames. Not only in criminal circles, but in the lower military grades, was the fashion largely adopted. Scarcely a sergeant or corporal but had his supplementary appellation, and " Brin-d'amour," " Bras-defer," " Va-de-Bon-Cœur," " La Douceur," " Chasselard," " La Rose," &c. &c., were plentiful as blackberries.

Become aware of the existence of an organized system of crime, Paris, alarmed, appealed to its natural protector, M. Argenson, head of the police, but found little consolation.

Police there were in rank abundance—*i. e.*, archers (horse and foot); exempts, forty-eight commissaries (as many as at present), and spies and agents by hundreds. But there was no controlling power, order, or system. Each worked for himself. They plundered the robber and the robbed alike. Of ten agents engaged in a common pursuit, perhaps but three obeyed the same superior. They were selected without reference to their antecedents, many having served in the galleys, and many more bearing the convict's brand on their shoulder. Miserably paid, they were perpetually exposed to the temptation of a bribe, until at length the sheep-dog had become almost as dangerous to the flock as the wolf him-self.

We have omitted to mention an important portion of the robber force, without whose aid many a brilliant exploit would have fallen flat; many a well-conceived project failed utterly in the execution—the ladies. The records glow and glisten with the well-known names of "La Catin," "La Bel-Air," "La Galette," "La Petite Poulaillière," "La Mion," "La Belle-Laitière," "Margot-Monsieur," "La Religieuse," "La Bonne," "La Blanche," "Tape-dru," &c. &c. But far beyond them all stands out, in rich relief, the name of that most celebrated, most accomplished, most devoted of all the (titular) wives of Cartouche—Big Jenny!

This remarkable woman was not descended from the highest stock. Her sire was believed to be an ostler, and it was probably owing in some degree to the associations of childhood that Big Jenny's first little misunderstanding with the laws arose from her connexion with a horse-stealing case, the result of which was that the young lady, whipped and branded, was exiled from Paris for the term of ten years. Jane, however, broke her *ban*, returned to her beloved city, and is found in 1720 ostensibly engaged in the peaceful profession of a fruiterer, but in reality flitting about from place to place, spying, plotting, drinking, fighting, robbing, and being robbed—the terror and admiration (according to the spectator's point of view) of every one that approached her.

It is with reluctance that, as faithful historians, we have to acknowledge the existence of a second (con-temporaneous) wife in " La Néron," who was parted with to M. Cartouche by her affectionate aunt, La Tanton, for the moderate consideration of a dinner at the cabaret Du Petit-Seau.

Let us glance for an instant at one of the excellent institutions at which, thanks to the administrative skill and energy of M. Cartouche, some of the most finished thieves of the time received the education they turned to such excellent account.

It is the largest of several huge caves sunk in the chalky sides of Montmartre, and lit by large iron sconces. From the centre of an arch spanning a deep recess, hangs by the neck the figure of a man. He is richly dressed; a laced hat is still clutched in his hand. By his side is a gold-hilted rapier, in his pockets a diamond snuff-box, a pocket-book, and a purse of gold. Within his portly person are bundles of hay. It is the *mannequin des épreuves*—the little Test-man.

To various points of this gentleman's person and attire are attached numerous little rattles and bells. To strip him without an alarm from these of every valuable disposed about him is the task to which the gang, crouched about him in various easy attitudes, one by one address themselves, each candidate as he fails being driven off by his fellows under a shower of playful, but by no means contemptible, buffets.

One alone succeeds. It is the master himself, the incomparable Cartouche, and tears come into the eyes of the admiring band as they watch the indolent ease with which those unrivalled fingers gradually, but surely, reduce the pendant beau literally to a "man of straw."

It was in 1720 that the terror inspired by the Cartouchian band, and the laxity of the police, reached its climax. They held virtual possession of the capital, especially by night. And their depredations were conducted with the military order and precision so much inculcated by their great leader.

A party would assemble quietly before some rich mansion. Then some huge fellow—very frequently, one Simon Once, a gigantic ex-porter—would offer his mighty shoulders as the base of a living pyramid which, formed of the lighter and more agile members of the gang, speedily reached to the lower windows. Some panes were adroitly removed, the apartments entered, and the most attractive objects began to glide down a chain of ready hands, till the pillage was complete.

It was thus that, in September, 1720, the band invaded the residence of the Spanish ambassador, Rue de Tournon, and nearly stripped the chamber of the ambassadress, seizing a magnificent pearl necklace, a brooch with twenty-seven large diamonds, a rich table-service, and the entire wardrobe of the lady.

About this period the South Sea bubble had introduced Law to the Paris public, and enormous profits resulted from the pressure and tumult among the high-born mob who daily besieged the offices of the great financier.  On one occasion a certain Lord Dermott is recorded to have lost shares to the value of 1,300,000—*now* nearly equal to 12,000,000—livres!

It was, however, only at the beginning of 1721 that the dreaded name of Cartouche became familiar to the Parisians.  "This Cartouche, the robber of whom I have before spoken," writes Barbier, "is not yet taken."  He certainly was *not*.

The exploits of the gang at this time read like a battle-page from Homer.

"Va-de-Bon-Cœur" stole in the Palais-Royal two silver flambeaux, enamelled with the Regent's arms.

At the Louvre, Louison (Cartouche's brother) possessed himself of the sword and mantle of the Prince Soubise.

The buckles and silver-hilted swords disappeared like magic, and the Regent himself was robbed, on leaving the Opera. But here the laugh was on the other side, the Regent, purposely to deceive the robbers, having caused his hilt to be richly chased— in steel!

The note-book of the receiver, Tanton, showed among other things, "Three large flagons of silver, from the palace."

It was only when the very highest society began to feel the inconvenience of such a state of things that the Government set themselves seriously to the task of reform. A notorious murder in 1721 determined the Regent once for all to exterminate the banditti of the capital. This was, perhaps, the more necessary, since the Regent himself, a man of many vices, and well described by Louis XIV. as "*le fanfaron de crimes,*" had been suspected by the Paris public to be in league with the robber band!

It so happened that a worthless scribbler of the day, dubbed "poet," and forced into notice by Racine, had published a series of rhymed philippics, in which the Regent was branded with every conceivable crime, murder and incest included. As in the composition of these unworthy diatribes the author had displayed an amount of talent he had never brought to bear on anything else, the work obtained a wide circulation, and quickly reached the eye of the Regent himself.

That royal gentleman did not, it was reported, even knit his brows at the imputation of murder—murder, that is, of any ordinary type. At the history of his unbridled debaucheries he laughed with a cynical enjoyment. But when, as he proceeded, he found himself depicted as the rival of Voisin and Brinvilliers, concocting at the laboratory of the chemist Homborg, slow-acting poisons destined for the Dauphin, the Duke of Burgundy, and all who stood between the " round and top of sovereignty," and himself—*then,* it is said, a tear of honest rage and shame gushed from his eye, little accustomed to such a visitor; he flung the book away, and vowed that the slanderer De la Grange-Chancel should feel his vengeance.

Nothing would have been easier than to cause the wretched rhymester to be put to death in some secret dungeon of the Bastile; but, strange to say, the furious prince so far controlled his wounded feelings on *this* occasion as to merely send him prisoner to the Isle Ste. Marguerite. Even from this penalty a poem, couched in a tone of humble laudation, sufficed to set him free. He fled to Holland, and at that safe distance recommenced the work of calumny.

Paris was still discussing these slanders, when one May morning, 1721, some labourers came upon the body of a man recently murdered. It proved to be that of another obscure poet, one Vergier; but so little were these men known to any but their own immediate companions, that for a time the corpse was believed to be that of De la Grange-Chancel.

" Kill a poet!" shouted the public. " *Why?* Not to rob, surely. These sort of folks are not robbable! It must have been an act of vengeance. And *whose* vengeance ? The Regent's, of course !"

And now about the assassins. Cartouchians, you may be sure. These fellows are all in the Regent's pay. The rumour and the reasoning spread like wildfire.

Cartouche was loudly demanded of the authorities,

but the request was more easily made than complied with. One of his most illustrious followers, however, was forthcoming, and the arrest of this man, Jean Rozy, *alias* the Chevalier, *alias* the Cracksman, was sufficiently curious to be worth giving in detail.

The banditti of Paris at this time were divided into cliques, or associations, between which, notwithstanding that they frequently acted in concert, there existed considerable jealousy. A province, for example, would send to the capital from time to time gangs of smugglers, highwaymen—men superior in strength and daring even to the highest class of Parisian robbers—being, in fact, the very aristocracy of crime. These rural practitioners were so numerous as in some districts to approach the dimensions of a veritable army. Barbier writes that in 1718 a force of nearly five thousand, chiefly smugglers of salt, held possession of the country round Paris, under the command of two retired officers—Colingry and Rasoir. So well were these levies organized and disciplined, that the Cardinal Alberoni is said to have regarded them in the light of regular troops when calculating the military resources of France.

Some days after the murder of Vergier, one of these provincial gentlemen, Dubourquct, *alias* the Notary, happened to be strolling in the Tuileries, and was recognised by two Cartouchians—the Cracksman and one Duplessis—who, hungry and with empty pockets, were lurking for prey. Now, Mons. Dubourquet was richly attired, wore a silver-hilted rapier, and regaled his nose from time to time with snuff from a box of the same rich material. This aspect of luxury stirred the bile of the famishing professors. They resolved on the plunder of their provincial brother.

Meeting him at the gate, they denounced him as a spy of the police, employed to watch themselves. Dubourquet, afraid of a disturbance in so public a place, spoke them fair, but was only suffered to escape on the forfeiture of his sword, purse, and snuff-box.

Mad for revenge, Dubourquet went straight to the authorities, and under the name of Sarost, a retired officer, informed against the Cracksman and his companion. The former was arrested. But Captain Sarost had gained his end, and never appeared to substantiate his complaint.

A second murder now occurred to redouble the public agitation. Cartouche himself with certain of his band were carousing at a cabaret, and listening to the performance of a strolling fiddler. The latter, having received a few sous, was departing, when he was pushed roughly back by a member of the gang, and ordered to continue. Some workmen at a neighbouring table, incensed at this tyranny, took part with the assaulted man. A row ensued. Swords and pistols were freely used. The police rushed in, and one of these, Mondelot, fell dead from a shot fired, it was declared, by a female Cartouchian named Manon-le-Roy. It is at least certain that this distinguished lady always carried arms, and equally so that when some time afterwards she was arrested, in company with two more amiable persons, Mesdames Chauvelot and Madeleine Beaulieu, she entrenched herself behind her bed, and for half an hour kept the whole body of " exempts " at bay.

The murders of Vergier and Mondelot brought the name of Cartouche prominently before the public. Henceforward, every audacious crime went forth stamped as it were with his name and authority. Some attempts were made to entrap the formidable thief, and one police-agent held him in such hot pursuit, that Cartouche resolved to give him a lesson.

One evening, on an occasion of a public fête, when a large body of archers and police were assembled in the Rue de Tournon, Cartouche was aware of his enemy stealthily following, and evidently waiting only a favourable moment to raise the hue-and-cry. Suddenly the chief wheels round, seizes him by the throat, and, having thus stopped his utterance, beats the poor wretch almost into a jelly with his cane; then flinging him back among the advancing archers, darts down an alley, changes coat and wig, and quietly re-appears in the very midst of those who were eagerly hunting him.

The gallantries of Cartouche would occasionally betray him into an awkward predicament. Married as he was in a certain fashion to Big Jenny, that lady was not without rivals, of whom, however, the amiable lady took but little heed. We have already mentioned La Néron. To her succeeded the fair flower-maiden, Manon-le-Roy, who, whipped, branded, and placed in the House of Correction, left the field open for Marie-Jeanne Bonnefoi, a pretty lemonade-seller, known as the Little Grey Sister, or Margot the Nun, so called from her demure aspect and modest attire.

One evening in August, 1720, the police were alarmed by a tumult that declared itself at the humble dwelling of the little nun. On effecting an entrance, they found a little man, half drunk, shouting, dancing, breaking furniture, and discharging pistols right and left among an admiring audience of both sexes. The excited performer was forthwith conducted to the guardhouse; but no complainant appeared against him, and after a while the little gentleman humbly represented that he was an honest chocolate-seller in the Rue Comédie-Français, Grisel by name, who had unfortunately drank a cup of wine beyond his usual modest allowance.

"Allons!" remarked a good-natured sergeant, "you have done nothing for which one would whip a cat. Be off about your business, but leave something with us in case we want you."

The little gentleman deposited 100 livres and his snuff-box, which articles he was allowed to reclaim next day.   It was Cartouche.

A fearful affair now occurred.  A woman of the gang, called La Blanche, one of their most approved spies and receivers, was murdered in her lodging by the male Cartouchian, Dautreques-Duplessis.  What was to be done with the body?  Duplessis confided his little difficulty to the chief.  The two wretches conveyed the corpse to a garret, divided it into as many portions as time allowed, placed the latter in a huge scuttle obtained at a broker's, and, marching through Paris in broad day, deposited their hideous burden in the Seine, Cartouche, pistol in hand, keeping curious observers at a distance till all was done. The wife of the miscreant Duplessis waited till dark; then placing the head of the murdered woman in her apron, carried that also to a place of concealment.

In December, 1720, Cartouche was fairly captured and confined in Fort l'Evêque; but spite of the terror inspired by this redoubtable robber, so slight were the precautions taken respecting him, that on the 2nd of March, 1721, he contrived to effect his escape. By this time it had become known that he was personally concerned in the affair of the murder of Mondelot, and the authorities roused themselves to unusual efforts for his recapture. Hereupon an odd incident occurred.

As the officer of the Criminal Court was uttering the usual proclamation, with sound of trumpet and "outcry," calling upon Cartouche to appear within eight days and answer to the charge of murder, and had come to the words, "In the King's name and those of nos seigneurs of the Parliament, we do command the person called ' Cartouche'———"

" *Present, Cartouche !*" shouted a voice in the centre of the crowd, that turned the whole body—archers, trumpeters, citizens and all—into a frenzy of rage and

17

agitation.   It was Cartouche himself, but he had vanished.

Two persons now entered into a solemn league and covenant to pursue the impalpable robber without rest or respite until he should be slain or taken.   One of these was an exempt named Huron, a bold and clever officer.   The other was the archer Pepin, a man of equal resolution.

The chase opened ill for our hero.   Huron tracked him so hotly as actually to exchange pistol-shots with him, by which Cartouche was said to have been seriously wounded.   It is certain that either to escape this persevering foe, or to recover from his alleged hurts, Cartouche disappeared for three entire months from criminal history.   It is stated by Grandval that he paid a visit to England, and became personally known to his great British prototype, Jack Sheppard.

Another historian affirms that he journeyed in company with his lieutenant, Balagny, into Champagne, where, at a cottage belonging to the last-named illustrious person, he led an innocent and pastoral life until his complete restoration urged him once more to the field of fame.

The police, who exultingly assured the public that Cartouche had been driven from the capital, were soon painfully aware of his return. A very large reward was set upon his head, and a great body of exempts—Huron and Pepin among the foremost—devoted themselves almost exclusively to the pursuit.

The zeal of both these officers proved fatal to them. They had one evening tracked Cartouche to a notorious robber-haunt. Finding themselves likely to be surrounded, five of the robbers threw themselves at once upon Huron and his followers. The officer received several pistol-shots, and was then cut down by Cartouche himself.

A few days later, Cartouche, while taking a quiet stroll with Madeleine, perceived Pepin on his heels. Turning suddenly on their pursuer, Madeleine attacked him with large stones, while Cartouche ran the unfortunate archer through the body.

These misadventures almost daunted the police, while they renewed public anxiety to a painful degree. The name of Cartouche was in every mouth.

"No more compliments and chat *now*," wrote Le Grand. "We merely say 'good morning,' and then add, 'What of Cartouche ?—have they got him ?'"

A regularly organized attempt was next made, under the direction of an aide-major of the Gardes Françaises—Pékom—who selected ninety of his most trusted and intrepid men, and sent them in various disguises, but well armed, in quest of the single robber chief.

The first result of this step was to awaken mistrust on the part of Cartouche and his companions. They saw themselves beset with disguised foes, and suspected every strange face that crossed their way. The Regent, moreover, issued a proclamation increasing the reward for the capture of Cartouche, promising pardon to any accomplice who should deliver him up, and severe punishment to any who gave him refuge.

At this critical period of our hero's fortunes occurred what was known as the affair of the hôtel Desmarets.

Nicolas Desmarets, nephew of the great Colbert, died on the 6th of May, at his hotel, Rue des Petits Augustins. This wealthy residence Cartouche resolved should be thoroughly pillaged.

A chosen band, commanded by the chief in person, forced an entrance, and were busily at work in the rich saloons and chambers, when one of their look-outs, "Ratichon," who usually dressed as an abbé, rushed in breathless, announcing the approach of an absolute army of archers, under the exempts Bourlon and Pannetier.

The danger-signal had hardly been given before the enemy appear. A fierce fight commences—from room to room, from stair to stair. The robbers fight stoutly; but some have fallen under the determined assault of an enemy whose numbers increase every moment. Ammunition fails. It is a *sauve qui peut.* Cartouche escapes by a chimney, gains the roof, and descends at some distance in the garret of a good-natured mechanic, to whom he represents himself as a man pursued by his merciless creditors. His host sympathizes, provides him with a disguise, and once more the lion has escaped the toils.

That distrust existed in the brigand band at this time is demonstrated by a ghastly incident related by Barbier. A body, fearfully mutilated, was found behind the Chartreux. A card affixed to the breast bore this inscription :—

"Here lies Jean Labaty, who has met a well-deserved fate. Let those who are guilty of the like treason, expect the like punishment."

Barbier mistook "Labaty" for "Rebaté"—in slang language, assassinated—and the corpse was subsequently ascertained to have been that of one Jean Lefebvre, a Garde Française in league with the gang.

The murder of Lefebvre was followed by that of Tanton, a cousin of Cartouche, who, suspecting him of treachery, decoyed him to a retired spot, stabbed him to the heart, and buried him in a dung-heap.

But now, at length, the hour of retribution was at hand.

Gruthus Duchâtelet—next to Cartouche the most ferocious of these human tigers—acknowledged to himself that the game was nearly up. Plunged as he was in the deepest and deadliest crime, he saw that but one chance of safety remained to him. He must denounce his chief.

No sooner resolved than done. On the 13th of October the traitor called on Pékom, the aide-major of the Gardes Françaises, made his offer, obtained his conditions, and, to make all sure, procured the ratification of the latter, not only by the minister Le Blanc, but by the Regent himself.

On being satisfactorily arranged, Péhom sent for a brave veteran sergeant, Jean Courtades, and confided to him—attended by a picked band of archers—the dangerous duty on hand, directing him to follow the guidance of Duchâtelet; but on the least suspicious movement of the latter, to blow out his brains.

The party, consisting of forty men, marching at ten

paces distance from each other, started at break of day. The place indicated by Duchâtelet was the cabaret "Du Pistolet," Rue de Ménilmontant, kept by one Germain Savard.

"Is any one above?" asked the traitor guide.

"No," was the answer.

"Are the four women there?"

"Come up."

Leaving some men below to watch Savard, Courtades led his band upstairs. In the chamber they found the four chief bandits; Balagny and Limosin drinking by the fire, Gaillard in bed, and Cartouche, seated on a couch, in the act of drawing on his pantaloons. The surprise was complete, and but a few minutes elapsed before the four prisoners, securely bound, were on their way, in coaches, to the hotel of the Minister of War.

Barbier writes exultingly :—

"Great news in Paris ! — Cartouche, the famous robber-chief, sought so long in vain that men began to doubt of his actual existence, is a prisoner ! He was sold and delivered by an ex-soldier of the guard, one of the gang. This soldier deserves to be broken on the wheel as richly as any ; but the fellow was cool

enough.   Cartouche had gone to bed at six this morning at a cabaret in La Courtille, with six pistols ready
to his hand.   He was conducted to the Ministry of
War, and from thence, on foot, to the Châtelet.   He
was insolent, as if despising his captors, declaring that
they would not dare to execute him, and would not
keep him long."

Cartouche had been taken *en chemise*.   His captors
refused to permit him even to finish dressing, and in
this condition he was presented to the public whom
he had held so long in abject terror.   He, however,
never lost his coolness.   On alighting from the carriage, he was compelled to step down barefooted into
the mud.   An archer rudely pushed him forward.
Cartouche dashed his mud-soiled foot into the man's
face, exclaiming—

"*Imbecile!*   You durst not have touched me
yesterday for your life!"

The process advanced quickly.   Duchâtelet, though
he had been promised pardon, was kept under surveillance—it being intended to try and condemn him,
though not to execute his sentence.   Certain of re-
prieve, he confessed, without hesitation, certain
burglaries in which Cartouche had personally taken
part—not to mention the murder of Lefebvre, in

which himself (Duchâtelet), Cartouche, Gaillard, Balagny, and Limosin had participated.

Notwithstanding these confessions, Cartouche continued to deny his identity, calling himself one Jean Bourguignon, a countryman. His celebrity seemed to call for an exceptional treatment. At all events, Barbier writes,—

" He is very well cared for. He has at dinner, soup, a good bouilli, with a little entrée, and three flasks of wine. He receives crowds of distinguished visitors, and the gaolers make a good thing of it. Fashionable ladies attend his levees. The Regent's mistress, Mdme. de Parabère, came in disguise, among others, to visit the hero of the day."

But the most distinguished of his visitors was the Maréchale de Boufflers, the widow of the hero who so gloriously lost the battle of Malplaquet.

It was not their first interview.

One warm summer night in July, 1721, just as the lady had retired to bed, leaving her window a little open for air, roused by a slight noise, she drew the curtain aside, and, to her horror, saw a man's face close to her own. She made a snatch at the bell, but two quick hands closed her lips and imprisoned her hands.

"No noise, madame!" said the visitor; "I am Louis Dominique Cartouche. I need say no more."

After a moment's pause, the robber resumed :—

"The street is guarded. They are on my traces, but no one saw me climb your balcony. I am safe if you keep quiet. If you will *not*——" He opened his blouse and displayed a rich but faded costume, with a complete armoury of silver-mounted pistols and knives. "But escape is not all I seek," continued her visitor. "I have not been in bed for a week. I am tired out, and hungry. You must provide me supper and a bed!"

The Maréchale gave a start and shudder.

"Compose yourself, madame," said Cartouche; "the devil is not so black as he is painted. I know how to behave to a lady. *Any* couch will serve for my bed. As for supper, a chicken, some fruit, and a bottle of champagne, is all I require. Ring for your maids; pretend a *fringale* (sudden hunger); and when I have supped and slept I will make my bow."

The lady tremblingly obeyed; her visitor, ensconced behind the curtains, watching her every gesture. The repast was quickly served, and the maids withdrew, much marvelling at their mistress's sudden appetite.

In a few minutes Cartouche had left nothing but some bones and peel, and an empty bottle.

"Now, madame," he said, rising, "I will wish you good-night. I retire to the sofa in your dressing-room. Please to forget that I am so near a neighbour, for Cartouche, as you may be aware, sleeps only with one eye!"

At three o'clock the robber rose, much refreshed, offered polite acknowledgments, and retired as he had come.

The Maréchale sprang from her bed, closed the window, and alarmed her household. Search was made among the valuables, but not an article had been removed; even the costly silver used for the supper had been respected by the eccentric thief.

Some days later, Mdme. de Boufflers received a basket of excellent champagne. To be sure, the acknowledgment cost Cartouche but little. The wine had been abstracted from the vaults of the most popular dealer in Paris.

Hearing of his capture, the lady could not resist the inclination to visit her scrupulous visitor. Cartouche received her with great politeness, only regretting that circumstances at the moment forbade his offering a return of her hospitality. The Maréchale presented him with two louis.

It was hardly to be expected that such a man would calmly acquiesce in the decree of fate which seemed to have consigned him to a hopeless imprisonment, from which the only outlet was to the scaffold.

Cartouche only awaited his opportunity. It came sooner than he had expected.

He had been placed in one of the horrible subterranean dungeons destroyed in 1780 by the humane command of Louis the Sixteenth. He had a companion in trouble who had formerly worked as a stonemason. This man, having, unlike Cartouche, his arms and legs unfettered, had ascertained the existence of a ditch, or fosse, under their floor, connected with the sewerage of the prison. With his nails, and sometimes a limb of his companion's chair, he effected an entrance into this ditch, and from thence through a wall into another leading from the cellar of a neighbouring house. A breach effected in another wall, the adventurers found themselves safe in the cellar of an honest fruiterer. A short staircase led up into the shop; and now, as Barbier naïvely remarks, their escape would have been completed if, *par mal-heur*, it had not failed.

The shop-door was simply bolted within, but before the robbers could discover the latch, a slight noise made by Cartouche's fetters aroused a dog till then asleep under the counter. An alarm followed. Down rushed a maid-servant, screaming "Thieves! thieves!" followed by the master of the house bearing a lamp, which Cartouche at once struck down. Even now they had nearly escaped, for the bolt was found and the door flung open. But, unluckily, a patrol of four archers was passing at the critical moment. Seeing Cartouche in fetters, they forthwith arrested the pair, and reconducted them to the prison, where they were placed in stricter custody than before.

"Cartouche," writes Barbier, "has been transferred to the Conciergerie, and lodged in the Montgomery Tower, heavily ironed. The fellow who betrayed him is a well-born gentleman, but a worse miscreant than his leader. He was implicated in the Chartreux murder, and, it is asserted, washed his hands purposely in the blood of the victim. He has the Regent's pardon, signed and sealed, but will probably be imprisoned. Forty-seven of the band (men and women) have been arrested on his information."

In his new prison none were allowed access to the bandit chief except his guards, the curé of St. Barthélemy, and a priest of Sorbonne, selected for his confessor. He received his clerical visitors with respect, but declined confession; and when offered by the curé some religious books, declared he had never learned to read!

What is called the interrogatory *libre* (that which is unattended with torture), produced nothing from Cartouche. He simply denied everything, including his own identity, and affirmed that he could not comprehend what they were talking about.

The process went forward with unexampled rapidity, and on the 26th November, 1721, the Court decreed as follows :—

That "Le Camus," Louis Dominique Cartouche, *alias* Lamarc, *alias* Le Petit, *alias* Bourguignon, Jacques Maire, Jean-Pierre Balaguy (called the Capuchin), Gruthus Duchâtelet, and Charles Blanchard (called the Gaillard), should be broken alive on the wheel; that their legs, thighs, arms, and reins being thus broken, their bodies should be affixed to the wheel, face upward, *pour y finir leurs jours;* Madeleine and Messier to be hanged. The whole of the prisoners to be previously submitted to the question, ordinary and extraordinary, with the view of extorting confession.

Appended to this decree was a kind of postscript, called "*retentum.*" It ordered that Cartouche and Duchâtelet should be quietly strangled, after being placed on the wheel, broken as aforesaid; that Balagny and Maire should be strangled after receiving three strokes, and Blanchard without receiving any strokes at all.

The procès-verbal relating to Cartouche reports the application of the question in the form of the *brodequins*, or boots. These, as readers are possibly aware, were wooden frames fitted to the legs, into which wedges of increasing size were forcibly driven, until the legs of the sufferer were reduced to a pulp.

" Having been admonished to confess his robberies, murders, and the names of his accomplices—

" Answered that he had committed no such crimes, and had therefore no accomplices.

" On application of first, second, and third wedge, answered that he was innocent.

" At the fourth, answered that he knew not what they were speaking of.

" At the fifth, that he was innocent—was dying.

"At the sixth, that he had done all that was required of him ; had done no wrong ; was dying.

"At the seventh, was innocent ; no accomplices.

"At the eighth and last, was innocent.

"Released and laid on a mattress, we renewed the
interrogatory, but without result.

(Signed) &c."

The execution followed hard upon the preliminary
torture, the disgrace of those days. On the same
afternoon, November 27th, 1721, our unfortunate hero
was led forth to the scene of his final earthly punishment.

The Place de la Grève was one mass of humanity,
every window commanding a view of the scaffold
being let for a large sum. The patience of the
audience had been severely tried, for the execution
was announced for noon; and it was five o'clock
before the redoubted malefactor was led into the
square.

To add to the disgust and disappointment of the
assembled multitude, especially those who had paid,
the officers, entering the Place about four o'clock, had
ruthlessly removed four of the five wheels, leaving
only one. Cartouche himself expressed considerable

annoyance at finding himself the sole object of interest, and it was this circumstance that probably influenced the confessions he made during the last minutes of his life. The removal of the wheels was, however, only caused by the lateness of the hour, the execution having been deferred thus long to enable Cartouche to complete his reluctant revelations.

Arrived in the square, the criminal threw a fearless glance around, comprehending in it every portion of the packed assembly, many of whom had passed two entire days and nights in anticipation of the moment now arrived—eating, drinking, shouting, singing, and sleeping by turns.

In all that human sea the robber recognised no familiar face—nothing that afforded the faintest hope of the rescue he had still deemed possible, but which it needed hearts as dauntless as his own to attempt. He glanced at the compact body of the two hundred archers who hedged the scaffold, and from that moment resigned himself to die.

Sending once more for the officials, he confessed that he was indeed Louis Dominique Cartouche, the robber, although his parents and his brother were, and had always been, honest and guiltless persons. He avowed that he had murdered Pepin in the Rue des

Petits Augustins, as also Tanton and Bidel. He had taken part also in the murder of Huron and of Mondelot. If there were more, it was done without premeditation, and to protect his own person. He added that in all his life he had never robbed *in a church*, though repeatedly incited to do so by Duchâtelet.

Cartouche certainly showed himself, in his confessions, *un bon camarade*, and a man by no means devoid of generous feelings. He absolved his own family with especial earnestness from any share in his misdoings. He refrained from denunciations even of those who had deserted or betrayed him, excepting only Duchâtel, towards whom he evinced intense scorn and hatred. But, in revenge, he was unsparing in respect to the spies and receivers of the gang, whom he denounced by the score. He avowed himself the head and chief of the numerous band, so long the terror of the capital—an assertion which, if any one feel inclined to doubt, was speedily confirmed by the confusions and indiscipline which on his decease became suddenly perceptible in the ranks of crime.

To the two last questions addressed to him, whether any person of condition belonged to his band, and whether he had ever accepted bribes to murder, he replied emphatically in the negative.

His confessions completed, Cartouche calmly surrendered himself to the executioners.

The procès-verbal, signed by the Greffier Drouet, announces :—

" The said Cartouche, borne upon the scaffold, and there bound and affixed to St. Andrew's cross, I for the last time demanded if he had anything else to declare, exhorting him to remember the necessity of making his peace with God, before whom he was about to appear. He replied that he had nothing to add to the avowals already made. The *Salve* was then chanted; the criminal, in accordance with the *retentum*, was at once strangled and executed; and I withdrew, attended by the officers whose names appear below."

On the 2nd December, Balagny (*alias* the Capuchin) was broken on the wheel. Like his chief, it was only when in sight of the scaffold that he made any full confession. He denounced twelve more notorious members of the band.

The 28th of March Louis Marcant was executed.

In June Barbier writes : " They are continuing the process against the Cartouchians, and have a hundred and fifty prisoners at the Conciergerie. On the eve of the Fête-Dieu they executed Rozy, *alias* the Chevalier

As they were about to leave the prison he began to *jaboter* (prattle), and denounced so many accomplices that in the course of the night and following day eighty persons were apprehended, among them two police exempts, Roux and Bourlon."

In July the diarist writes: "Nothing but hangings and breakings on the wheel! Every day some Cartouchian executed. Yesterday they despatched (*expédia*) Mademoiselle Neron, the chief's mistress, a very pretty brunette. She was hanged at one o'clock."

On the 24th July, 1722, it came to the turn of "La Grande Jeanneton." Big Jenny had used her tongue to such purpose that the police arrested, on her information, fifty-two persons, chiefly innkeepers and proprietors of wine shops, some of them well to do and highly respected. Among those apprehended were two ladies who occupied rich apartments, and kept their carriage and horses. Confronted with Big Jenny, the latter denied their acquaintance. It was "une méprise de nom." The ladies were politely re-conducted to their dwelling, under a guard of twenty archers, to keep the amused spectators at bay.

Poor Jenny had had to undergo the question, the *brodequins*. Strong and courageous, the girl (she was

only twenty-five) preserved her fortitude till the introduction of the third wedge; but then, breaking
silence, she denounced more of the band than any
had done yet, delivering up to justice innumerable
receivers, including three sisters of a good family, the
Saint-Bigors, one of them the wife of an officer in the
Luxembourg regiment.

On the 31st July a very strange execution took
place. The young brother of Cartouche, *le petit*
Louison, was hung in the Place de Grève, but only
by the armpits, for it was not intended that the boy
should die.

He cried out very loudly at first, and begged that
he might be put out of pain at once, as the weight
of his body seemed to force every drop of blood down
to his feet. " *Ce-qui*" (adds Barbier) " *est la souffrance
des pendus.*"

Later, his tongue protruded, and he spoke no more.
Without waiting for the ordained two hours to expire,
the lad was taken down and placed in medical care;
but it was too late. He was already dead. "He was
very wicked for his years," says Barbier, "and had
been an accomplice of his brother from a very
early age."

The same day was executed Tanton, uncle of the

chief.  He was the compiler of a kind of "Thieves'
Directory," containing the *real* names and addresses
of all distinguished robbers of the day.

Several executions followed, and it might well be
thought that Paris was now rid of her worst foes.
But no.

"In spite," writes our friend the diarist, "of the
executions at La Grève, there are more thieves than
ever in Paris.  Cartouche has died on the wheel; but
his name and memory engender robbers."  The organization he is supposed to have given to crime was, in
reality, only the disorganization of society.

X.

# THE SKELETON OF THE RUE VAUGIRARD.

ON the twenty-sixth of April, 1833, a singular party arrived, in two carriages, at the door of No. 81, Rue de Vaugirard, Paris. From the first alighted a man of middle age, of shrewd, determined aspect, bearing in his hand an official-looking bag, crammed with papers. He was followed by a short, stout man, well dressed, and wearing an enormous pair of green spectacles; and the rear was brought up by another individual, tall and thin, apparently a mechanic of the better class, whose air was gloomy and downcast in the extreme. The last two persons on descending from the carriage were surrounded by a municipal guard and some followers, who appeared to be awaiting their arrival.

The second vehicle brought a gentleman who carried a case of surgical instruments, and respectfully made way for his companion, no other than the celebrated analytical chemist, M. Orfila.

"Monsieur the Attorney-General," said the latter, in his grave, musical voice, as he cordially shook hands with the personage we have first described, "my colleague, Dumoutier, and I await your directions. What is the business?—poison?—autopsy?"

"Neither," was the answer, with a smile. "Archæology."

With this ambiguous answer, he conducted the party, by a small back door, into the damp and weed-grown garden of the house, and towards a table covered with black cloth, which had been placed under an aged mulberry tree, and displayed writing materials, &c., as if in preparation for an official inquiry.

The party now surrounding the table was composed of the magistrate, with M. Orfila, and the surgeon, a clerk, the municipal officer, and his two assistants, each of whom kept a careful grasp upon one of the men in custody. At the distance of a pace or two, close to an apricot tree, which was trained upon the wall, stood two labourers, spade and pickaxe in hand, apparently awaiting orders.

The magistrate ran his finger across a plan that lay on the table before him, and, pausing at a .red cross, and glancing thence to the apricot tree, said, quietly, " Begin *there*."

The men dug. After working a few minutes the pickaxe of one of them sank into an excavation ; at this, the short prisoner with the green spectacles made a sudden movement, and even into the dull dead eyes of his companion there came a momentary glitter. The officers, as if involuntarily, tightened their grasp, as the magistrate, addressing the labourers, desired them to proceed with the greatest caution, so as to injure nothing.

Carefully trenching the soil, they presently came upon a bed of lime, forming a sort of hard coat. It was into this the pick had penetrated. Removed in fragments, it gave to view a narrow grave, about four feet from the surface, and at the bottom of the grave a skeleton, perfect in all respects, the teeth and hair complete as in life. Around the neck was a four-times knotted cord. Upon the marriage finger appeared the golden ring.

" It is quicklime," remarked M. Orfila, " but they have forgotten the necessary moisture, and what was no doubt intended to destroy, has only preserved. The flesh has disappeared, but the skeleton is perfect. Well, monsieur the magistrate, what do you wish us to do?"

"A miracle, gentlemen," was the answer, "and I offer you the assistance of these two gentlemen, Doctors Marc and De Loury" (who entered as he spoke), "in effecting it. I wish you to reclothe these bones with flesh, to tell me to whom they once belonged—the sex, the age, and exactly how long they have rested in this hitherto unknown grave."

"Nothing is easier for my colleagues," replied the able anatomist Dumoutier, "and my assistance would be of little benefit, but for one circumstance. I could, if you desire it, determine from merely examining the skull, what were the peculiar habits, thoughts, passions, vices, and virtues of the soul by which it was animated."

The physicians could hardly repress a smile. Dumoutier was one of the earliest and most enthusiastic disciples of the then nascent philosophy of Gall and Spurzheim.

Meanwhile the skeleton had been lifted from its earthy bed and placed on a table in the dining-room, which could be entered from the garden. The lime and subjacent earth were also collected, and placed in coffers for the analysis, to which the professional gentlemen now addressed themselves.

They arrived at an unanimous conclusion : they had

before them the remains of a female about four feet eight inches in height, of advanced age. The teeth were singularly perfect for her years, and during life must have been larger and longer than common. The hands were small, and the perfect nails gave evidence that the deceased had never been accustomed to hard personal toil. They fixed her age at seventy.

The magistrate's face grew brighter as each successive conclusion was announced. He could scarcely have relished more the gradual unrolling of an Egyptian mummy.

" But, gentlemen," he presently remarked, " that is not all. I must now know the date of death."

" That is more difficult," answered De Loury; " a few years since such a question would have been asked in vain. *Now*, experience supplies us with approximative solutions."

Reasons were then adduced for pronouncing the death to have occurred from ten to twelve years since. That the cause was unquestionably strangulation, the fatal cord remaining laced four times round the neck, and circumstances placing the idea of suicide out of consideration, and that (in view of the folding up of ' the lower members) burial must have followed within a few hours, that is, before rigidity commenced.

The magistrate turned towards the prisoners :—

" Well, Bastien and Robert, these gentlemen knew nothing of the matter for which they were invited hither. Yet, in two hours, they have drawn the perfect picture of your victim. They have, as it were, made us present at the very crime. There needs but one word more—the victim's name. I add it. The widow Houet."

" And," put in Dumoutier," I will tell you what was the character of her whose remains lie here, and who was known by that name. She was avaricious, distrustful, timid, and passionate."

He must have been right; for, as if these words had placed the dead before them, the impassible Robert started and recoiled, as if stricken with a sudden fear. The perspiration broke from his forehead—his teeth chattered—his moving hands seemed to feel for something on which to lean. In doing so he touched his companion ; but, instantly starting back, as with disgust and horror, regained with a strong effort his self-command.

" The identity is established; the proofs are complete," said the magistrate. " Gentlemen, I asked a miracle of you. It is performed."

Such was the scene that first drew public attention

to a case, the earlier incidents of which occurred twelve years before, and which we now proceed to give in a more condensed and intelligible form than a mere report of the judicial proceedings would allow.

On the 13th September, 1821, the widow Houet, a woman of sixty-eight, disappeared from her residence, Rue des Maturins. She possessed a fortune of 43,000 francs, and had two children—a son almost an idiot, and a daughter married to one Robert, a wine merchant, and an engraver of crystals. To this daughter, M. Lebrun, a brother of Madame Houet, had given a dower.

From the period of this marriage a bad understanding had existed between Madame Houet and her son-in-law Robert, and the old lady had been heard to declare that she should one day die by his hands.

At six in the morning of the 13th September Robert called at the house of his mother-in-law, and invited her to breakfast, to which she consented. Towards seven, a day-servant—Jusson—employed by her, made her appearance, and was scolded for being late. Madame Houet was dressed to go out, appeared agitated, talked to herself, and presently hurried away. She was last seen crossing the Rue de la Harpe, in the direction of a house in that street, inhabited by the Roberts.

Towards eleven, the woman Robert came to inquire for her mother, who had not come to her appointment, but nothing had been heard of her.

The next morning some one called on Robert to inform him of the continued absence of his mother-in-law. He was alone, and only replied :—"Do not speak of it to my wife. It will only make her uneasy. I shall not tell her till Sunday."

Two days later a letter purporting to be from Mdme. Houet, was received by a M. Hérolle, stating that she was about to take a journey, and should be absent some days.

Another letter addressed to a tenant of hers at Versailles, one Vincent, hinted at her intention to commit suicide.

Both letters were strongly suspected of being forgeries.

It was suspected that a crime had been committed. But where, when, and by whom ?

A perquisition was made in the widow's house, and six notes of 1000 francs each were found, besides 710 francs in specie. She had not then, it seemed, been murdered for the purpose of robbery.

Suspicion naturally fell on Robert. He had failed in business, and sold his wine establishment for 1800 francs, which, save an annuity of 168 in right of his wife, was all that now remained to him. ·But there were stronger grounds than the presumption that he would be a gainer by the death of the old lady. Robert had been noticed by several persons about the hour when she was last seen, watching at the door of his house, as if he expected some one ; while, subsequently to her disappearance, he, instead of displaying uneasiness or aiding in inquiry, only sought to conceal it from his wife, and affected to believe that the misfortune was irreparable.

For the present justice was baffled. Presumptions are not proofs; and accordingly, in 1822, the Tribune of First Instance decided that there was, for the time, no room for further investigation.

Meanwhile Robert had quitted Paris, and established himself with his wife at Dannemoine. But in 1823 he returned, accompanied by a man named Véron, and the two reoccupied an apartment that had always been reserved by Robert in his old house in the Rue de la Harpe. Here scenes occurred which tended to reawaken all the former suspicions.

A person named Bastien, coming one day by appointment to the house, received from Véron, on the part of Robert, a note for 250 francs. Some days later Bastien called again, demanding a personal interview with Robert. The two were closeted together, and an animated conversation was heard to ensue. Loud and violent exclamations and hasty steps somewhat alarmed Véron, who listened, and presently heard a struggle, and the voice of Robert, as if half strangled, exclaiming, " Thieves! thieves! murder," &c.

Bursting into the room, he found the pair engaged in a deadly struggle, Robert half suffocated, Bastien pale and menacing.

At sight of Véron, however, they started asunder; and Bastien, snatching his hat, slunk away. While the other occupied himself in adjusting his disordered dress, Véron's quick eye detected lying on the table a bond for 20,000 francs, apparently awaiting signature —a pen ready filled lying beside it.

Recommended to place himself under the protection of the law, Robert at once refused, alleging that the quarrel concerned losses at play, and was their own private affair; but when alone with Véron, who appeared to be a gentleman not easily startled at crime, Robert confided to him that Bastien's exactions were becoming intolerable, and coolly proposed that he should be lured into the house at Versailles, assassinated, and buried in the garden!

Concerning this same Bastien, it was known that he had failed in business at Grenoble, and to escape his creditors came to Paris. Robert being at this time in the wine shop, Bastien frequented the shop as a customer, and after the disappearance of Madame Houet, became an intimate friend of Robert.

Not long after the scene above described, Robert and Véron returned to Versailles. One day the former, who had made a visit of a few hours to Paris, came back much excited, and informed Véron that the villain Bastien had, by holding a pistol to his throat, compelled him to affix his signature to a bond for 30,000 francs.

Again, Véron, who was not fully in the confidence of his friend, urged him to avail himself of the law's protection; and again Robert, who had his own reasons for keeping the law as long as possible at arm's length, positively declined, declaring that he preferred flight to the scandal that would be occasioned, and with this view withdrew once more to Dannemoine.

Here he remained unmolested till 1827, when his persecutor suddenly pounced upon his retreat, and at the first visit compelled the Roberts to accept twelve bills, amounting in all to 6000 francs. Robert had been upon the point of changing his residence; and his wife, who had gone before to prepare their new abode at Villeneuve-le-Roi, had to be brought back to Germiny to sign the required acceptances.

A stormy interview was overheard by the inn-keeper at Germiny, who slept in the adjoining chamber.

" *Voyons,*" roared the voice of Bastien. " Did I do this business, or did I not?"

" Yes, you did," growled Robert.

" Pay me, then."

" Hèlas, mon Dieu! I *must,*" said the other, gloomily.

Nevertheless, he resisted. It was daybreak, and the acceptances remained unsigned.

Later, Robert sought out the host, and finding him alone, gave him a crown, saying—

" There is a fellow here who wants money that I cannot afford to give him. When you see us together presently, I shall tell him I have not a sous in the world, unless I borrow it. Then you shall lend me this crown."

The host, however, declined the part assigned him

in this little comedy, and even revealed the proposition to Bastien.

"Ah, c'est comme ça!" said the latter. "Tell him, then, that there is not a wisp of straw in his house that I cannot demand—nay, if I choose, I may turn him out of doors to beg his bread."

Ultimately, Robert paid the general bill, and the parties left the house together.

Scenes of this description had already attracted the notice of the police; and it should be mentioned that, in 1825, on the receipt of an anonymous communication, accusing Robert and Bastien of the murder of Mdme. Houet, a second inquiry had been instituted, the two men being placed under surveillance the while. It proved as fruitless as the former. The absence of the *corps du délit*—in this case represented by the body of the missing woman—paralysed the arm of justice, and a second decree of "non-lieu" (no ground for further inquiry) was reluctantly issued.

By some means never explained, Robert contrived for a time to give his enemy the slip. He retired to Villeneuve, and for five years was left in peace. But one fatal day Bastien knocked at the door. He was tired of rambling about the world, felt himself declining in years; wished to settle down as a quiet country gentleman ; and could he wish to find a more suitable home than at Villeneuve, close to his faithful old friend ?   Meanwhile, he desired to inaugurate this renewal of their intimacy by requiring his friend's signature to a little bond of 40,000 francs.

*Then* burst out the secret that had made one of the miscreants so long the slave of the other.

"*Assassin!*" thundered Bastien, incensed at Robert's refusal.   " Do you wish me to mount the roof of your house, and proclaim to every passer-by that Robert is the murderer of his mother-in-law ?"

Without a word Robert turned and staggered down-stairs, with no thought but immediate escape ; but in doing so he encountered a friend and neighbour, one Fleury, who had been alarmed by the disturbance. This man proposed at once to summon the police, and give this *coquin* (Bastien) into custody.

" No, no—for God's sake !" ejaculated the other, and, to the utter astonishment of Fleury, he dashed once more upstairs, from whence he escaped by a garret window into a loft, and so into the fields, while Bastien waited for him beside the street door.

Some weeks now elapsed.   Bastien had quitted Villeneuve, and Robert, warned by some means of the welcome fact, returned to his house.

Here he was shortly after waited on by a person named Gouvernant, in whom Bastien appeared to have placed great confidence, and who had, at all events, been given to understand by the latter that he (Bastien) had Robert at his mercy, on account of a concealed crime. His mission was to renew the money-claim, and his weapons for its enforcement were two slips of paper—the one containing certain names and addresses, the other the plan of a garden, in a corner of which there was traced a *red cross*.

At sight of these credentials Robert turned deadly pale; his knees trembled; he reeled into a chair.

" The villain ! the monster !" he exclaimed. " When he has stripped me of everything, who will assure me that he will not take my head also ?"

The visitor, finding him utterly prostrate with despair and terror, took his leave for the present, making an appointment, however, to meet him at a neighbouring inn.

Robert, rightly suspecting that Bastien intended to take part in the next interview, did not deem it advisable to attend. Upon this, Bastien, losing all self-control, furnished himself with a piece of chalk, and going direct to Robert's house, wrote upon the street door :—

"*Robert has murdered his mother-in-law, the widow Houet.*"

That night the Roberts disappeared from Ville-neuve-le-Roi.  They had fled into Burgundy, passing by Sens, towards Bourbonne-les-Bains.

Furious at this evasion, Bastien now gave himself wholly up to projects of revenge.  With judgment blinded by rage, he went at once to the representatives of the murdered woman, and denounced Robert as the author of that mysterious crime.  And this time justice struck effectually.  It was requisite, moreover, to strike at once, the French law forbidding to open a fresh inquiry after the lapse of ten years from the abandonment of the last.  A few months, and the murderers, however guilty, would be beyond the attaint of law.

The first step, rather to the amazement of the informer, was directed against his own precious person.  A decree commanded the immediate arrest of M. Bastien.  In his pocket-book were found several important papers.  Among others the following memorandum :—

" June, 1821.—M. Robert.

" Hired cellar, Rue des Deux-Portes.

" Rue de Vaugirard, small house, with good fruit garden.

"July, 1821.—Borrowed 700 francs.

"Later, received money to purchase spade, pick, and watering-can.

"Same day—bought (Place de la Grève) half a bushel of lime."

At the back of this memorandum was written :—

"Plan for murder of the Widow Houet by the Roberts', for which purpose we have hired the cellar, and afterwards the house, Rue de Vaugirard."

There were found also fragments of letters, one of which contained the following passage :—

"Unhappy Robert! is it then decreed that you shall not escape punishment for that crime you have described to the man you have involved in it as 're-volting?' Have you forgotten the Rue de Vaugirard, and the spot where your victim lies? Never. Believe that all is safe! Time and the remains (*débris*) still exist, undestroyed."

Another letter, or note, contained :—

"You and your wife —you are the murderers! Have you forgotten the cellar and the Rue de Vaugirard, and the disappearance of your mother-in-law, the 13th September, 1821? Do you fancy your crime is expiated? Man, your foot is on the scaffold!

Your idiot brother-in-law will enjoy the money.  For *you* there is only remorse !"

Annexed was a plan of the garden—Rue de Vaugirard—including the red cross before described.

The last paper was as follows :—

" The Court has decreed that, as regards Bastien, there is *non-lieu*" (no ground of process), " and as regards Robert, *non-lieu quant à présent.*  This decision is final for Bastien, according to the legal maxim, *Non bis in idem.*  Not so for Robert.  Even were Bastien to own himself guilty, he cannot again be prosecuted.  The judgment is irrevocable !"

This last note explains the man's audacity.  He doubtless believed his own safety as much assured as was Robert's destruction.

The new process was opened April 12th, 1833.

It was proved that the house and garden had in effect been hired by Bastien of a Madame Blanchard, from July, 1821, Bastien alleging that he wished to settle in Paris to superintend the education of his children.

One of his first acts had been to dismiss the gardener hitherto attached to the place.  No progress seemed to have been made in furnishing the residence ; and this circumstance, coupled with others of a doubtful character, such as strange nocturnal visitors, lights in the garden, &c., and finally, the apparent absence of everybody, awakened the suspicions of Madame Blanchard. Obtaining the aid of the police, she opened the doors and examined the premises, but without making any discovery. The next day, Bastien, made aware of the perquisition, returned Madame Blanchard the keys, and paying a second quarter in advance, announced that his wife had changed her mind, and abandoned the idea of a residence in Paris.

While the new inquiry was progressing, the Roberts had been arrested, the papers found on Bastien clearly implicating the woman in the crime, while they indicated at the same time an adulterous connexion with her. She was, however, subsequently released on a decree of "non-lieu."

The case came to hearing on the 12th of August, 1833, before the Assize Court of the Seine, presided over by M. Hardouin. An immense crowd filled the court and its approaches, and those who had obtained entrance gazed with awe and interest on the skeleton, which, prepared by Dumoutier, lay upon the table in the centre of the court, and formed the first terrible witness of the crime about to be revealed.

Bastien was attired in a sky-blue coat, his eyes

concealed by his immense green spectacles. He appeared, by turns, sullen and restless.

Robert was plainly dressed. His grey eyes were constantly fixed on one point beside the judge, and he seemed perfectly unconscious of the presence of those around, replying to the questions put to him in a low, confused voice. His age appeared to be about sixty-four. Bastien was fifty-one.

Bastien was interrogated first.

In his answers he admitted having learned the disappearance of Mdme. Houet very soon after it occurred, and had received at different times considerable sums of money from Robert, whom he suspected of having caused it.

(It was evident that his line of defence would be that he had detected, and profited by, a crime, although he had taken no part in its commission.)

He had had intimate relations with Robert, and, at the latter's request, had hired a cellar in the Rue des Deux-Portes, and also a house and garden, Rue de Vaugirard, in which to conceal contraband liquors.

Had he not in March, 1823, compelled Robert to sign a bond for 30,000 francs ?—He had.

In October, 1823, had he not written to Véron a letter containing threats against Robert, and declaring that the latter should give him whatever sums he chose to demand?—Possibly. He had received many sums from Robert, varying from 10 francs to 17,000, and all on the same ground—*i.e.*, hush-money.

*President.*—I will now tell you, Bastien, what has emboldened you to bring this charge against Robert thus openly—a thing you dared not do in 1823. You have been told by one Gouvernant that you have no longer anything to fear, being placed beyond the grasp of justice by the decree of " non-lieu." I have to warn you that that is a mistake.

*Bas.*—When I said I had nothing to fear, I meant that I had nothing to accuse myself of.

*Pres.*—Robert told you that he wanted the house in the Rue de Vaugirard for smuggling purposes, by which he hoped to make large profits, wherein you would doubtless expect to participate. Well, the house remained unused. There was no sign of clandestine commerce—not a single bottle of wine. Yet, you made no comment. Your companion not persisting in the fraud you speak of—why did he conceal his name behind yours?

No answer.

*Pres.*—You bought a spade and pickaxe. For

what purpose? The gardener must have possessed such tools.

*Bas.*—He had been dismissed.

*Pres.*—You purchased lime.   For what purpose?

*Bas.*—Robert told me it was to clean the kitchen.

(It was here shown from Bastien's notes that these purchases had been made immediately after the tenancy commenced, while the gardener was only dismissed a month later.)

A chemist then proved. that the quantity of lime covering the corpse amounted to two decalitres, exactly half a bushel, as mentioned in Bastien's papers.

*Pres.*—Bastien, this skeleton was found in a spot of the garden precisely corresponding with the red cross in your plan.   It is that of the widow Houet. Now, you have stated that she was strangled, and the cord around her neck confirms it.   How came you so well informed?

*Bas.*—Suspecting his secret, I one day said to him bluntly: "Tell me, unhappy wretch, is it not true that you are a murderer?   The soil here has been lately disturbed.   *What sort of seed have you planted here?*"   Throwing himself on his knees, he answered, "Monsieur Bastien, have pity on me.   I will give you whatever you ask. All I have is at your command." That is all that passed. I had the power to take his money, and, *ma foi*, I used it.

*Pres.*—How did you know the deceased was strangled?

*Bas.*—Robert told me everything.

*Pres.*—In one of your disputes with Robert, you were heard to say, "This is dangerous talk. It will cost *three* heads!" What did you mean by that?

*Bas.*—I meant *his* head, and—and his wife's—perhaps my own also; for I should have blown out Robert's brains, and then my own.

*Pres.*—A doubtful explanation. Why, at the inquiry in 1824, did you not reveal all this?

*Bas.*—It was against my interests. Robert was my *vache à lait* (milch cow).

The interrogation of Robert was commenced. The accused retained his downcast demeanour, and kept his eyes on the ground.

*Pres.*—Robert, you were on bad terms with your mother-in-law. She at one time forbade your visits; while, on the other hand, you complained of her extravagant habits, saying that she persisted in speculating in lotteries, and would have nothing to leave you and your wife at her death.

*Rob.*—I could not have said so, knowing nothing on the subject.

*Pres.*—She lent you various sums?

*Rob.*—About 10,000 francs in all—no more. I never asked her for a penny.

*Pres.*—Speak louder, if you please.

*Rob.*—My voice is naturally weak.

*Pres.*—Do you believe that your mother-in-law was murdered?

*Rob.*—I neither know nor believe it.

*Pres.*—You had an interest in her death. At that period you were a ruined man.

*Rob.*—I have never been ruined. I sold my business for 1800 francs, and I had goods to the value of 3000 more.

*Pres.*—By your mother-in-law's will, you have only recently come into actual possession of what you expected. Meantime, your income has not exceeded 1500 francs. In this condition, you actually signed a bond to Bastien for 20,000 francs. *Why?*

*Rob.*—I will explain the whole. I desired to place what money I had left in a certain manufactory. It was not sufficient. Walking one day with Bastien in the Palais Royal, he observed to me that if we could raise a little money we could do a very good stroke of business. Presently we met a gentleman, then two others—to all of whom Bastien spoke. Then he said to me, "One of these men will give us 6000 francs, another 3000. This looks well for the manufactory." It was now late, and I wished to go home. Bastien detained me, saying it was *not* late. "It is ten o'clock," said I. "I bet it is nothing of the kind," said he. "I accept it," was my answer. "Five hundred—ten thousand francs," he shouted. "Twenty thousand!" I replied, thinking the whole a jest. It turned out that I was wrong, and, because I would not pay 20,000 francs he called me rascal and cheat. Next day he came and demanded a bond for that sum. I refused. "Beware," he said; "this will cost three lives." I ran from him. He followed, calling out that he would put up with the wrong— that he had behaved badly. But he had bought some wood and had not the means to pay for it. How much did he need, I asked. "Three thousand francs." I gave it, and later, 4000 more. And that ended the affair.

*Pres.*—One hardly pays such sums for a bet of such a kind.

*Rob.* (with some quickness).—Monsieur, to judge of that, one must know the people.

*Pres.*—Attend, Robert.  It seems more probable that you incited some one to this crime, than that you committed it yourself.

*Rob.*—Ah, monsieur—impossible !

*Pres.*—Of what, then, were you afraid?

*Rob.*—Of all these people—Bastien, Gouvernant, Véron, believing them to belong to the band of Vidocq (the well-known agent of police).

*Bas.*—I deny it altogether.

*Pres.*—Did you, Robert, send money to Bastien in prison ?

*Rob.*—Never, monsieur.

*Pres.*—Bastien, what say you ?

*Bas.*—He sent me ten, twenty, and sometimes a hundred francs at a time.

At this answer of his co-accused, Robert entered into a long and confused explanation, made still more unintelligible by his weak voice; at the close of which witnesses were called.

A laundress, Esprit, deposed that she had heard Mdme. Houet declare that she would die by the hand of her son-in-law.  After the disappearance, Robert came to the house as if to make inquiries.  Witness replied bluntly that *he* knew most about it, and would do better to follow up the inquiry without seeking to inculpate his idiot brother-in-law. "You suspect me?"

"As I was about to answer," continued the witness, "he hastily begged me to speak lower, which I, having no cause to fear being overheard, refused to do." On this he hastened away.

Chevenaux, a porter, testified that within a few days of the disappearance Robert came to his lodge, and observed, "If ever you are summoned, you will be able to bear witness that I was at home."

Madame Lecoq had seen Robert watching at his house-door on the day of the disappearance. When it was announced to him, he remarked to witness: "My little neighbour, this misfortune happened that very day we had that pleasant chat together. You remember? So that if they should question you about me, you will be able to say that you saw me at work in the coal-yard. But" (added witness), "I could not say that, for I was uneasy at Robert's strange manner, and went away on pretence of taking my husband his dinner."

*Pres.*—These are singular precautions, Robert.

*Rob.*—It is possible; but I remember nothing of the sort.

At this point of the inquiry the medical professors

came forward, and were requested to uncover the skeleton. As the white sheet and green veil concealing the object were slowly withdrawn, revealing the remains of the murdered woman, with the bones and even the cartilages completely displayed, a lively agitation pervaded the crowded assembly. The accused men alone preserved their composure.

*Pres.*—Accused, look on these remains. Do you recognise them?

Bastien replied: "We have seen them."

Robert turned away his head.

The doctors repeated the description already given, adding that the deceased had been murdered by strangulation without suspension.

Véron, the friend of Robert, in 1823, related the quarrel between the latter and Bastien:—"You owe me 20,000 francs," said Bastien; "pay me, or if not——" When Robert and witness went out together, Robert said: "I am a wretched man. Are you my friend? If you are, assist me now. We will make an appointment with Bastien in the Rue de Montreiul, kill the fellow, and bury him in the garden." "But," I replied, "we are necessary to our families. Such an act would never pass unpunished." A little while after Bastien came to me, and said: "Are you aware that Robert has murdered his mother-in-law?" Such a communication, coupled with Robert's refusal to appeal to the protection of the police, appeared to me," the witness concluded, "*assez drôle*" (odd enough).

*Pres.*—In spite of this *assez drôle* proposal of murder, you remained on friendly terms with Robert?

*Wit.*—I merely continued to work with him as before.

Noquet, a mason, stated, that being employed in the house at Versailles once belonging to the deceased, now her daughter's, Bastien came in, and, inviting him to drink, questioned him concerning the widow's property. Witness told him Robert had inherited a portion. "Ah!" said Bastien, "I thought he took the whole." At that moment Robert appears. Bastien and he have a fierce quarrel. The police are called in; the case is heard; and both men declare that their dispute merely concerns a bet. They are discharged.

Lebœuf, another witness of the quarrel, gave the dialogue more precisely, as thus:—

*Rob.*—I owe you nothing, I tell you.

*Bas.*—Liar and cheat!

*Wit.*—Come, come, my children, what does all this mean?

*Bas.*—That this fellow is a rascal!

*Wit.*—Bon! *V'là du mic-mac.*

*Rob.*—It is as much as life is worth to have to do with a man like this!

*Wit.*—One doesn't risk life on such a squabble as this. What *are* your dealings with the citizen?

*Bas.*—Take care, Robert. Three heads are in danger!

"I know that *mine* was all right," concluded the witness, slowly and distinctly, "and I said:—

"'*Tiens*, the business is that you have bribed this man to murder your mother-in-law. *A child might see that!*'"

One Masson, a master mason, stated that at this point of the quarrel he had interposed, saying:—

"Well, well, *père* Robert, come and eat a cutlet. This man means to kill you, and himself also; nevertheless, a cutlet first!"

As they were eating, Robert dropped his napkin. Witness picked it up, and called Robert's attention to the fact that it was not a napkin, but part of a chemise that had belonged to the deceased woman.

"*Ah, laissez donc ça!*" exclaimed Robert, much agitated. "Do not disinter the dead!"

One Diensin deposed that he had lodged for some time with Gouvernant, whom Bastien visited. One day Gouvernant took him aside: "You see that big fellow there!" pointing to Bastien. "He was accused of a well-known murder. *Ah, diable! il s'en a ensauvé*" (he has scraped through it). They could not bring it home. He's a lucky one—*ce gaillard là!*"

The examination of Gouvernant, the man so often referred to by the other witnesses, created much interest. This worthy, who called himself by the elastic title of "agent," was at present a convict. Though disqualified by law from giving testimony on oath, he was admitted as a witness without it, his evidence being taken for what it was worth.

Speaking with much assurance, he stated that he had been on intimate terms with both the "messieurs" accused. "One day," he continued, "Bastien came to me and said, 'I know all about the widow Houet, and the author of it. They are searching in the *garden.* So long as they keep away from *the spot*, I shall be silent, for I hold a bond of 17,000 francs on Robert, and that would become worthless. But if they "burn," I will confess all.'" Bastien was very anxious and uneasy during the researches.

"I lost sight of both messieurs," continued the witness, "until 1827, when I fell in with Bastien. He told me things were going badly with him, and related his adventures in pursuit of Robert, who had absconded, but whom he had now traced to Villeneuve-le-Roi. He then proposed to me to visit Robert, and try to extort something from him. I consented, on condition that he (Bastien) should not himself enter the town, because everybody, children and all, would run after him, calling out, '*Here's Robert's man! Robert's man's come!*'

"He then gave me, as credentials, a plan of the garden, having a red cross in one part, which he made with a drop of rabbit's blood.

" I went to Robert, and asked—

"'Are you the murderer, or are you not ?—yes or no ?'

"'I don't know what you mean.'

"'Well, I'll tell you.' So saying, I placed the garden plan before him. '*Now* tell me, have you murdered the Widow Houet or not?'

"'What do you require of me ?' he asked. 'This Bastien is such a miscreant, that when he has got all I possess, he is as likely as not to take my life.'

" ' Don't fear that.  When he has got all he can, he'll let you alone.'

" ' Give me an hour to consider of it.'

" When we left the house we found a crowd assembled, Bastien in the midst, crying out, ' Robert is a murderer !'

" ' How !' shouted the crowd;  ' Robert !—a householder !—a *rentier !*—a man who played at bowls !—a man of substance !   *C'est-il possible ?'*

" ' Well ?' cried Bastien, seeing me.

" ' He has asked for an hour.'

" ' Ah !  An hour !  I understand.  See here !'

" It was then that he went and wrote on the house door :—

" ' *Robert murdered his mother-in-law, Sept.* 13*th,* 1821.'

"Some days after Bastien came to me, and said, ' How does this matter stand ?  The decree of *non-lieu* was only conditional as regards *him* ; for *me* it is final—eh ?'

"I gave it as my opinion that they could still prosecute him ; but only upon fresh testimony.

" Bastien seemed to consider that he had nothing to

fear; but I warned him more than once that in implicating Robert he might seriously compromise himself.

"'I am inclined,' said he, 'to denounce him to the widow's representatives, and claim a reward.'

"'How will that help you? If the wife is declared innocent, you will get nothing from *them.*'

"'She is guilty—as guilty as her husband. I could procure the condemnation of both as easily as drink a glass of water.'

"'Perhaps,' I objected, 'the body is decomposed, bones and all, by this time.'

"'In that case,' returned Bastien, 'I engage to find at least *a wedding-ring.*'"

*Pres.* (to Bastien).—Bastien, how did you know there would be a ring? According to you, Robert never told you.

*Bas.*—He must have done so. Besides, one might guess that a woman wore a ring.

The witness Gouvernant continued, and alleged that Bastien had declared that the woman had been strangled.

*Pres.*—Explain this, Bastien.

*Bas.*—Robert told me. He said he had strangled his mother-in-law, and buried her on the spot.

*Pres.*—Who prepared the grave?

*Bas.*—He himself, *the night before.*

Robert here interposed.

" It is all false, I swear.   There is an understanding between the witnesses.   Gouvernant is an agent of police, first-class.   Bastien is an agent of Vidocq. Give me ten minutes, and I will explain everything."

" This monsieur," remarked Gouvernant, demurely, " calls me *mouchard* (police-spy).   He takes every one that approaches him for a gendarme or a spy."

*Pres.*—With respect to the ring?

The witness Diensin, already examined, deposed that Gouvernant told him that Bastien wore on his little finger the ring of the murdered woman.

This exhausted the list of witnesses.

The accused Robert, who had manifested great impatience to be heard, now commenced his defence. This consisted of a rather more minute than interesting narrative of his early life, from which it appeared that he had been a man so devoted to honest labour, that he frequently painted, glazed, and plumbed, for nothing.  " *Faites excuse,*" said Robert, checking himself at this point, " I once accepted a bottle of wine, and in vintage-time I——"

Recalled by the President to the case at issue,

Robert proposed to favour the Court with a few details concerning his early disputes with his mother-in-law. These, however, the President pronounced irrelevant to the process, and Robert sat down, apparently not ill-satisfied with the impression he had made.

The Court now announced its intention to leave to the jury this question—Had Robert, by gifts or promises, procured the murder of the deceased Widow Houet.

" *Incapable, mon cher Monsieur,*" said Robert. " Incapable of anything of the kind! I am not a man to say one thing and mean another."

The Advocate-General Bayeux summed up the evidence in a speech that neither for its eloquence nor its lucidity would repay the reproduction. The case, however, was too precise and clear to be injured by any shortcomings in its advocate. He included both the accused in his denunciation, and confidently demanded their conviction.

The advocates for the defence did their best to shift from one prisoner to the other the weight of guilt, after which the President charged the jury, who retired, and remained in deliberation during two hours and a half.

On reappearing, their verdict established the fact

of murder. Bastien was pronounced *guilty* of the crime with premeditation.

Robert was found *guilty* of having procured the murder; but acquitted of actual participation in it.

To the astonishment of every one, including the judges, attenuating circumstances were admitted.

The prisoners were brought in. Bastien was calm. His companion's face betrayed poignant anxiety, and on hearing his comparative acquittal, he staggered, and would have fallen, had not a bystander supported his trembling form.

Both were sentenced to exposure on a scaffold, and *travaux forcés* for life.

At the moment of passing sentence Bastien had made a slight movement, but without the slightest change of feature. However, on being conducted to his cell, he turned suddenly pale, and sank on a seat. On examination his hand was found covered with blood, and convulsively clutching a pair of scissors, with which he had stabbed himself in the left breast. The wound was slight.

The two convicts appealed; but their appeal was rejected, and November 26th they underwent " exposition " in the Square before the Palais de Justice.

The crowd uttered ferocious cries and ribald jests: "Down with the murderers!" "To the guillotine with them!" "Monsters! the law is too gentle for such as you!" &c. &c.

Public opinion sometimes corrects the decision of an enlightened jury!

## XI.

## A FRENCH WOLF.

IN March, 1862, the chance of continental travel brought under the writer's personal notice the consummation of a history of horror not perhaps to be surpassed in the most carefully elaborated page of French romance. The narrative of facts so frightful would indeed be a barren as well as painful task, did not the case in question present certain novel aspects worthy of attention.

The neighbourhood of Montluel—a small town about twelve miles from Lyons, on the road to Geneva—enjoys a traditionary ill repute. Across the plain of Valbonne, on which it stands, may be seen the glimmer of two white houses—the Great and Little Dangerous—so called from having been in former days the scene of many deeds of lawless violence. The country around is broken, sparsely inhabited, and dotted with patches of dense and sombre woodland, sometimes reaching almost to the dimensions of forests.  A better locality no robber could desire.

Now, for six years, dating from February, 'fifty-five, the ancient bad reputation of this precinct had been resuscitated.  On the 8th of · February, 'fifty-five, some sportsmen, threading the thickets of Montaverne, came on the corpse of a young female, covered with blood, which had proceeded from six terrible wounds in the head and face.  The body was stripped, and had been subjected to gross outrage.  A handkerchief, collar, black-lace cap, and a pair of shoes, were picked up close at hand.  By the aid of these things, the deceased was soon identified as Marie Baday, late a servant at Lyons, which city she had quitted three days before.  She had stated as the reason for her departure, that a man from the country had offered her a good situation in the neighbourhood, provided she could take it at once.  Precisely similar proposals had been made, on the very same day, to another servant girl, Marie Cart: the agent being a country-looking man, aged about fifty, and having a noticeable scar or swelling on the upper lip.  Marie Cart postponed her answer until the 4th of March : a circumstance which probably induced the suspected person to address himself, in the interim, to Marie Baday.

On the 4th of March, the same man called again upon Marie Cart, who finally declined his offer, but introduced him to a friend of hers, Olympe Alabert—also a servant—who, tempted with what she considered an advantageous proposal, closed with it, and left Lyons under the guidance of the supposed countryman. Night was falling as they entered the wood of Montaverne, in which, a few days before,. the body of Marie Baday had been found. Acting on a sudden impulse, induced, perhaps, by the gloomy solitude of the place, the girl quitted her conductor, and sought refuge in a neighbouring farm.

At this point—strange as it seems, considering on what a stratum of crime they had touched—the discoveries of the police ended for that time.

In the month of September following, a man, answering in every point to the former description, induced a girl, named Josephte Charlety, to accompany him to a pretended situation as a domestic servant, and both left the city together. Their way led through cross roads; until, night coming on, the girl—like Olympe Alabert—oppressed with a nameless terror, fled to the nearest house.

On the 31st of October, the wolf again visited the fold, and selected Jeanne Bourgeois, another servant girl. But once more an opportune misgiving saved the intended prey. In the succeeding month, the wolf made choice of one Victorine Perrin; but, on this occasion, being crossed by some travellers, it was the wolf who took to flight, carrying with him the girl's trunk, containing all her clothes and money. None of these incidents seemed to have provoked much attention from the authorities; and horrible deeds actually in course of commission were only brought to light by the almost miraculous escape of another proposed victim, Marie Pichon.

On the 26th of May, '61, at eleven o'clock at night, a woman knocked wildly at the door of a farm, in the village of Balan, demanding help against an assassin. Her bruised and wounded face, torn garments, shoeless feet, all bore testimony to the imminence of the danger from which she had escaped. Conducted to the brigade of gendarmerie at Montluel, she made the following statement: listened to at the subsequent trial with breathless interest: "To-day, at two o'clock, I was crossing the bridge La Guillotière, at Lyons, when a man I had not before observed, but who must have been following me, plucked my dress and asked if I could tell him in what street the Servants' Office was situated. I mentioned two, adding that I was myself about to visit the latter. He asked if I were in search of a place. 'Yes.' 'Then,' said he, 'I have exactly the thing to suit you. I am gardener at a château near Montluel, and my mistress has sent me to Lyons with positive orders to bring back a house-servant, cost what it may.' He enumerated the advantages I should enjoy, and said that the work would be very light, and the wages two hundred and fifty francs, besides many Christmas-boxes. A married daughter of his mistress paid her frequent visits, and always left five francs on the mantelpiece for the maid. He added, that I should be expected to attend mass regularly.

"The appearance, language, and manner of the man gave me so strong an impression of good faith, that, without a minute's hesitation, I accepted his offer, and we accordingly left by the train, which arrived at Montluel about nightfall—half-past seven Placing my trunk upon his shoulder he desired me to follow, saying we had now a walk of an hour and a half, but that, by taking cross paths, we should quickly reach our destination. I carried in one hand a little box: in the other, my basket and umbrella. We crossed the railway and walked for some distance along the parallel road, when the man turned suddenly to the left and led me down a steep descent, skirted on both sides by thick bushes. Presently he faced round, saying that my trunk fatigued him ; that he would conceal it in a thicket, and come back for it with a carriage on the morrow. We then abandoned the path altogether, crossed several fields, and came to a coppice, in which he hid the trunk, saying we should presently see the château. After this, we traversed other fields, twice crossing over places that looked like dried-up watercourses, and finally, through very difficult ways, rather scrambling than walking, arrived at the summit of a little hill.

"I must mention something that had attracted my attention. Throughout the walk my guide seemed remarkably attentive, constantly cautioning me to mind my steps, and assisted me carefully over every obstacle. Immediately after crossing the hill I spoke of, his movements began to give me uneasiness. In passing some vines he tried to pull up a large stake. It, however, resisted his efforts, and, as I was following close on his heels, he did not persevere. A little farther, he stooped down and seemed to be endeavouring to pick up one of the large stones that lay about. Though now seriously alarmed, I asked, with all the indifference I could command, what he was looking for. He made an unintelligible reply, and presently repeated the manœuvre. Again I inquired what he was looking for,—Had he lost anything? 'Nothing, nothing,' he replied; 'it was only a plant I meant to pick for my garden.' Other singular movements kept me in a state of feverish alarm. I observed that he several times lagged behind, and, whenever he did so, moved his hands about under his blouse, as though in search of a weapon. I was frozen with terror. Run away I durst not, for I felt he would pursue me ; but I constantly urged him to lead the way, assuring him I would follow.

"In this way we reached the top of another small hill, on which stood a half-built cottage. There was a cabbage-garden and a good wheel-road. My very fear now gave me the necessary courage. I resolved to go no farther, and at once said, 'I see you have led me wrong. I shall stop here.' Hardly had the words left my mouth when he turned sharply round, stretched his arms above my head, and let fall a cord with a running noose. We were at this moment almost in contact. Instinctively, I let fall everything I carried, and with both hands seized the man's two arms, pushing him from me with all my strength. This movement saved me. The cord, which was already round my head, only caught and pulled off my cap. I shrieked out, 'My God! my God! I am lost!'

"I was too much agitated to observe why the assassin did not repeat his attack. All I recollect is that the cord was still in his hand. I caught up my box and umbrella, and flew down the hill. In crossing a little ditch, I fell and bruised myself severely, losing my umbrella. Fear, however, gave me strength. I heard the heavy steps of the murderer in pursuit, and was on my legs again in an instant, running for life. At that moment, the moon rose above the trees on my left, and I saw the glimmer of a white house on the plain. Towards this I flew, crossing the railway, and falling repeatedly in my headlong course. Soon I saw lights. It was Balan. I stopped at the first house. A man ran out, and I was saved."

Such was Marie Pichon's narrative. The authorities, now fully aroused, at once commenced a searching inquiry. Ultimately, the eye of justice rested on a certain small house in the little hamlet of Dumollard. Village gossip spoke unreservedly of the skulking nocturnal habits of its master—the stern, unsocial manners of his wife. Their name was the same as the village, Dumollard: a very common name in that district. The man had a peculiar scar or tumour on his upper lip.

The magistrates at once waited upon Dumollard, and requested an explanation of the employment of his time on the day and night of the 28th of May. The answers being evasive, and certain articles in the house wearing a very suspicious look, Dumollard was given into custody, conveyed to Trevoux, and instantly identified by Marie Pichon as her assailant. Meanwhile, a search in his house resulted in the discovery of an immense accumulation of articles, evidently the produce of plunder—clothes, linen, pieces of lace, ribbons, gowns, handkerchiefs, shoes—in a word, every species of articles that might have belonged to girls of the servant class. Very many of these bore traces of blood: others had been roughly washed and wrung out. These objects amounted in all to twelve hundred and fifty. "The man must have a charnel somewhere," said one of the searchers.

It was next ascertained that, in November, '58, Dumollard was seen to alight one evening at the station of Montluel, accompanied by a young woman, whose luggage he deposited in the office, saying that he would call for it next day. It was never claimed.

"On the night you mean," said the wife of Dumollard—who, after the search in the house, had been likewise taken into custody, and now showed a disposition to confess—"Dumollard came home very late, bringing a silver watch and some blood-stained clothes. He gave me the latter to wash, only saying, in his short way, 'I have killed a girl in Montmain Wood, and I am going back to bury her.' He took his pickaxe, and went out. The next day he wanted to claim the girl's luggage, but I dissuaded him from doing so."

In order to verify this statement, the magistrates, on the 31st of July, '61, repaired to Montmain Wood, taking with them the two accused. For some hours all their searches proved fruitless, the woman declaring her inability to point out the precise spot, and the man preserving a stolid silence. At length some appearance of a tumulus was detected among the bushes, and a few strokes of the pickaxe made visible some bones. A circular trench was then carefully dug, and a perfect female skeleton uncovered. The skull presented a frightful fracture. Under it was found some brown hair and a large double hair-pin.

The prisoners were now brought forward, and confronted with the silent witness.

The woman having volunteered further confession, the party now proceeded to the wood Communes, also near Montluel; but night coming on, investigation was deferred till the next day. A great part of the next day was passed in fruitless search, when, just as the party prepared to return to Montluel with the view of organizing explorations on a larger scale, Dumollard suddenly declared that he would himself point out the place they sought.

He thereupon guided them to a spot about fifty yards deep in the wood. Here they laboured for another hour with no better success, until one of the officers noticed a slight displacement of the soil, presenting some small fissures, from whence flies were issuing. Above this spot two little shrubs, evidently placed by design, had taken feeble root.

A stroke of the spade laid visible the back of a human hand. Presently the body of a young female, in complete preservation (owing to the character of the soil), was exposed to view. The corpse lay on its back, the left hand on the bosom, the fingers clutching a clod of earth. Appearances favoured the frightful conclusion that the victim had been buried while yet alive and conscious.

The bearing of Dumollard in the presence of this

new and terrible accuser, was as calm as ever. Not the slightest trace of emotion was perceptible on his stolid features. It was observed, nevertheless, that he studiously avoided looking, as it were, on the face of his victim. The magistrates seized the moment to impress upon him the inutility of any further attempt to evade justice, and invited him to make a full confession. After a few moments of seeming irresolution, he commenced the following recital :—

"One day in December, '53, I was accosted in Lyons by two individuals of the farmer class, whose manner and appearance won my unlimited confidence. After treating me to wine at a neighbouring tavern, they invited me to stroll on the quay, asked me a multitude of questions, and finally proposed to me to enter their service. I inquired the nature of the work required of me. 'The abduction of young women,' was the reply. 'You shall have forty francs for every " prize," and if you remain with us twenty years, we will guarantee you a hundred thousand francs.'

" Such a proposal seemed far too advantageous to be treated lightly," continued Dumollard. " They gave me the necessary instructions, which were simple enough. I was merely to look out for young females in search of situations, offer them first-rate wages, and conduct them beyond the town.

"A week later, we commenced operations on the Place de la Charité. My first attempt failed ; but the second woman I accosted listened to my story, accepted the pretended situation, and accompanied me from the town. At the end of the suburbs my two employers met me. I pretended to have forgotten something, and, telling the girl these gentlemen were friends of mine, requested her to go on with them, promising to overtake them at Neyron. I lingered about the spot for three hours, when the men returned, and handed me a parcel, saying it was a present for my wife. Opening it, I found a gown and chemise, both stained with blood. I recognised the dress of the woman I had brought, and demanded what had become of her. ' You will not see her again,' was the only reply.

" On the way home I washed the clothes in the fountain at Neyron, and gave them to my wife, saying I had purchased them at Lyons.

"I never knew the exact place in which they mur-dered the girl, but I think it must have been near the bridge Du Barre, and that they flung the body into the Rhone. I think so, because one day in the ensuing summer, while crossing that bridge in their company, one of · them remarked, 'We have sent two bodies under this bridge already.' And this I understood to imply two other murders, anterior to that I have mentioned.

"Nothing remarkable happened until February, '55, when my two friends met me by appointment at a wine-shop, and brought with them a young female of dark complexion, with whom and the men I set forth, and proceeded as far as the road leading from Miribel to Romaneche, which passes through the wood. Here I sat down, declaring I would go no farther. They tried to persuade me to proceed, but finding me determined, presently pursued their way, taking with them the girl.

"I waited two hours. No cry reached my ears. Still I had a presentiment of something wrong. The men returned alone, saying they had left the girl at a farm. As they brought no clothes with them, I was inclined to believe their story. We then parted, and I returned home."

[This was, no doubt, the unfortunate Marie Baday.]

"Nothing occurred for two years, during which I had occasional interviews with my two friends; at length, in December, '58, I fell in with them on the

Quai de Perrache. They told me they had something on hand, would I come? I consented, and they left me; presently returning with a young girl, with whom we started by the rail for Montluel. It was dark when we arrived, and the men, taking me aside, requested me to guide them to some secluded spot, indicating the wood of Choisey. I told them it was too close to the high road; it would be better to go on farther. Presently we reached the edge of Montmain Wood. *That*, I told them, would do.

"They left me seated by the roadside. Soon I heard one loud scream, about three hundred yards distant; then profound silence. In a few minutes the men returned, bringing a silver watch and some clothes. I told them I had heard a scream, and asked if she had suffered much? 'No,' they answered; 'we gave her one blow on the head, and another in the side, and that did the business.'

"We knew that the body of Marie Baday had been found, and it was judged prudent to bury this new corpse. I therefore ran to my house for the tools, and at the same time gave my wife the watch, and the clothes, which were stained with blood. She asked me whence they came? Thinking that if I accused others she would not believe me, and relying, like a fool, on her discretion, I replied that they had belonged to a girl I had killed, and was about to bury, in Montmain Wood. I then went back to my friends, who dug a shallow grave, and concealed the body, while I sat by."

[This was the victim—never identified—whose skeleton was exhumed, as before mentioned, on the 31st July, '61.]

Dumollard referred to certain other attempts, which had failed, owing to the suspicions of the intended victims, and continued—

"I must speak now of this girl, Marie Eulalie Bussod, whose body lies before us. I accosted her one day on the bridge La Guillotière, and asked her if she would accept a good place in the country, offering two hundred francs. She required two hundred and ten, and we went to the residence of her sister to discuss the matter, where I agreed to her terms. At the end of a week I returned, and escorted her to the station at Brotteaux, where I had, in the interim, desired my two employers to meet me. They came, and I introduced them to Marie Bussod as friends and neighbours of mine, who would accompany us some little distance after quitting the rail.

"It was dark when we reached Montluel, and I had

to act as guide, carrying the girl's trunk. 'What a lovely creature!' whispered one of my friends to me as we set out.

"I led the way towards the wood Communes—a wild, retired spot—following a path, almost oblite-rated, towards Croix-Martel. Here I hid the trunk among some bushes, assuring the girl I would return for it in the morning.

"Somehow, at this point, my courage failed me. I told my friends I could go no farther; at the same time, however, pointing out to them Communes Wood, which lay but a few paces distant. In two hours the men returned, bringing some clothes and a pair of gold ear-rings, which they gave me for my wife. I inquired what they had done with the girl? 'Oh,' said one, 'she got two blows on the head, and one in the stomach. She made no great outcry.' I then went home for a spade, and the men buried her here, as you see.

"Marie Pichon would inevitably have suffered the same fate, had not my two employers failed me at the appointed place. I did not wish to do her any harm. On the contrary, finding the men absent, I wished to get rid of her, and, to frighten her, threw my arms (not a cord, as she affirms) round her neck. I was glad to see her run away. 'At least,' I thought, 'they'll not get *this* one !'

"Some days later, finding an inquiry on foot, I judged it prudent to destroy the effects of the girl Bussod, and those of Pichon, and, assisted by my wife, buried them accordingly in the wood des Rouillonnes.

"Now I have told all. I have nothing more to add."

It is almost needless to mention that the two mysterious persons on whom he affected to lay the burden of these atrocious crimes had no real existence. Unable to resist the proof of his own complicity, Dumollard, as Rush did before him, saw no hope of escape, save in conjuring up some individual more guilty than himself.

The account against him now stood as follows :

Three women, unknown, murdered and flung into the Rhone.

Murder of Marie Baday; body found in Montaverne.

Murder of a girl unknown ; skeleton found in Montmain wood.

Murder of Marie Bussod ; body found in Communes Wood.

Attempts at robbery and assassination on the persons of the women Charlety, Alabert, Bourgeois,

Perrin, Fargat, Michel, Pichon, and three others unidentified.

Nor is it to be supposed that he confessed to *all* the victims. Without dwelling on opinions which carried the number of those actually murdered to twelve, sixteen, eighteen, it may be gathered from hints let fall at intervals by the female prisoner, as well as from the vast accumulation of clothes and the like (among which were numerous articles which must have belonged to children of nine or ten years old), that these intermediate periods described by Dumollard as presenting "nothing remarkable," were stained with deeds as horrible as those confessed to: deeds, perhaps, never to be revealed on earth.

The trial commenced on the twenty-ninth of January, 1862, at the assizes of the Ain, sitting at Bourg: the woman Dumollard being included in the act of accusation. It lasted four days. Through the politeness of the officials it was not difficult for a stranger to obtain an excellent place in the crowded hall, and the temptation of witnessing an important French criminal trial was too great to be resisted by the passing traveller who writes this account of it.

The proceedings commenced at ten o'clock, under

the presidency of M. Marillat, of the Imperial Court of Lyons : the Procureur-General on his right, the Procureur-Imperial on his left ; and the magistrates of Bourg, Trevoux, and Montluel on the bench behind.

A short pause, and the prisoner appeared, escorted by four gendarmes, his wife following.

" There he is !  There he is !" murmured the assembly.

" Yes, here I am !" retorted the prisoner, waving his hat, as a popular candidate might at an election.

He was placed on a bench at a little distance from his wife, and had the appearance of a hale rustic of fifty or thereabouts ; his hair, beard, and moustache, thick and dark ; his nose aquiline ; eyes blue, round, and very prominent ; his whole expression singularly calm and self-possessed.  The swelling on his upper lip, by which he had been more than once identified, was very apparent.  He had told the jailer that it was occasioned by the sting of a poisonous fly.

The phrenological development of this man presented some extraordinary traits.  The skull, enormously large at the base, sloped upward and backward, until it terminated almost in a cone—a point too acute to be appreciated without passing the hand through his thick hair.  The organs of destructiveness, circumspection, and self-reliance, exhibited the most marked development. In front, the skull rapidly receding, presented, indeed, a "forehead villainous low." From the root of the nose to the root of the hair, it did not exceed three inches. The organs of comparison, causality, ideality, &c., were all but imperceptible; nay, in some instances, presented an actual depression. In a word, the cruel, brute-like character of this head was due rather to the absence of almost *every* good feature, than to the extreme development of the bad. It was a type of skull commonly found among nations yet beyond the pale of civilization.

The jury having been impannelled, and two supplementary jurors having been chosen by lot to supply the places of any who might, from illness or other cause, be disqualified from sitting out the trial, the indictment was read.

Scarcely had the last word dropped from the officer's lips than Dumollard rose, and beckoned eagerly to his counsel, M. Lardière. The latter approached.

"There is a draught of air somewhere," said the prisoner, "which really annoys me excessively. Can nothing be done to remedy it?"

This important matter arranged to the prisoner's

satisfaction, the list of witnesses—seventy in number—
was read aloud—all (save one, deceased) answering to
their names.

Next came the interrogatory; that doubtful feature
in the otherwise excellent system of French criminal
procedure.   It was conducted, however, in the present
instance, with dignity and fairness.   Dumollard was
questioned on his domestic relations.

" Your father was a Hungarian ?"

" Yes."

" What became of him ?"

"I cannot say." (Then, hesitatingly:) " If you insist
upon my explaining, I will."

" Certainly.   You are here to explain."

" My father was well-to-do in his own land.   My
mother told me that, in 1814, we went into Italy—
to Padua.   There my father was taken prisoner by
the Austrians.   We never saw him again."

[A horrible story, but resting on very substantial
proof, and fully credited at Trevoux, held that Dumollard's father had been implicated in a plot against
the life of the Emperor of Austria.   On being recognised at Padua, the unhappy man was hastily tried,
and subjected to the punishment of " écartelément,"

—*i.e.*, the culprit being attached to four horses, is dismembered.]

"It is said you have been accustomed to ill-treat your wife?"

"Never. Well, sometimes, when she has plagued me very much, I may have forgotten myself for a moment."

"You have been convicted of many offences?"

"Once, only."

"How, once only? We have here the record of two convictions, at least. You have no means, yet you do no work. You have borne the character of a vagabond at war with society."

"Since I became the associate of those two wretches" (the fictitious persons), "it has, indeed, been as you say."

"You live in singular privacy, forbidding your wife to know her neighbours :—a rule so well observed that, before your arrest, the mayor of your commune knew nothing of you. You returned to your house at unusual hours, using a password, 'Hardi,' as one of your neighbours will prove."

"I may have done so, but not in the sense you mean."

Questioned as to Mary Pichon, the prisoner's

account corroborated hers, except that he reiterated his assertion that his only object was to frighten her.

"But she declares you strove to strangle her with a cord."

"That is false. If I had had such a purpose, I should not have led her to a place where any alarm might be heard."

"But why lead her thither at all?"

"My employers said to me, 'Eyes are upon you of which you know nothing. If you betray us you are lost.' That alarmed me."

"You have destroyed many of the effects of your several victims. Why have you allowed so many to remain?"

"I preserved those articles," replied the prisoner, with perfect gravity, "for the sake of the relations of the deceased."

Dumollard being removed, his wife was brought forward. There was nothing noticeable in her appearance or demeanour.

She stated, in reply to various questions, that her husband had twice brought her articles of dress which he described as having been the property of women murdered by him. She had noticed the blood marks, but said nothing to her husband, with whom she lived on indifferent terms. He was frequently absent at night, returning before dawn and using a watchword, as stated. Though cognisant of his guilty practices, she continued to live with him, being completely cowed by his menaces.

The production in court of the stolen effects was the next scene of the legal drama. These were brought forward in two immense chests bound with iron clasps, and sealed.

"*Ah, tiens!*" murmured the assembly. "Now for the wardrobe of M. Dumollard!"

The articles were sorted, and placed, "chronologically," in heaps. There were seventy handkerchiefs, fifty-seven pairs of stockings, twenty-eight scarves, thirty-eight caps, ten corsets, nine gowns, and a multitude of miscellaneous objects.

Witness after witness then entered the box, and delivered their testimony with surprising terseness and lucidity. Until the evidence of each was complete, no interruption was offered, unless when the President, observing that the witness was merely corroborating matters already amply deposed to, recalled the speaker to facts bearing more immediately on the case.

Owing to this, and perhaps in some degree to the

French facilities of expression, the trial proceeded with great rapidity.

The sixth witness, Louis Cochet, was an odd-looking little man, with a very excited manner. He was Dumollard's next-door neigbour. He stated that he had seen the prisoner come home at two in the morning carrying a trunk.

"He muttered 'Hardi! hardi!' at the door, and was let in. The next day, he said to Madame (the female prisoner), 'Aha! I have got the watchword! I avail myself of Monsieur's absence to call when it suits me!' Then I asked what he did abroad so late? She grew red, and said drily, 'He has his own affairs.' Oh, messieurs!" said the impressionable little witness, bursting into tears, "I'm fifty-one. I never was in a court of justice before. Now, indeed, I know what frightful 'affairs' this neighbour of mine dealt in!"

The seventeenth witness, Dr. Montvenoux, detailed the autopsy of the body of Marie Bussod, stating his belief that she had been buried alive.

Hereupon the prisoner's counsel rose for the first time.

"1 desire," he said, "to know the witness's precise reasons for this presumption. We have horrors enough to contend with, without this crowning atrocity. The opinion of the medical witnesses has already created a most painful sensation."

Dr. Montvenoux alleged, as his chief reasons, that the wound was not mortal, nor even severe; that a clod of the outer earth—not that which formed the subsoil—was grasped in the hand; and that the teeth were set, as if in agony.

The court now adjourned for a few minutes. Dumollard took a huge lump of bread-and-cheese from his pocket, and began devouring it with the appetite of an ogre. At this moment his eye happened to fall on Marie Pichon, who was moving through the court. Faithful to his plan of defence, he called out to her :—

" Ah, *malheureuse!* But for *me*, you would not have been here now. Come and thank me for rescuing you from those villains."

The girl made no reply ; but her sister, who accompanied her, retorted with such warmth and volubility that the dialogue was checked by the officer of the court. A curious little episode occurred in the waiting-room. Marie Pichon, who was evidently regarded as the heroine of the hour, and was distinguished by a very pleasing countenance and ingenuous manner, had been prevailed upon by a photographer sent from Paris to sit for her picture. Just as she had taken her position, a respectably-dressed woman forced her way through the crowd, and running up to Pichon, implored her to forbear, reminding her, in accordance with a popular belief which it seems existed, that all women who have become associated in a marked manner with great criminal processes—such as Nina Lassave, Fieschi's mistress, "Madame" Lacenaire, and others—came to some melancholy end.

Maria Pichon started: "Ah, *mon Dieu!* monsieur, spare me! Do not put me beside that wretch!" she exclaimed, and was instantly lost in the crowd.

The examination of the fifty-third witness produced a most painful scene. This was Josephte Bussod, sister of the murdered girl, who, with two other sisters, appeared in deep mourning, and testified the most profound grief. It was necessary that she should identify the clothes of the deceased; and as each familiar garment stained with her blood was in turn held up, the tears and sobs of the witnesses redoubled, and deeply affected the auditory. The prisoners alone preserved their calmness.

"Do you recollect this dress?" asked the President of Dumollard.

"Oh, perfectly."

"And you, Marianne Dumollard?"

"Of course; I have worn it."

"Have you not also worn a cap with marks of blood?"

"Certainly not. I should have *washed* it," said the woman.

"You fully recognise the prisoner?" asked the President of the weeping witness.

"Recognise him!" shrieked the poor girl, wringing her hands with wild passion. "The miscreant! the monster! He killed my sister—my poor Eulalie! But it is I, too—*I* that am guilty. O, *mon Dieu! mon Dieu!* I believed him! I trusted him! I made her go with him—to death—to death! And *what* a death!"

She was carried out fainting. A gentleman sitting near stated that since the discovery of her sister's fate she had never ceased to accuse herself in this manner as a sort of accomplice.

The Procureur-General gave a brief summary of the case, claiming the extreme penalty of the law against both the prisoners.

"*One,*" he concluded, "as the participator in all the robberies, the confederate of all the horrors that

had preceded them. The other, as an habitual professed assassin, whose life has been one long outrage
and defiance of all laws, divine and human. Steeped
in infamy—enemy alike of the living and of the dead
—he has made no single pause in his career of crime,
nor can any penalty of man's enactment attain the
standard of his desert."

Dumollard's advocate, M. Lardière, followed, and
commenced his address in a manner decidedly
French.

" In the secluded village of Dagneux, lately so
obscure, to-day so notorious, there stands, fronting
the church, a modest tomb, wherein repose all that is
mortal of those I loved best on earth—my father and
my mother. Since the period that the exigencies of
my professional career have forbidden me to kneel at
that cherished shrine, memory has daily pictured to
me those happy shades, that simple, quiet community,
among whom the soft joys of earlier youth were
tasted."

The excellent advocate, in less euphonious phrase,
proceeded to explain that Dumollard, recollecting his
name in connexion with the place, had written to
him, entreating him to undertake his defence.

"Perhaps it is a first expiation on the part of this

unhappy man," remarked Monsieur L., with almost overweening modesty, "that he should have selected *my* weak aid, instead of that of some more distinguished member of that bar whose hospitality I am now enjoying."

Monsieur L. made no effort to rebut the evidence, resting his defence on the ground of those social defects which cast men like Dumollard, unheeded, unreclaimed, loose upon the world, from their cradles; while, at the same time, the growing aversion to capital punishment weakens the sole barrier by which the passions of such men are restrained. Shall, then, society wreak mortal vengeance upon a deed for which it is itself, in some measure, responsible?

The counsel of the female prisoner, M. Villeneuve, delivered a long and very eloquent address, and, having better materials to work with, made a decided impression on the court and jury.

The President gave an impartial summing up, and concluded by submitting to the jury twenty-eight distinct questions, bearing upon the various acts of murder, robbery, &c., charged in the indictment.

It was four o'clock on the fourth day when the jury withdrew to their consultations. The prisoners were removed, and groups forming in every part of the court, eagerly discussed the case.  No doubt was felt as to Dumollard.  The strongest opponents of capital punishment seemed on this occasion to have laid aside their prejudices.  As an illustration of this, a gentleman who had been summoned among the jury, but was not one of those on whom the lot fell, observed—

"I have never been able to condemn a man to death, but in spite of the scruples I have always felt and expressed as to the inviolability of human life, I would, in *this* instance, have signed *with both hands* for the guillotine."

In the meantime the individual most nearly concerned was taking refreshment and chatting easily with those around him; but he neither addressed nor even looked at his wife, who sat at a little distance, weeping bitterly.

Two hours and a half had elapsed, when the door leading to the jury-chamber swung open, and the twelve re-entered, the foreman carrying a large scroll, which he handed to the President.  There was no need to proclaim silence, when, placing his hand on his heart, the foreman began—

"On my honour and my conscience, before God and men, our verdict, is——"

"Stay, gentlemen," said the President; "here is

something irregular. You have not only to pronounce upon the principal charges, but also to answer ' Yes ' or ' No ' to each of the aggravating circumstances. Have the goodness to retire and do this."

It took some little time to rectify this informality, and then the jury once more made their appearance. The twenty-eight chief questions were for the most part supplemented by other questions, each requiring a separate answer, such as :—

" With violence ?"

" During the night ?"

" With premeditation ?"

" On the public highway ?"   And like questions.

In all there proved to be sixty-seven affirmative and seventeen negative answers—the former embracing all the material charges.

The effect of this complicated verdict was the conviction of both prisoners, with (by a majority) extenuating circumstances in favour of the woman.

For the first time during the proceedings, Dumollard's coolness seemed to desert him. His countenance became perfectly livid; his eyes glared wildly round. At this moment, perhaps, the full horror of his position first revealed itself to his stubborn intelligence. There occurred, too, one of those dramatic pauses which give time for a scene of peculiar interest and solemnity to impress itself ineffaceably on the memory. Throughout the dimly-lighted court nothing was to be seen but bowed heads or stern still faces, waiting for the word of doom; not without a sense of that humiliation which even in the very act of justice confesses with reluctance the possibility of guilt so monstrous in the human form. Hunger makes the wolf savage, "yet with his kind he gently doth consort." Here was a man who, to pamper the lowest passions of which nature is susceptible, had literally waded in the blood of the most helpless and innocent of his kind.

It was the voice of the Procureur-General that broke the hush, praying the court to grant the application of certain articles of the penal code. The prisoners, called upon to add what they pleased to their defence, made no reply.

Then the President, after reading the articles applicable to the case, pronounced the fatal judgment. Martin Dumollard to the pain of death, the execution to take place at Montluel; Marianne Dumollard to twenty years' imprisonment and hard labour.

That night the condemned murderer slept tranquilly, though for the preceding four his rest had been broken by convulsive tossings to and fro.

"Well, Dumollard, how goes it?" said his advocate, entering his cell next morning.

"As one who expects to die," was the answer.

"It remains then to make a good end; let that be the first expiation of your crimes."

Neither to such exhortations, nor to the earnest counsels of the excellent Abbé Beroud, vicar of Bourg, who paid him many visits, did the unhappy wretch give any heed.

"I shall do nothing with him," said the good priest, mournfully. "The mind is too coarse and brutified. It is not with him as with others, where darkness and light are at least mingled in the soul. Here it is one profound obscurity."

Nevertheless, he did not relax his efforts; and, as Dumollard exercised his right of appeal to the Court of Cassation, opportunity was not wanting.

Dumollard's cell was shared by four or five others, condemned to different terms of imprisonment. These sometimes flattered him with hopes of success in his appeal.

"In twenty days," he answered, "I shall either lose my head, or be set at liberty; but I would rather die than be sent to Cayenne or even kept in prison."

This speech betrayed two misapprehensions on the criminal's part. One, that a certain time must elapse before the execution of a capital sentence, whereas the law assigns none; the other, that a favourable decision of the Appeal Court ends all proceedings, and sets a prisoner free. Whereas it merely remits the case to a new jury.

On the 27th of February his appeal was rejected; the report being accompanied by that recommendation to mercy without which no capital sentence in France is carried into execution.

The report was then submitted to the minister and to the Emperor, who wrote upon it, " *Il n'y a lieu* "— there is no room (*i.e.* for pardon)—and the magistrates and officials of Montluel received orders to execute the sentence within twenty-four hours. The executioner of Grenoble was directed to assist his colleague of Lyons.

On Friday evening, the 7th of March, the guillotine was taken from the vaults below the Palais de Justice, placed upon an immense car, and transported to Montluel: whither a large detachment of Lancers had already proceeded, to preserve order among the immense multitudes that came flocking from every part of the country. At four o'clock that same evening, the criminal received intimation that he was to die on the morrow. He turned deadly pale; but soon recovered his habitual indifference, and only replied that it was what he had expected. His confessor was then introduced, and remained with him half an hour. About to leave, he suggested to the condemned man that the time had arrived when, if ever, he should exchange forgiveness and reconciliation with his wife, offering at the same time to obtain permission for his release from irons.

Dumollard assented, and the interview took place immediately—the male prisoner remaining calm and unmoved as ever—the woman deeply agitated. After this, the two sat down to partake of their last meal together: an abundant supper, provided at the cost of the good priest, who, though it was fast day, permitted them, "in the present conjuncture of circumstances," to eat what they pleased. Of this license Dumollard (again like Rush) availed himself to the utmost limit of human appetite. Beef, pork, cutlets, and especially puddings, disappeared under his efforts with a rapidity that struck with amazement the spectators of that gloomy feast. He seemed to consider the time too precious to be wasted in conversation; but, nevertheless, found opportunity now and then to address a word of comfort to his wife, whose sobs interrupted the repast.

"Patience, patience; you are fretting about me; but it is a waste of grief; you see *I* don't care. As for you, you have to remain twenty years in prison. Be careful of the little money I shall leave you. Take some wine now and then. But mind! on your liberation, do not go back to Dagneux, where your family would not welcome you. Remain at Dijon. By-the-bye," he added, as if an important idea had struck him; "don't forget to reckon with Berthet—she owes you for so many days' work; that will be seventeen francs, less five sous."

At half-past ten at night, the vehicle which was to convey Dumollard to Montluel arrived at the prison. Embracing his wife for the last time, he quietly mounted, accompanied by his confessor, and escorted by two gendarmes.

"Ho là!" said the criminal, who seemed to have a peculiar aversion to cold air. "This is very annoying. I am chilled to death."

"Here, père Dumollard," said a good-natured gendarme, "by a lucky foresight I brought my blanket."

Once made comfortable, the prisoner seemed to desire nothing more. Through the whole length of that ghastly journey, his was the only unruffled spirit of the party. He conversed incessantly, but without effort or bravado, describing the localities, the distance from point to point of places mentioned at the trial, &c., &c., with a cool minuteness which, under the circumstances, and with the accompaniment of sickly moon-gleams, the howling March wind, and the dull rumble of the carriage that bore the culprit nearer and nearer to his doom, struck his companions with awe.

It was half-past one in the morning as they entered Chalamont, a mile or two short of Montluel, and here the crowd had become so dense as to create some difficulty in passing. Yells and execrations resounded on every side. Some women forced their way up to the vehicle, flashing their lanterns into the face of the criminal. The Abbé Beroud warmly remonstrated, rebuking their indecent curiosity, and exhorting them to be satisfied with the act of justice about to be done. Thus, through masses of living beings, miles in length, the *cortége* approached Montluel.

The scaffold had been erected during the night in the widest piece of public ground—the Place

Bourgeat—and now stood ready, in the centre of a perfect forest of bayonets and drawn sabres. Beyond the military square every visible inch, from ground to chimney-top, was packed with living beings. How some of these points of vantage were gained at all, or how descended from, were questions only to be resolved by those who saw the process. We were informed that thousands had been content to pass the long chill night in these positions.

Dumollard had alighted at the town-hall, and was warming himself comfortably at the fire in the council-chamber. A magistrate present exhorted him to confess whatever remained upon his mind in reference to the crimes for which he was to suffer. The criminal made no other reply than :

" I am innocent. It is unlucky, but I am sacrificed for the guilt of others."

M. Carrel, the curé of Montluel, entered.

" Ah, good morning, M. Carrel !" said Dumollard. "I have heard much good of you. It was from your hands that, at sixteen, I received my first communion."

Some further futile efforts were made to induce him to confess. One singular answer was noted :

"If others have buried bodies in my vineyard, I am not responsible for that."

He was offered some refreshment, and took some coffee and Madeira; after which the executioners were introduced, and the "toilette" commenced. The prisoner himself took off his blouse, and sat down.

His feet were tied, but not sufficiently to prevent his walking, and his arms secured. They then cut off his hair and the neck of his shirt. As the steel of the shears touched him, he gave a convulsive shudder, but quickly regained his self-command. One final effort to obtain confession, or at least admission of his guilt, met with the former result, and this extra-ordinary offender, persevering to the last in his war with justice and society, marched forth to his doom.

The shout that rent the air as he appeared might have been heard for miles. The silence that succeeded was the more appalling. Dumollard's lips moved as though in prayer. The priests bent forward, caught, and earnestly re-echoed the solitary accents:

"Jésus! Marie! Pray for me!"

He knelt for a moment on the lower steps of the scaffold, and the Abbé Beroud offered to his white lips the symbol of divine mercy. Then the executioners helped him up the remaining steps, tied him to the plank, pushed the latter to its place. Quick as lightning the axe descended, and in a few seconds head and body lay together in a rude coffin ; the body to be interred in an obscure nook of the cemetery at Montluel, the head to be sent to the phrenological professors at Lyons. There was scarcely time for a trace of blood to become visible. Never was the merciful death of the guillotine more skilfully administered. Never was death punishment more richly deserved, than by the French wolf, Dumollard.

## XII.

## THE MARTYR-WIFE.

THERE occur in the life of society, as in the lives of its individual members, sinister and distressing periods, intended—it might almost be believed—by Providence to confound the most assured calculations of mankind, and to sap the very basis of that which seemed constructed to endure for ever. At such times nature herself appears to partake the general disorder, the seasons change their character—poverty, hunger, and want of work — those counsellors to crime—affect moral order, and, as if such examples must find their echo in the circles removed, one might suppose, from the same debasing temptations, strange and horrible crimes declare themselves among the rich and honoured of the world.

Such a crisis as this was experienced in France in 1847—a period almost unexampled in these later days for social crime, and culminating in a deed which sent a thrill of horror throughout the land.

The murder of the Duchesse de Praslin by her

husband was judged in different lights. As regards its brutal and cowardly nature, there could, of course, be no two opinions; but there was considerable divergence as to the source to which it might be traced. To calm, just minds it presented only another terrible instance of the passions which, from time to time, reveal themselves in our fallen nature, and are identical in all conditions of men. To those of strong political bias it offered a new pretext for passionate invectives against an order of things which had been too indifferent to—if it had not actually fostered—vice and crime among the classes least exposed to temptation.

Let us be content with the moral lessons that may be derived from a perusal of this strange dark passage in the history of Parisian crime.

On the 17th August, 1847, the Duchesse de Choiseul-Praslin, only daughter of the Marshal Count Sebastiani, returned from the magnificent Château de Vaux-Praslin, near Melun, to Paris, on their way to bathing quarters at Dieppe. The family alighted at the Hotel Sebastiani, their usual metropolitan residence, one side of which faces the Faubourg St. Honoré (No. 55), the other the Avenue Gabriel, Champs-Elysées.

On their arrival the Duke and Duchess parted, the former proceeding, in company with his daughters, to pay some visits; the latter, with her sons, retiring to their apartments. It was by this time half-past nine at night.

About eleven the Duke returned, conducted his daughters to their chamber, and then descended to his own, situated in the rez-de-chaussée, and separated by a vestibule from that of his wife.

By midnight sleep and silence seemed to reign throughout the mansion.

At half-past four fearful outcries, compared by one of the hearers to the yells of a mad person, proceeding from Madame de Praslin's chamber, alarmed the house. They were followed by violent and irregular ringing of the bell; and Auguste Charpentier, the Duke's valet, and Madame Leclerc, lady's maid, hastily dressing, flew to obey the summons. Their attempts to enter by an antechamber at the foot of the great staircase were baffled, nor could their joint efforts force the door, which, contrary to usage, was bolted as well as locked within. Strange intermittent cries continued to be heard, and the terrified servants thought they could distinguish the hasty trampling as of one pursued, mingled with dull blows. Hastening round to another door opening from the grand saloon, they found that also secured within. In vain they knocked and entreated, "*Madame! Madame!*" There was no reply.

They now rushed into the garden, into which the Duchess's apartment looked, but the casements were closed as usual. Arrived, however, at the end of the house, they noticed that the door of a wooden staircase leading to an antechamber which separated the Duke's apartment from his wife's—was open. The doors of the dressing-room and of the antechamber opening into the Duchess's chamber were also open. The valet entered. All was dark and silent; but there was, as the man declared, a smell of blood!

More and more alarmed, Charpentier ran to the apartment of one Merville, valet de chambre of the Duchess of Orleans, and aroused him with an account of what he feared had happened.

Merville sprang from his bed, seized a large stick, gave Charpentier a sword, and, taking a lamp, hastened to the scene of murder, through the doors that had been found open.

They found the body of the unfortunate lady, clad only in her night-dress, lying on the floor, her head supported on an ottoman. She was literally bathed in blood.

Horror-stricken at the spectacle, they staggered back into the garden, and when there observed smoke ascending from the chimney of the Duke's room. The windows were closed, and it now struck them as somewhat strange that, despite the alarms, the Duke had not made his appearance.

The next minute the two servants were joined by the porter, Briffard, and several other persons, and the party prepared to return to the house.

At that moment the Duke opened the door of communication between the saloon and the Duchess's chamber. He wore his grey dressing-gown, and appeared much agitated.

"What is the matter? what has happened?" he gasped out.

At the moment, a servant threw open one of the windows, and, admitting the light, exhibited the corpse of the unhappy lady—a mass of wounds and blood.

"My God! my God!" exclaimed the Duke; "what a misfortune! what a crime! Who has done this? Help! help! Bring surgeons."

Briffard's wife gently raised the body; others brought water to wash the wounds. It was thought by some that she breathed once or twice, but this was doubtful. The surgeon on arriving pronounced her lifeless.

The Duke, on hearing this, placed his hands on the bloodstained shoulders.

"Poor soul! poor soul!—what monster has done this?" he exclaimed. Then, flinging himself on the bed, he tore his hair, crying, "My children! my poor children!—who shall tell them they have no longer a mother? Poor Marshal!" (Sebastiani).

The commissaries of police, Pruy and Bruzelin, were quickly on the spot, and commenced an inquiry.

The medical men reported that they discovered on the back of the head five wounds reaching to the bone, one of these affecting the vertebræ; and on the front of the head eight wounds, all but one incised like the former. On the neck, two wounds; under the jaw a wound that left bare the carotid artery and jugular vein, besides many slight stabs and scratches. Both hands were mutilated by many wounds, as though they had repeatedly grasped a two-edged cutting instrument which had been drawn through them. The face, besides superficial cuts, presented excoriations apparently made by the nails of the murderer seeking to stifle the cries of the victim, while he completed his fearful crime.

The state of the room bore testimony to the terrible nature of the struggle that had occurred there. Lighted by a single window, looking on the garden, this apartment was about twenty-one feet by eighteen. It contained a large bed raised on a platform, at the head of which hung the bell. Upon the mattrass was visible a large stain of blood. The embroidered muslin curtains and the pillow were dashed' and sprinkled with the same crimson stains. The door opening on the saloon was marked with blood, and the print of a bleeding hand was visibly imprinted in the neighbourhood of the lock. The door opening into the boudoir was stained in like manner, and hair, evidently torn from the victim's head, was scattered on the floor. An ottoman placed near the fireplace, on which the body was found leaning, was literally striped with blood. A chair, upset in the centre of the room, bore similar marks; beside this lay a book, an English novel —"Mrs. Armytage"—marked with blood, and numberless other traces around the apartment gave melancholy witness to the severity and duration of the death-struggle between the unhappy lady and her assassin.

And who *was* the assassin? Whoever he was, he could have entered only by the door of the little wooden staircase, leading to the garden. The only trace of his presence was a pistol found on the floor. It had blood-stains on the barrel, and on the butt and lock, hairs, and a fragment of skin.

Having concluded these examinations, the commissaries received the declaration of the Duke.

M. de Praslin, with an emotion which, under the circumstances, seemed natural enough, explained that the pistol was his own. He had caught it up on the first alarm, and the stains of blood were probably imparted by his own hands, marked as they must have been by lifting up the body of his murdered wife.

Towards eight o'clock the Prefect of Police, the Attorney-General, and M. Aristide Broussais, Juge d'Instruction, accompanied by General Sebastiani, arrived at the mansion. So much was the latter gentleman overcome by the sight, that, all soldier as he was, he fainted outright.

Seeing this, the valet Charpentier ran into the Duke's chamber for a glass of water. On doing so he observed that the room was in great disorder. The hearth was laden with tinder from articles lately consumed. A tub was in the middle of the room, from which Charpentier offered to take some water, when the Duke, hastily interposing, told him that the water was foul, and bade him throw it out of the window.

As the authorities were about to *consigner*—place in a sort of custody—the servants of the house—

"They had much better," remarked Charpentier, quietly, " pursue their investigations in the chamber of Monsieur le Duc."

They did in effect examine the Duke's clothes, and found on his dressing-gown several stains of blood. In the grate were quantities of ashes of burnt paper and of a large handkerchief. The dressing-gown, however, had been newly washed in certain places. All these objects were taken possession of by the magistrates, and the Juge d'Instruction interrogated the Duke anew.

His statement was in substance as follows :—

That after arriving at Paris he never saw his wife, who had gone straight to her apartments. That on returning home with his daughters he had retired to bed, without sending for his valet, whose services he frequently dispensed with. That at some hour, which appeared to him about dawn, he was awakened by confused cries; but these being not unusual in the Champs Elysées, he had not risen immediately. Hearing, however, voices in the garden, he sprang up, and arming himself with a pistol, went straight to the Duchess' chamber, through her dressing-room. That he had called out "Fanny! Fanny!" but receiving no answer had returned to the dressing-room, and after lighting a lamp re-entered the chamber, where he found the Duchess in the state before described. That he had barely time to lift up the bleeding head before a loud knocking at the door apprised him that help was at hand. That he had hastened to unbolt the door, and give access to several of the servants, while his valet, Charpentier, had already effected entrance by another door. That during the succeeding half-hour he had many times been in contact with the corpse, and thus acquired the stains of blood upon his hands and dressing-gown, all which he strove to remove in order not to shock his children. Finally, that his first act was to summon both the surgeon and the commissary of police.

Asked as to the use he had been making of the pistol, the Duke replied that he had taken it for his own protection, and had, in his horror at the sight of his murdered wife, let it fall he knew not where.

How did he explain the ashes of a burned handkerchief and many papers found in his grate?

On retiring to bed he had selected the handkerchief for a nightcap, but finding it soiled, flung it into the grate, already full of papers. The latter took fire from a match with which, on the alarm, he had lighted his lamp.

But there was a clean handkerchief purposely laid by his bedside?

Could not explain the not using it, nor afford any explanations more precise than those already given.

To what cause did he attribute the murder? Had the Duchess any known enemies?

None, to his knowledge. The crime must have been committed by robbers, not till then become aware of the family's return.

What account could he give of five pieces of cord, one of them stained with blood, found that morning in the pocket of his dressing-gown?

Could give no account of the cord. As to the blood, he might have received some stain on his hands while supporting the body.

"I have now to call your attention, M. le Duc," said M. Broussais, " to a very grave circumstance. On a table in the Duchess's room was found a pistol, stained with blood on the butt and barrel, and having hairs and a bit of skin adhering to the lock. This was the same weapon with which you acknowledge to have been armed. I beg you to explain this fact, which at present certainly points directly to yourself as the author of this murder."

The Duke clasped and hung his head, as if in despair or weariness, and was silent. Exhorted to make some reply, he at last said :

"I ought to have denied at once that the pistol found in my wife's room was the same as that with which I armed myself. I do so now, and add, that neither with that or any other did I assail her. As to the hairs and skin, if the fact be really so, I cannot explain it."

On examining the Duke's hands they were found to bear some slight scratches. On the right was the trace of a bite, on the left distinct nail marks. The left leg displayed a large recent bruise.

No sign of an entrance having been effected from without could be detected in any part of the house.

During the progress of the inquiry it had become known that a bad understanding had for some time existed between the Duke and Duchess, dating, as it seemed, from the entrance into the family, as governess, of a young lady named Deluzy. After a stay of six years her departure had been agreed upon, and was to have taken place about two months previous to the murder, the Marshal Sebastiani having insisted on this concession to his daughter's wishes being no longer deferred. Some unexplained reason had, however, occasioned a further delay, during which scandals most injurious to the character both of Mdlle. Deluzy and the Duke were very persistent and widely-spread.

The valet, Charpentier, confirmed these reports, and stated that, since the departure of the governess, his master never failed to visit her in his visits to Paris.

Euphémia Merville, lady's-maid to the Duchess, stated that for seventeen years, that is, up to the arrival of Mdlle. Deluzy, in 1841, complete domestic harmony prevailed. She had, indeed, seen her mistress shed tears, and had heard the Duke contradict her; but he never appeared actually harsh. After Mdlle. Deluzy appeared matters became worse. The Duchess seemed hurt by the authority exercised by her, and it was a matter of observation among the servants that an attempt was being made to weaken the bonds of affection that had hitherto existed between Mdme. de Praslin and her children. The Duchess never spoke of this, but the witness had frequently seen her weep bitterly, and had found her lady's handkerchiefs soaked with tears. It was known to the household, in short, that the Duchess was not happy, and believed by them that their master intrigued with Mdlle. Deluzy.

"From the first moment," added the witness boldly, " I believed that my lady was murdered by the Duke. I would not *say* so, but I am convinced that it is so."

Briffard, the porter, had been aware that a misunderstanding existed between the Duke and Duchess, but knew nothing of its origin.

His wife, with less reticence, vowed that it was well known to be due to the fatal influence of Mdlle. Deluzy, who (the witness added emphatically) was a bad woman, for whom she had always the greatest aversion. She—Mdlle. Deluzy—had once treated it as a matter of reproach to the Duchess that the latter had not shed tears on the departure of her married daughter for Italy. Witness had replied that those who do not weep frequently suffer more than those who do. Mdme. Briffard avowed her belief that the murder was the work, or at least at the instigation of *cette horrible femme.*

By this time Mdlle. Deluzy was in custody. She had been found residing in the house of M. Rémy, literary professor. Her interrogatory was in substance as follows :

Describing herself as Henriette Deluzy-Desportes, aged thirty-five, she stated that, having resided for a time as governess in the family of Lady Hislop, near London, she entered that of the Duke de Praslin in March, 1841. She had board, lodging, and 2000 francs (80*l*.) a year.

The first question was couched in the most pronounced style of French interrogatory :

Had she not for a long time committed grave offences against the deceased lady, not only failing in due respect and deference, but seeking to deprive her of the affection of her husband and children ?

The witness replied, earnestly :

" Never ! never ! When I joined the family things were already on a painful footing. The Duke wished to direct his children's education alone. They had had several governesses, with none of whom the Duchess could agree. The Duke informed me that I should take my meals alone with the children, and inhabit a separate part of the mansion, where only their mother would see them. I told him that I could not agree to these conditions, and they were abandoned, it being understood that the children should be under my exclusive tutelage, although we should associate generally with those in the house. Some time elapsed, when the Duchess expressed her intention of taking part in our readings and lessons; but on the Duke objecting she refrained. At Praslin, I lived with my pupils much apart, but never sought to alienate them from their mother. There were causes of dissension between the Duke and Duchess, which it was not in my power to remove."

" What were these causes ?"

" The desire on the part of the Duchess to rule both her husband and children, and on the Duke's part a determined, but not ungentle, resistance."

" It is ascertained that Mdme. de Praslin had conceived a certain jealousy of you, and suspicions of a grave nature as to your relations with her husband."

" Never!   At all events she never expressed them to *me*."

" Where did you pass the night of the 17th August ?"

" In my apartment at Mdme. Lemaire's."

" Alone ?"

" Yes.   But surrounded by other lodgers, who could have heard all my movements."

"You are aware that there is strong evidence to connect M. de Praslin with this murder?"

"Ah! no—no! Impossible! He? He, who could not bear to see one of his children in pain? Oh, gentlemen, this cannot be!"

The witness fell on her knees, wringing her hands, and continued, in the wildest agitation :

"I say I cannot believe him capable of such a deed. But if it be so, I am the guiltier. *I* who loved, adored my pupils. I wrote letters to him. You can see all. I told them I should die. I am a poor friendless woman, without relation in the world, excepting my stern old grandfather, who grudged me even the poor aid he has sometimes been compelled to afford. Alas! alas! I ought to have resigned myself more to the difficulties of my situation, forgotten my own feelings, and the desire of my pupils' love, and thought only of their mother. Now I am punished. When I was dismissed I thought I should have died at once. But no. Then I drank laudanum; but, unhappily, not enough. They restored me to my miserable life. I was so happy those six years with my darlings, and without them life seemed purposeless. Yes, it is *I* who am guilty. The Duke must have pitied me, and

asked for my recal.  *She* refused it, perhaps—and—
ah! mon Dieu——"

"There appears to be some exaggeration in this
despair?  Is it only to the children that you wrote in
such a tone?"

"Can you not understand, gentlemen, that affection
of *any* kind may reach despair?  As for M. de
Praslin, it could hardly be that, loving his children
so fondly, I should be wholly indifferent to *him*.
But I am no mischief-maker, no adulteress.  I could
not have kissed those innocent faces with such a stain
upon my soul."

"This tender feeling then, found some echo in M.
de Praslin?"

"Not in the least. He thought only of his children.
He felt for them, because their mother was unkind."

"Do you mean to say that he would have murdered their mother, to save them from her harshness?"

"No.  His motive—if indeed he be guilty—must
have been the fear of the separation with which the
Duchess perpetually threatened him, and which
would have been the ruin of his children's future."

"There must have been very serious dissensions
indeed to necessitate separation.  Let us deal with
*that.*  Your dismissal was not the result of a *first*

jealous apprehension. The Duke took your part against his wife, so that it became necessary for her father, Marshal Sebastiani, to interpose on her behalf."

"Mons. de Praslin was always my friend," said the witness, steadily; "never my lover."

"It is now a month since you quitted the house. In that interval are included these passionate letters to the children, and several visits—three at least—from the Duke. He invited you to call at his house as yesterday—and yesterday morning the Duchess was murdered!"

"I can only declare that there was no connexion between us in the past, nor any scheme for the future. If the Duke had been free and could have loved me, I would have refused a marriage so unequal, and therefore so disadvantageous to his children; though I might, I cannot say otherwise, have been willing to sacrifice my honour—my life—for him. But I would not, either as husband or lover, have possessed him at the cost of one hair from his wife's head."

"Listen. In one of your letters to the children we find an unfinished sentence. You say, 'You do not tell me about your father. I trust he retains both health and courage. It seems to me that I

should be less miserable if I felt that I was suffering . . . .' Will you complete the sentence?"

" I should perhaps have added 'alone,' or 'for you
all.' The sentiment was perhaps expressed more forcibly than it was felt. At any rate, it was an honest
one, and not unnatural, since we had passed six years
in the closest companionship."

The interrogatory was here adjourned.

Owing to some misapprehension as to their powers,
the accused being a peer, the authorities contented
themselves with placing the Duke under the surveillance of the police agents at his own residence,
an express being despatched to the King, Louis
Philippe, then at Eu, to obtain the convocation of
the Chamber of Peers by special order.

But an incident now declared itself, which rendered
a closer custody necessary.

The Duke, who, while undergoing the corporal
examination mentioned above, had exhibited no sign
of suffering, became suddenly ill. Fearful vomiting
and an almost imperceptible pulse, alarmed the
medical attendants, and Dr. Louis, who was summoned
to a consultation, pronounced it an attack of cholera.
In a few hours the patient had become so weak as to
require being lifted from his bed to the sofa. On

the next day, the Duke being no better, M. Andral was sent for, and that experienced practitioner at once decided that he was suffering from the effects of poison, and a course of treatment in accordance with this opinion was at once entered upon.

An order for the convocation of the Peers' Chamber appeared in the *Moniteur* of Saturday, the 21st, and on the same day M. de Praslin was conveyed in a carriage to the Luxembourg, great precautions being taken to secure his undisturbed passage—such being rendered necessary by the menacing aspect of the groups that had been assembled from daybreak around the Hotel Sebastiani.

At the moment of departure there was found on the person of the prisoner a vial containing a mixture of arsenic and laudanum.

The commission, under the presidency of the Chancellor, M. de Pasquier, was composed of the Duc Decazes, le Comte de Pontécoulant, le Comte de St. Aulaire, Cousin, Laplagne-Barris, and Vincent St. Laurent.

The prisoner was arraigned as Charles Laure Hugues Theobald, Duc de Choiseul-Praslin, peer of France, aged forty-three, born at Paris.

The president, Pasquier, began :—

"You are aware of the crime imputed to you, and of the evidence adduced to substantiate the accusation. I invite you, accused, to shorten the fatigue, for which you seem unfitted, by confessing what it seems you will hardly dare to deny."

"I have no strength to answer. Very long explanations would be necessary."

"Say rather 'Yes' or 'No.' That is simple."

"It needs sometimes a strong mental effort to say either."

"At what hour did you part with your children on the night of the murder?"

"At half-past ten, or thereabouts."

"Whither did you go?"

"To my chamber—to my bed."

"You slept?"

"I did."

"On being aroused, what was your impression?"

"I thought I had been awakened by a cry in the house, and rushed to the room of my wife. I beg," added the Duke, "that you will observe my condition, and adjourn the interrogatory."

"You entered your wife's room several times that morning. On the first occasion, did you find her in bed?"

"No. Unhappily she was lying stretched on the floor."

"*As when you dealt her the last blow?*"

"How can you address such a question to me?"

"Can you explain the scratches on your hands?"

"These were made in packing at Praslin."

"And that bite?"

"Is not one at all."

"It must have been a trying moment, when, retiring to your own room, you found yourself covered with your victim's blood, and employed yourself in effacing the stains!"

"How could I have shown myself to the children without doing so?"

"Have not some evil counsels urged you to this deed?"

"I have received no such counsels."

"Do you experience no feelings of remorse, that might be in some measure soothed by confession?"

"I have no strength to-day."

"You have only been required to say 'yes' or 'no.' Silence under such circumstances looks like guilt."

"You have begun with the conviction that I am guilty. I cannot change it."

"Yes; if you will give us reasons to believe the

contrary.; if you can explain that which can only explain *itself* on the assumption of your guilt. While committing this crime, did you ever think of your children?"

" For the crime—I did not commit it. As to my children, I think of nothing else."

" Once for all, will you positively deny that you committed this murder?"

The Duke hung his head for a few moments in silence. Then he said in a low voice:

" I cannot reply to such a question."

The weakness of the prisoner now became so manifest, that the examination was, of necessity, adjourned. He was conveyed to his bed, which he was not again destined to leave—the symptoms becoming hourly more aggravated, and leaving no doubt whatever that the unhappy man was suffering from the effects of deadly poison.

A secret *séance* of the Chamber of Peers decided on the continuance of the inquiry, despite the absence of the prisoner, and the interrogatory of Mdlle. Deluzy was at once resumed.

" When you entered this family, a good understanding existed between the Duke and Duchess?"

"Not exactly that. The governess—my predecessor—had warned me that my position between them would be a difficult one."

"Did you find it so?"

"Not for some time. I lived much apart, with the children, and observed nothing."

"When did the situation alter?"

"As the girls grew up their father was more with them, and therefore unavoidably with me. Mdme. de Praslin went much into society, and was often at her father's. In the country she stayed much in her own apartment."

"Did it not occur to you as your duty to draw the mother and her daughters into closer union?"

"I tried repeatedly to come to an understanding with Mdme. de Praslin on that subject, but could not succeed. She told me that she disapproved the course of education prescribed by her husband, but that she had promised to abstain from any interference. She gave me no instructions concerning her daughters, save in regard to dress; never sent for, and rarely spoke to them. They rather feared her, but were at all times affectionate and deferential in demeanour."

"Did you not perceive that this separation from her children in all that most nearly concerned them, was a subject of discord between the Duchess and her husband ?"

"On the contrary, I thought that Mdme. de Praslin—more attached to her husband than to her children—kept them aloof, in order to have him more to herself, and when he was absent observed the same rule of conduct, that she might be able to reproach him with the misdirection of their education. When the Duke, while playing with his children, happened to make her a short or careless answer, it was her habit to quit the room."

" In whatever you say you appear to cast all the blame upon Mdme. de Praslin. Surely the lamentable occurrence we are investigating should make you gentler in your judgment. Your manner creates a great doubt whether you did actually use the empire you had acquired over the children's minds, as testified by your letters and theirs, for the purpose of bringing them into nearer relations with their mother."

" I would not for the world show disrespect to the memory of Mdme. de Praslin; but you enjoin me to speak the truth, and all the truth. I do not speak of her heart, or feelings, or principles, only of her temper, at times uncertain and irritable, which rendered her less fit for the control of children whose characters were precisely the reverse. She did not, moreover, evince that tenderness which appeals so readily to youthful hearts. She was peevish in small matters; and then, by way of compensation, over-indulgent where firmness was required."

"In effect, not only authority but affection had passed from Mdme. Praslin to *you*. Even if you could have effected nothing, you cannot have been ignorant of the state of affairs, and thus we are forced to the conclusion that your fatal indifference has had a considerable share in producing this catastrophe."

"I never sought to transfer the children's love from their mother to myself," replied the witness, warmly; "I loved them and devoted myself wholly to them. Their pleasures and their pains were mine also. For six years I watched over them with a solicitude no one has denied; and in return they loved me with all the ardour and constancy which belong to children of their age thus treated."

"You have intimated that the Duke associated much with his children, and yourself?"

"In the country, certainly, he frequently walked with us. In Paris, where the Duchess spent much time with her father or in society, the Duke would pass the evenings in our study. The children were only allowed to stay a few minutes with their grandfather, and Mdme. de Praslin never sent for us to her own sitting-room."

" You persist, then, in casting all the blame on Mdme. de Praslin. It is painful to see that, when we refer to the two letters addressed to you by that excellent woman, one at the new year, where she generously offers to forget all causes of disagreement between herself and you, pardoning (though she spares you that word) all that has passed. The other, written at the period of your dismissal, when she assures you of her good wishes, promises her protection, and confers on you a pension of 1500 francs, in recompense of your services to her family."

" So far as regarded myself personally, Mdme. de Praslin's conduct was much as it was to all else, even to those she liked best, rather uncertain, and sometimes a little incomprehensible. For example, she would at one time reproach me with the influence I exercised in the family, at another urge me to use that very influence in favour of some design of her own. Often after a dispute she would make me some handsome present. In the last days of my residence, even when she had refused to allow me to dine in her company, she would meet me with all her former kindness, and send me books, &c., to amuse my mind."

" These are, indeed, strong proofs of the generosity which was known to belong to her character. As for her irritability and uneasiness, have you not contri- buted to these, and to the want of harmony between herself and the Duke by your correspondence with him and the children after your dismissal?"

" Alas! I declare that I had no evil design in that correspondence. I was in despair, and might have expressed my wounded feelings too strongly. If Mdme. de Praslin had condescended to come to an understanding with me, had taken our correspondence under her own direction, had promised that my pupils and I might occasionally be brought once more together, the suffering would have been lessened, and its expression toned down."

" Always blaming the unhappy lady!"

" I am sorry to say what I must say," replied the witness, bursting into tears. " She is dead. Would that I could recal her, not only at the cost of my own life, but of tortures worse than death!"

Mdlle. Deluzy then proceeded to explain that since quitting the family she had seen the Duke three times, once with his younger children, the second time alone, when he had desired her to ask for him at the door, the third time, on the 17th August (the night of the murder), with three of his daughters and his son. On occasion of the second interview their conversation turned upon the system of education to be followed with regard to the third daughter, Marie.

At the last visit much time was spent at first in tears and embraces. After this, the witness affirmed, embarrassed as she was by having to speak before the children, she briefly informed the Duke that her hostess, Mdme. Lemaire, had offered her a situation, but having heard injurious reports concerning her, required as a condition that Mdme. de Praslin should write a letter of recommendation and "rehabilitation" in her behalf. She, however, begged the Duke not to press the matter with his lady, as Mdme. Lemaire probably made more of it than was really necessary, in order to justify the moderate salary she had offered to the witness.

"Mons. de Praslin," witness added, "then took leave, fearing that the Duchess might reproach him and the children for their visit. Our last words were ' till to-morrow,' it having been agreed that I should

call at two o'clock and pay a visit of respect and con-
ciliation to Mdme. de Praslin."

"Had M. de Praslin held out hopes of obtaining
the letter of rehabilitation from his lady?"

"He told Mdme. Lemaire it might be difficult, as
the Duchess wished me to leave France entirely."

"Was the Duke excited on taking leave?"

"No. He had simply said, 'I am truly sorry for
you. I play a sad part in this affair.' But he was as
calm as usual."

"He said or did nothing to excite a suspicion of
the fearful extremities to which he intended to go?"

"Nothing—nothing! I know not if I may be
allowed to mention something that shows that violence
was not always on *his* side. I have several times
heard Mdme. de Praslin threaten suicide. At Vaudreuil she did attempt it. The Duke in depriving her
of a weapon received a slight wound in the hand.
Again, at Dieppe, after a quarrel which was overheard in our chamber by the children and myself, she
rushed into the street, intending to throw herself into
the sea. It may show her instability of temperament,
that the Duke found her, some hours later, shopping,
and perfectly composed."

"Were you aware that there was a project of

separation on foot which distressed Mdme. de Praslin ?"

"I was. L'Abbé Gallard, who, on the part of Marshal Sebastiani, came to request me to leave, alluded to the scandal that would ensue should I refuse. As if I *should* refuse! And M. Riant, Madame's notary, told me that the Duchess had conceived the project of separation, though the Duke believed it to be only a passing fancy."

" Did the Duke himself never speak to you on that subject? Reflect."

"When he came to tell me that his efforts to procure my stay had failed, I wept bitterly ; and then he said, 'Give way I beg of you with a good grace, for the scandal they speak of can only mean a process of separation, and then I should lose my children."

"There is reference made in your letters to certain calumnies respecting you. *What* calumnies?"

"MM. Gallard and Riant only said that an impression unfavourable to my character had been caused by my intimate association with the Duke. After leaving the house a sort of fatality still pursued me, and several persons repeated these calumnies to Madame Lemaire."

Thus ended this singular and painful, but not uninteresting interrogatory.

Further researches in the Hotel Sebastiani, and at Vaux-Praslin, had meanwhile brought to light a number of letters which completely revealed the progress of that domestic discord which resulted in a fearful crime. Those which bore the signature of the ill-fated lady, deserved all the eulogy pronounced on them by the president, Pasquier.

"Precious relics," he called them, "of one of the most beautiful spirits ever created by the Almighty for the honour of our age—an eternal memorial of the perversity of one of the guiltiest of men, but at the same time suggesting the consoling reflection that Providence has sometimes seen fit to place beside the vilest natures their most angelic opposite, so that eyes, wearied and offended with gazing on such guilt, may find thus close at hand a reassuring solace."

On the 24th of August the condition of the Duke was such that the Curé de St. Jacques and L'Abbé Bourgoin were summoned to his bedside, and administered to the dying man the comforts of religion.

After this he appeared calmer and stronger, and received a visit from the *grand référendaire*, to whom he confessed that he had taken poison as soon as he saw that suspicion rested upon him.

"But," remarked his visitor, " suicide in presence

of such a charge is tantamount to admission of its justice."

The Duke was silent for a moment, then declared that no other person was cognisant of the intended crime. His speech was interrupted by acute pains.

The grand referendary reminded him that the sufferings of the soul were worse than any that could befal the body, and entreated the dying man to seek some alleviation of these in expressions of repentance, adding that his family were willing to believe that the deed he had committed was wrought in a moment of madness.

The Duke raised his eyes to heaven, and murmured, half inaudibly, " Yes, yes, I do repeat it !"

Pressed for some further explanations, the grand referendary offering either to summon the Chancellor, or to be himself the recipient of any such avowals, the Duke became violently agitated; and, after a minute of silence, answered that he felt at the moment too fatigued and suffering, but would willingly receive the Chancellor on the morrow.

It was impossible to question him further. He was, in fact, sinking rapidly; and some hours later, at half-past four, the Duke de Praslin breathed his last sigh.

The official report was completely affirmative as to the guilt of the unhappy man.

"The presumption," remarked M. Pasquier, "was but too well-founded. The Duke de Praslin has judged and condemned himself. Seven days and a half after sacrificing his pure and innocent victim, he has avenged her on himself."

Human justice had no more claim on this unhappy offender; but it became necessary to pursue the inquiry as regarded Mdlle. Deluzy, and accordingly a requisition from the Procureur-General demanded that the case be referred to the Court of First Instance in Paris in order to complete the investigation.

In the interval took place the funeral ceremony of the unhappy pair, but under very different circumstances.

The Duchess was interred in the vaults of the Château Vaux. It was a solemn and touching ceremonial, for the Duchess was adored by all the numerous dependents of the family, as well as the neighbouring poor for miles around. Her charities, never revealed in her lifetime, were found noted in a locked volume, in which she affected to record the expenses of her toilette.

The Duke was buried as secretly as possible on the

night of the 26th August. At midnight a travelling hearse was brought into the garden of the Luxembourg, and up to the inner entrance of the prison. The coffin being placed within, the melancholy procession set forth, under the escort of a brigade of sergens-de-ville, passing by the Rue Vaugirard, through the Barrière du Maine. Through the dark and stormy night, it reached the Cemetery du Sud, wherein some labourers had dug a grave for they knew not whom.

In the morning those who visited the cemetery might have noticed a fresh mound in the remotest corner, shaded by cypress and yew, undistinguished even by the black cross that crowns the meanest grave. That was the last resting-place of one of the noblest peers of France, the Duke de Choiseul-Praslin.

The inquiry concerning Mademoiselle Deluzy, lasting over many days, failed to reveal any legal grounds for a criminal proceeding against her. A writ of *non-lieu* was consequently issued, and she was at once set at liberty.

We will now throw together, as briefly as possible, the facts of this most melancholy domestic drama, as elicited in the prolonged and minute inquiry.

It appeared that in October, 1824, Madame de Praslin became the wife of the Duke (then Marquis) of that name. In March, 1841, Mademoiselle Deluzy entered the family as governess. In this interval of seventeen years Madame de Praslin had borne ten children, of whom she lost only one.

If during that period there may be traceable in the correspondence of the young wife some slight tokens of jealousy, there was certainly nothing to indicate real uneasiness, or any want of harmony in the domestic circle.

Succeeding by the death of his father to the property of Vaux-Praslin, the Duke expended large sums in improving his magnificent domain; but with this new wealth and splendour, happiness seemed to take wing. The affection that had lasted seventeen years suddenly cooled. The Duke not only ceased to make his young wife the sharer of his plans and pleasures, he suddenly announced that each should occupy a separate range of apartments, and furthermore expressed his desire that Madame de Praslin should not herself any longer direct the education of the children.

It is to this period that this letter refers. Eloquent, impassioned, diffuse, as love's language frequently is, it is the wail of a repulsed, but innocent and loving wife, whose only fault is jealousy—in such a case, another name for love.

"Ah, why," she writes, "my well-beloved, refuse to allow your mind and spirit to accord with mine? By this course you deprive our lives of their greatest charm. You call me ' exacting' because I desire to partake your troubles. You hide them from me as if I were a stranger; and to make me more completely so, condemn me to isolation and the sense of your indifference. How long will it take for me to follow this example? My heart would break long before it had attained that end. You do not like to see me suffer, yet you will afford me none of the consolation that only *you* can bring. I see that you yourself are unhappy. I feel that I have within me treasures of love and pity, to give you comfort, and yet you repulse me from you! Am I not the companion of your life— half your very self? entitled, therefore, to share your griefs and troubles, as well as your happiness and prosperity? Who *should* help and soothe you but she whom Providence itself has purposely placed at your side?

"It does not need an intelligence like yours to comprehend how much a really loving nature requires. It may be that my occasional warmth of manner has made you unwilling to confide too much to me; that I may have repelled you by a jealous, suspicious, or too imperious bearing. Ah, believe me, Theobald, four months of grief and repentance have wrought a change! It is to console and soothe you—not to irritate—that I desire a return of your confidence. Ah! I swear to you I will never more seek to control you. I acknowledge your superior reason; and in desiring to be, as formerly, the true partner of your life, it is only that I may pour balm into its every wound. Again I swear to you, in the name of my love— of your own—of all that is dearest and most sacred to us both— that I require only your love and trust! I will be guided solely by you. I will torment you no more with my jealousy. I will arrogate to myself no right of rebuke or counsel. My penitence is too sincere—my suffering has been too great—to admit of my being ever again guilty of the faults that have cost me so dear!

" We are very young, Theobald. Ah! do not let us be separated all our lives to come! Give me only trust and tenderness! I will be the loving, but passive half of your existence.

" Take back your Fanny! Prove her, once more, with your confidence and affection. You will find yourself happier *thus* than separate from her. You seek for distractions, but do they restore you to real happiness? Ah—no! not with such a heart as yours, and with the life we are leading now. Ah! do not be deaf to my prayers, my repentance, my vows, for I love you, and my life shall be spent in love and gratitude to you!

" You treat me as if I had been absolutely guilty. You banish me from your heart and bed. What more could you do, even had I been unfaithful? I weep day and night. I stand at your door, and dare not enter. Of what do you accuse me? My suspicions, my impatience? Have I ever displayed anger, such as one caress, one word of tenderness, would not at once dispel?

" My well-beloved, believe me, and restore me my lost happiness. If you knew what delight I feel in hearing your praises— what pleasure it gave me to hear my father this evening remarking how much you could accomplish, and with ease, when it pleased you to try! Ah! I was proud and happy, but not surprised, for all that *I* knew a long time ago.

" My friend, my friend, you who once loved me so fondly, forgive me! You will never regret your goodness. When you shall tell me of your troubles, your head upon my bosom, your hands in mine, your lips on my brow, you will be happier, believe me, than *now!* Life is short, and we have already wasted so much in separation. Very soon I shall lose courage to make advances perpetually repelled. For you, it is not in your nature to take the lead in such a matter. You *will* not stir—your wife *dare* not! Thus life will waste away, yourself unhappy, and your wife dying of pain and sorrow! Ah! then, return, return to me!"

It would seem that the reconciliation so touchingly

courted was for the time effected.  But it was only a
brief interval of peace.  Too soon reappears on the
scene, revealed by the letters we are quoting, the sad
procession of well-founded jealousies, suspicions,
wrongs, dissensions.  Mdme. de Praslin evidently
strove to disbelieve the suggestions of her own heart
and reason ; but the world would not leave her that
solace.  The scandal was too widely spread.  The
very servants knew the truth, and at length the pride
of the outraged wife rose in open revolt.

The 20th May, 1841, witnessed a fearful scene of
reproach and defiance.  Words, never to be forgotten
either by the speaker or hearer, were uttered, and
Mdme. de Praslin, broken-hearted, retired to her own
apartments, and wrote as follows to her husband :

"Do not be surprised, my dear Theobald, at my fear to be alone
with you.  We are separated for ever—you have said so.  While
I entertained any hope of a complete reconciliation, I was agitated,
day by day, with alternate hopes and fears, which may, without
doubt, have affected my demeanour.  But now all is over !  The
sacrifice is made !  You may be at ease.  Nothing before the world,
our children, or the household, shall betray to them that my happiness is gone for ever !

" To be alone with you is, at present, more than I can bear.  I
must weep alone—must collect myself—and study carefully the new
and cold aspect that I must henceforth wear.  Time may calm my
sorrow, and habit give me strength for what at this moment appears
to me impossible.  *Then*, be assured, instead of avoiding you, you
will be, as formerly and for ever, my most welcome companion. . .

"It will be a labour to forget the past; to forget, besides, my later hopes and illusions. Time and custom can alone teach me to separate, in my thoughts, Theobald from Mons. de Praslin, and reduce the former to a mysterious recollection.

"Ah that what I suffer, and have yet to suffer, may at least secure your happiness! Come without fear to Vaudreuil. Stay much among your children. You shall never find me in your path.

"Farewell! Ah! that with this word all your troubles might end! Farewell! You loved me *once!* Farewell once more! .We shall meet again in heaven—*that*—the only appointment I shall henceforth make with you (*le seul rendezvous que je te donnerai désormais*)—you dare not refuse! Think of this sometimes. I love you ever.

SEBASTIANI PRASLIN."

With this bitter cry the unhappy wife retired to her solitary couch, and sought such relief as tears can give, biting her pillow as she lay, in the vain endeavour to keep down the sobs and signs of grief that might else have brought intruders into that chamber of sorrow.

At length, rèst being impossible, she rose, and opening the secret journal in which she was used to record her trials and troubles, continued the mournful narrative. The first few leaves were found to have been torn away:

"Twice before these pages have been covered with the recital of my griefs. I destroyed them in a moment of hope, desiring to retain nothing that might bear testimony to the wrongs I had suffered.

"Two years have passed. My hopes are dead for ever, and I only feel the sad necessity of making you comprehend a heart that had centred in *you* all its hopes of happiness.

"Your conduct must have been dictated by some•thing more than indifference. You have a good heart, and would hardly treat one who so fondly loved you with such cruelty, without a stronger motive. Nothing short of absolute aversion could induce you to deprive me of all the privileges of a wife and mother.

"Can you believe that I should mislead our children? Impossible! You know my purity of heart and life. Do you suppose I do not love them? Great Heaven! Then you believe me a being without a soul—worse than a beast of prey!

"True, I may have been indolent, perhaps incompetent, but that was my misfortune. And now I see, too plainly, that your affection is gone, since you take my children from me, only to entrust them to a young, light woman, without religious principles, of whom eight months ago you had never heard.

"Once I believed that I occupied the first place in

your heart, but I discovered my mistake, and submitted. Next I had to learn that you preferred your
independence to my affection; and again, after a
painful struggle, I yielded. The death of your
excellent father, whom I loved with all my heart, was
the occasion of proving to me that I held only the
fourth place in your regard. Ah that I could
persuade myself that I retain it still !"

A melancholy truce seems to have succeeded this
outbreak, the conditions of which must have been
violated by Monsieur de Praslin, for under the date
of January 25th, 1842, she writes :

"Until this year I might always feel sure of
meeting you once a day, when you came home. I
had permission even to visit you whenever I pleased ;
but now you pass almost all your evenings in your
own apartment, whether alone or not I cannot say,
and supper is brought to you there.

" Ah, my Theobald ! are your promises come to
*this ?* You had said, 'If you don't visit *me* I shall be
always seeking *you*, and in the end we shall be
reunited, not to part again.' Well, I have adhered
to *my* promise—but *thou ?* You said, ' Do not
question me, and I will tell you everything.' Years
have gone by since I have forborne the least inquiry,

even into that which interests me most deeply, yet you have never vouchsafed me the slightest information to comfort and reassure me.

"You said, 'Leave the care of the children to me, and I will consult you in everything that concerns them, always preserving a seemly attitude in regard to their governesses.' Ah! how have these pledges been observed?"

About this time the Duke appears to have experienced something like a return of affection for his neglected wife. There was reason, however, to doubt its reality, and the poor wife finds herself compelled, against her fondest desire, to suspect some hidden motive.

"Last night, to my great surprise I must allow, you loaded me with caresses—you made me the most kind and tender promises. This evening, I teased you to go to the theatre, to distract your mind; you answered that it was too late. Then you talked of using a hired carriage for the evenings, as if you had not always a carriage at your orders. You seem to dread that I should know whither you go. And, in reality, whither *do* you go, and whom do you visit?

"You have just gone out, at ten o'clock, on foot. You have no relations now in Paris; who then do

you visit, in such a manner, at such a time?
You think me suspicious, but surrounded with so
much that is mysterious, how can it be otherwise?
My beloved Theobald, to *me* this is not life. Alas,
am I to be always kept in ignorance of everything
that concerns you?"

Fresh explanations were entered into, and from
these Mdme. de Praslin seems to have become convinced
of the fact that her husband required of her nothing
less than a tacit sanction of whatever he chose to do—
that she should, in short, lend herself to a state of
things which, as wife and mother, must soon have
become intolerable to her.

"Does he understand," she writes, in May, 1842,
"that I cannot be happy without his exclusive confidence?—without resuming my position as mistress
of the house and directress of my children? Will
he concede that? Will he venture to signify it to
Mdlle. Deluzy? I doubt it. She will say, 'Choose
then between your wife and me.' And she will be
the conqueror."

On the 12th May, 1842, the Duchess had an explanation with Mdlle. Deluzy, and writes her impressions to her husband.

"I find that she does not insist upon being

directed only by *you.* I believe that she would remain if all went on as it was before, and I do not think she desires to alienate my children from me. She declares that you constantly tell them that my health alone prevents my taking the direction of their education. Ah, why did you not tell me you had done so, and save me the pain of believing that they thought me indifferent to them ?"

The discord makes fatal progress. On the 22nd May the Duchess writes in her journal:

" All is over. We are hopelessly divided. How, oh, how can he have conceived this hatred of one who loved him so purely—so tenderly? Ah, it is a cruel fate for me !"

The next entry reveals a terrible scene.

" To-day," she addresses him, " disgusted at seeing you so long in company with Mdlle. Deluzy, I thought I could best avoid a scene, and at the same time mark my displeasure, by leaving you without a word. How could I foresee the fury that succeeded! Could you push your violence farther than to follow me upstairs with reproaches and insulting gestures, break my china vase, and take away the two objects I valued most ?

" Is it true, then, oh, my God! that his love is

wholly gone? Sometimes I would fain doubt it, and consider his conduct as a plan he has conceived to correct my faults of character. But, alas! this has lasted five years. I know I have faults. I suffer too much not to remember that.

"He has not uttered one word of regret for his violence, for the destruction of the things I prized so highly. He smiles when I speak of it. I had hoped that his passion was half assumed.

"How sad is the influence exercised upon him! How changed he is! Once so truthful, I detect him now in a hundred falsehoods. Once so pure, he passes his life in I know not what unworthy company. His manners, once so dignified, are become gross and vulgar. His language, once so polished, betrays the society he now frequents. Ah, Theobald! thou art no more thyself—no longer the man I loved."

Four months later is recorded another outburst of grief. But this time she is less the wife than the outraged mother:

"Paris, September 15, 1842.

"You cannot, Theobald, be conscious of your own cruelty, and the sufferings you inflict on me. Grief, believe me, is a slow and painful death. Ah, Theobald, how I loved you! How I loved our children! I had nothing else in the world. Now, nothing is left me of all I had, even your name. I live alone, abandoned, despised.

I that have a husband and nine children! Another woman before my very eyes enjoys all that is most precious to me, and you expect me to be content! My God! what crime has brought upon me such a penalty? Ah, Theobald, you had no right to deprive me of my children, to give them over to a woman without modesty, without principle, without discretion! Ah that you should be thus weak and blind!

"Mdlle. Deluzy is entirely mistress. Never before has the position she holds been so provocative of scandal. And what an example to give the young, to show them that it is a common thing to visit, at any hour and in any dress, a man's apartment, to receive him in one's dressing-gown, to arrange journeys, parties of pleasure, &c., &c., and to pass entire evenings alone with him! Has she not had the insolence to say to me, 'I am sorry, madame, that it is out of my power to mediate between yourself and your husband? But in your own interests I strongly advise you to treat me as your friend. No doubt it must be painful to you to be separated from your children; but seeing the resolution the Duke has come to with regard to this, I feel that he must have serious reasons for what he has decided upon.' Is it possible that your wife, who has been always pure and affectionate, should be subjected to such an insult from a hired governess whom you hardly know? What must I feel to see my children in the hands of one who avows her contempt of me, and establishes her ascendancy by causing me to be hated and repulsed by my husband?"

Another year has passed, and the Duchess finds herself in the same isolated condition.

### *Letter, undated, found at Praslin.*

"On arriving here I hoped for at least some short period of truce—of tranquillity. The illusion was brief. Before the steps of the carriage were let down, I read in your icy looks—in the faces of my children—in the *little green eyes* that glittered behind your shoulder, that I should have to undergo treatment so painful and humiliating that 1 cannot express it in language. Be assured, Theobald, if I struggle yet, it is from a sense of the duty imposed on me to neglect nothing that may restore even an apparent peace, while I cannot by my silence give seeming approval to a state of things as regards the children which I feel to be detestable in the present, and most pernicious in the future. I know very well that you are master—can act as you please with regard to me, but this is a matter in which a wife's rights are almost equal to those of her husband. You must be aware that did I appeal to the law, it would decide in my favour. You know well that I shall *not* do so; but is that a reason for abusing your power? You desire at any cost to retain Mdlle. Deluzy. You think the loss would be irremediable. *You*, who find it so simple and easy to supplant a *mother*, deem it impossible to find a substitute for a governess!! She might have proved a good one, but you have demoralized (*dénaturé*) her office. How should it *not* affect her to hear you say more clearly than in words, 'I have a wife, but I prefer *your* society—your affection and care? My children have a mother, but I have greater confidence in *your* devotion, *your* care, discretion, judgment, tenderness—although you are young and almost a stranger. Take my wife's place, then—command, direct. Whoever is worthy to guide my children must be supreme *here.*'

"Theobald, you have not the right to condemn me to this civil death. My children must suspect me of some guilt. Ask yourself frankly what *you* would feel were you to be deprived at once of a wife you fondly loved, and your children, and doomed to see the latter delivered up to every kind of false and dangerous impression. When I was weak enough, in excess of love for you, to make the sacrifice of resigning the care of my children in the vain hope of regaining your lost affection, I committed a great fault. I confess it. I ought to have rather died. It was a false calculation, and has given you a bad opinion of my judgment and principles—even of my heart. But my tenderness confounded all our rights in *one.* I regarded you as a part of myself. But oh, how weak you are!

You have reached a point at which you *dare* not take a manly step with regard to your wife and children. You must have the sanction of *that person* for all you do. You are such a slave to her that you dare not stir without her. You are constantly at her side, and your wife—the mother of your nine children—must live and die alone."

Other letters, too painful to transcribe, might be introduced here, but we must hasten towards the close of one of the saddest episodes of modern social life.

It would seem that whenever M. de Praslin returned answers to these mournful appeals, they contained little beyond attempted recriminations, cruel reproaches, and hints of a separation. To one of these the unhappy wife rejoins:

"My dear Theobald,—No more illusions. I feel my brain beginning to give way. In the name of your children, have pity on their mother. Do not drive me absolutely mad. Is it possible that you can take a cruel pleasure in speaking before all the world of projects, all the more painful to me because I love you, and yet feel that they are intended for my punishment? Why will you always torment me with an affectation of mysteries with which I am to have nothing to do? You say that you desire a temporary separation—to return to me, perhaps, hereafter, with renewed affection when we shall have lost the habit of quarrelling. But do you not see that the more I suffer, the more bitter will my feelings become? Kindness may cure me—but pain and sorrow drive me beyond myself. If, when you returned to me after a long separation, you should find me cold, apathetic, habituated to that melancholy independence—would it not grieve and disappoint you? All I entreat is that you would abandon these ideas of separation, and spare me this pretence of mysteries I do not share. If we become reconciled, you shall torment me thus as much as you please, but *now——*"

The irritation still augments. Mdme. de Praslin begins to feel that as wife and mother she can remain no longer in the cruel and humiliating position assigned her.

[*Written in pencil ; found at Praslin, in the Duke's secretary.*]

"You have the rare and precious gift of poisoning everything. If by your doubtful words and menaces you mean to imply that I disapprove of the control exercised in our house by a person I utterly despise, and who deserves neither your confidence nor mine, you are right. The very presence of a woman who so conducts herself near my children, is a shameful scandal. I know very well that you have other connexions (*liaisons*), and that *she* does not absorb you entirely—but, at any rate, she gives herself the air of doing so. I have the right to tell you that, in placing young people in the hands of a woman who disregards all appearances, and is entirely devoid of self-respect, you are committing a very grievous error. You are at liberty to act as you please ; but you are, in fact, training up my children to expose them hereafter to the desertion and contempt that have been the portion of their mother. You abandon them to a woman who misleads you, and whose principles are most corrupt. So long as I had a husband, children, and a home, I was happy, and never dreamed of separating myself from them for a day. Now that you have deprived me of all, I own that I do desire to escape from what you have made a hell."

(*Later date.*)

"You will not be surprised, sir, if after such an insult, I refuse to remain under the same roof with the person to whom I am indebted for it. For a long time I have been seeking to have some definite explanation with you. I have done all in my power to obtain it. You refuse. I therefore, in order to avoid greater scandal still, demand your permission to travel. During the interval you can reflect upon the course you will take. I shall not remain in Paris, but shall visit Lower Normandy. It will be supposed that I go to the sea-baths. The day will come, Theobald, when you will regain your reason, and comprehend your cruelty and injustice towards the mother of your children. I shall leave, if you think proper, the day after to-morrow. Endeavour to spare me a carriage. I shall not go by Paris. You have treated me like a guilty wife. God forgive you for it."

In a letter written on the eve of departure, the Duchess writes :

"Adieu, Theobald. If a sentiment of false shame hinders you from hereafter repairing the wrong you have done me, God is my witness that I leave you with my heart broken, but with ardent prayers for your happiness. I know that, however you may one day regret what you have made me endure, your ideas of dignity will not permit you fully to atone for it. It is, therefore, solely for the interests of my children that I implore you to open your eyes. They are in the worst hands. Farewell, farewell. Have pity on your children."

The year 1846 brought a gleam of sunshine across these stormy skies. On New Year's Day Mdme. de Praslin made a touching advance towards reconciliation with the person who had been the source of all her misery. She sent her a bracelet, accompanied with the following letter :

"Paris, January 1st, 1846.

" If it is forbidden us to lie down to rest without having forgiven our enemies, it seems to me even more incumbent on us to bury with the old year all causes of dissension and discontent. It is, therefore, in all sincerity, Mademoiselle, that I offer you my hand, desiring, in order that we may henceforth live in harmony, that you will forget any painful moments I have caused you, while I, on my part, will banish all remembrance of what has on your side occasioned me pain and sorrow.

" I am satisfied of your sincere and tender attachment to my children, and no one, believe me, is so ready as I to feel both gratitude and affection for any one who devotes herself to their care, so that I am not condemned to the pain of seeing them alienated from their mother. In separation from me I lose my fitting place in their young hearts and lives, and the end will be that they will doubt my love; while I may even be so unhappy as to lose, without reason, their esteem and confidence.

" That cannot surely be your object, since you must be well aware that it is as harmful for children as it is distressing to a mother to destroy a bond so sacred. By degrees consequences are arrived at which were neither foreseen nor intended.

" I had purposed long ago writing to you at this time of reconciliation and good-will. It is, therefore, with double pleasure that I have received your pretty offering to-day, since it affords a proof that you are as desirous as myself to put an end to a state of things which must, I am certain, be annoying to the children, while it places *you* perpetually in false and disagreeable positions, and isolates *me* from all I hold most dear.

" Let us, therefore, wholly resign the course hitherto followed, and thus be free to adopt another and a happier one. I beg your acceptance of this little pledge of an agreement to which I trust you will cordially accede.

SEBASTIANI PRASLIN."

Some months now elapse. Mdlle. Deluzy is at

Turin, on a visit to the Duchess's eldest daughter, married in Italy.

Mdme. de Praslin replies to a letter from the governess in these terms:—

*"Praslin, 25th August, 1845.*

" I do not wish, Mademoiselle, to delay answering and thanking you for your kind letter, which afforded me lively pleasure, and which I could have wished twice as long.  It was indeed time that news should arrive.  Both my head and heart were becoming disquieted with this long silence.  Everybody seemed to be aware of that, for the factor himself, of his own accord, brought me my letters late at night.  Among them were Bertha's and your own.  The good Louis had gone to Melun, meaning to return to-morrow; but noticing among my letters the Turin postmark, forgot how tired he was, and ran back in triumph with the letter-bag to Praslin.  You see, it is good to have friends about one, and this incident will show you how quickly they observed my anxiety.  At last! *All's well that ends well.*

" To-day we heard mass at the Chapel de St. Louis.  My little ones are very good, and from eight in the morning till half-past nine at night we are rarely separate.  In the evening I read them selections from Molière, which delight them.

" Thank you a thousand times for the details you send me.  Pray continue these welcome communications.

" The children had prepared a fête for the distribution of prizes at the Sisters', and I intended to have conveyed them thither, but we had to give it up.  The Curé de Crisenay had strongly advised my doing so.  There was a kind of epidemic at Maincy, and there were many deaths among the very old and very young, while at Maisenay only women were attacked by it.

" We live shut in at Praslin; but, I assure you, not shut *up.* When it is fine we stay never less than four hours out in the park. My dear little things and I get on very well in our solitude.

"The council-general is on the 14th.   I think Mons. de Praslin
will be there.   In his place, *I* should.

"You say that Louise and Bertha speak much of me to Isabella.
It is perhaps to give me pleasure that you mentioned that.   At all
events, you have entirely succeeded.   I wept with joy.

"Once more, dear mademoiselle, I thank you from my heart for
your letter.   Do not let it be the last.

SEBASTIANI PRASLIN."

Mdme. de Praslin herself went to Italy, and on her
return had an almost friendly explanation with her
husband, when it was agreed that order should be
re-established in the disturbed family.   Unfortunately
nothing was actually effected.   Troubles reappeared,
and a new and terrible crisis was at hand.

(Found in the Duke's secretary.)

"Paris, January 15th, 1847.

"MY DEAR THEOBALD,—Up to this moment I have waited for the
fulfilment of your renewed promises.   At my return from Italy,
it was agreed that our domestic system should undergo a complete
change.   I feel it my duty to tell you that I could not return to
Praslin without resuming my due position as wife, mother, and
mistress, in the completest sense.

"The governess plan has never answered.   It is time to renounce
it altogether.

"Until my daughters are married I shall live constantly among
them, partake their occupations, accompany them everywhere.   My
plans are made, and I am sure that, on reflection, you will find as
much ground of confidence in trusting their education to a mother
as to any governess.   Masters can be had as easily at Praslin as at

Paris, and recourse has already been had to them. I have foreseen, and can arrange everything.

"My father has, I know, offered Mademoiselle Deluzy a handsome pension. With this and the exercise of her talents she can subsist honourably in England.

"You may fear that the children will miss her too much. It is a natural regret, but will be less lasting and profound than you imagine. I have good reasons for believing this. I have often heard you speak of her in a manner that convinced me you had begun to feel, at least in some degree, the grave inconvenience of her presence in the family.

"From a feeling of delicacy I have not sought any support out of your own family to disembarrass us of this painful source of dissension; but now, after years of patience, I feel that I must give way to my father's very natural desire to speak with you on a matter which so dearly concerns the interests of my children. Since *you*, my best support, have failed me, I can only appeal to my father. The first vexation passed, I am sure that you will learn to rejoice in a crisis that will have restored peace to our household.

"If you desire that Mademoiselle Deluzy should visit Praslin to collect her property, I will remain in Paris till she returns. If she only sends for them, I will proceed thither whenever you please. I have done my best, in spite of all that has occurred, to arrange for her, as you wished, an honourable retirement from her post.

"I have fulfilled my task. Duty to my children forbids me to delay any longer putting an end to a position of things most hurtful to us all.

"Do not be afraid of any painful recriminations. It is the interest of both to abstain from such. The first condition of domestic life should be peace and kind consideration.

"It is only on mature reflection that I have resolved to take this step. It is the advice of my father, and would have, I am sure, the assent of my uncle De Coigny, the representative of my mother.

My hope is that all can be arranged between my father, yourself, and me, without the interference of anyone beside.

"You have often, my dear Theobald, expressed your wish for this change, yet you as often shrink from making it. But now I rely on your assistance in this, as in everything else that concerns the happiness and welfare of our children.

FANNY SEBASTIANI PRASLIN."

The wretched and demoralized nature to which these lines were addressed remained untouched by the appeal.

"Death comes too slowly," writes the unhappy wife, later, "but it is coming. I cannot bear this profound misery. I have neither husband nor children. My place is occupied by others. What are independence, luxury, fortune to *me?* I want my husband and my children. I liked dress when I went abroad in your company. I liked parties, attended by *you.* I loved all curious and pretty objects when we lived in harmony together; but now all these only offend and weary me.

"If you knew what I suffer when I see happy wives, and hear them talking of their households! You tell me to make new acquaintances, but what right have I, repulsed by my husband and children, to claim love and friendship from those who move in a circle of duties and affections of their own? Might they not ask, 'What can you ask of us, you who have a husband and nine children of your own?'

"*Cher, bon* Theobald! Do not curse me in my grave, for I loved you all—*all*—my poor dear cherished ones! Alas! must I die before you will be reconciled to me?"

The poor soul turns to the only ear that is never deaf to the sufferer's cry. She kneels before the Holy

Book, and opens it at hazard. It is the second chapter of Ecclesiastes :—

" My son, when thou shalt engage in the service of the Lord, prepare thyself for trial and temptation, and strengthen thyself in the justice and the fear of God. Keep thy soul in humility, and abide in patience."

Refreshed by the sublime admonition, she rises and records her prayerful comment :—

" Take from me, Lord, if it be Thy pleasure, all my earthly blessings, the affections of all I love most fondly, and reunite us one day in Thy bosom. Save us, O God, to Thine eternal rest ; and for this our fleeting life deal with it as Thou wilt. Thou knowest I speak from my heart. What Thou wilt *I* will. Give me only strength and resignation to abide Thy pleasure."

In June, 1847, Marshal Sebastiani, becoming aware of the point at which matters had arrived, and of the daily-increasing scandals, determined to interpose. A violent scene was the consequence ; after which the Duke, Duchess, and the children, ceased to take their meals, as formerly, in the Marshal's apartments.

The annexed letter speaks for itself.

### *Marshal Sebastiani to the Duke de Praslin.*

"Mons. le Duc,—You have caused me very great pain. You have accused me of indifference in having closed my doors to you and your family. Do me justice. I have done all in my power to avert this separation. I have risked discredit in forcibly shutting my eyes to scandals which have been propagated in the newspapers, besides affecting disbelief of the reports with which all Paris is but too familiar.

"In recompense of my generosity, you have addressed to me reproaches as bitter as they were undeserved.

"I have never mentioned the name of Mdlle. Deluzy to any one. I am prepared to offer you certain testimony, which it is in your own interest to hear; but be just, and do not require from me what is manifestly impossible. If I cease to receive my daughter, it is that I may not embitter you more against her. You, therefore, it is who deprive me of the company of my grandchildren. I have not deserved this treatment at your hands.

"Try to understand the true interests of these young people. Have I ever done anything to you that could justify such conduct? But you are hardly yourself, and I can overlook it. Take counsel of your own heart, which is a good one, and will therefore do me justice.

H. Sebastiani.

"When you are as old as I am, you may perhaps regret having used me thus."

The old Marshal had, however, resolved, cost what it might, to put an end to this deplorable condition of things. His daughter had spoken of a separation. That scandal must be spared if possible.

The cause, real or apparent, of the disunion was Mdlle. Deluzy. The Marshal sent his notary, M.

Riant, to visit her, and explain to her the consequences that would result from her persistent residence in the family.

The Abbé Gallard also called upon her, and, in
somewhat sterner language, pointed out the necessity
for her immediate departure from a house in which
her presence was a perpetual cause both of dissension
and of scandal.

Mdlle. Deluzy acknowledged to herself that all was
over.   She consented to depart.

Great kindness and delicacy seem to have been
displayed towards this woman, who, whether rightly
or wrongly, had been the understood source of so
much discord and suffering.   Marshal Sebastiani
settled on her a pension of 1500 francs, only requiring that she should quit France altogether.

The two annexed letters bear upon this point :—

" *June* 18th, 1847.

" Madame la Duchesse,—I should have desired to express by
word of mouth the feelings which animate me, but under present
circumstances I find the task beyond my power.   Allow me then
to postpone until a calmer and happier time the thanks I owe you
for the generosity with which you reward my poor services.   In
quitting the children I love so tenderly your approbation afforded
me a certain comfort.

" I accept gratefully the recommendations you are good enough
to offer, and shall avail myself of them the moment circumstances

permit. The failing health of my grandfather compels me at this moment to remain with him.

"I shall beg leave to make you acquainted with my after proceedings; and meanwhile entreat you, Madame, to receive the expression of my profound respect.

H. DELUZY."

### Reply of Mdme. de Praslin.

"*June 19th,* 1847.

"MADEMOISELLE,—I regret much to hear that you are indisposed, and that in that state you incurred the fatigue of thanking me for what, remembering your devotion to my children, was nothing more than due. If regard for their true interests has hastened a separation which, a few days since, appeared to be much more distant, do not doubt but that it will only render me more anxious to serve you whenever you will afford me the opportunity.

"I hear that you propose to pay a visit to Lady Hislop. In that case I would offer you a letter to Lady Tankerville, who will, I am sure, unite with Lady Hislop in assisting your wishes to the best of their power. If you desire an introduction also to Mdme. de Flahaut and to Miss Elphinstone, pray say so.

"I remember that you wished to borrow a book of me at Praslin. I trust you will not refuse me the pleasure of offering it as a present.

"I can only repeat, Mademoiselle, that I shall be most eager to aid your wishes at any opportunity that may present itself, and trust that you will soon afford me that pleasure.

S. PRASLIN."


The victory was won!—a sad triumph—alas! and pregnant with a fearful sequel.

Mdme. de Praslin experiences a sense of impending misfortune. The Duke has muttered threats, and his cold and gloomy looks inspire her with a secret nameless apprehension.   Her journal contains the following passages, written on the eve of their departure for Praslin :—

"June 17th, 1847.

" I am obliged to tell myself again and again that in joining my efforts to those of my father to get rid of that woman, I have only accomplished a sacred duty.   It has cost me dear.   I hate *l'éclat*, but every one, and my own conscience also, approve the act.

"My God!   What will come of it?   (*Quel sera l'avenir?*)   How enraged he is!   One might suppose that *he* was not the most to blame.   Can he shut his eyes to that?   My God, open them!"

## (*Last Extract.*)

" He had been tired of this woman for a long time, but *was afraid of her*.   That is why he refused to dismiss her.   It is clearly so.   And now that he has got help his self-love revolts against it.   That is his *real* cause of annoyance; and in conjuring up within himself a fictitious grief he hopes to soothe it.   ' You have marred my whole life by this act.'   These were his words, spoken with suppressed fury.

" In what haste he seemed, yesterday, to leave for Praslin, and to cut the matter short (*couper court de suite*)!   Yes, I have, as they assure me, done him a real service; but, as concerns myself, *he will never forgive it—never!   He will be revenged on me.*   Day by day, hour by hour, minute by minute, he will revenge himself for the good I have done him, for my having been right when he was wrong.   The gulf between us will grow deeper day by day.   The more he broods on this the more he feels conscious of his own error, the more will he wreak his vengeance on me.   The future appals me—I shudder in the contemplation (*L'avenir m'effraie; je tremble en y songeant*)."

The rest is known.

One month later Mdme. de Praslin wrote the following paper. It was found in her cabinet, sealed, and marked—

"*Mes Impressions.*

"*July* 13*th*, 1847.

"It is long since I have written a line, but nothing is changed.

"She is to leave, they say, when we go to Praslin; in the meantime she exercises the same influence over both my husband and children. I can understand her conduct, if indeed she be quite devoid of shame, but *his* remains a mystery. He condemns the scandal, yet every day he supplies it with fresh food. He pretends that his relatives have been assailed, and makes public his quarrel with my father as the consequence of it. He breaks with *us*, while he is perpetually with *her*. It is the most incomprehensible character I have ever known.

"What *can* have given her this empire over him? It must surely be the influence of fear.

"Poor man! I heartily pity him. What a life! what a future! If at forty-two he can be so easily fooled by an *intriguante*, what will become of him when old?

"How I loved him once! He must, perforce, have been changed by these debasing associations; for, viewing him as he appears *now*, I cannot understand my own passionate love. It is *not* the same man; how suspicious he has grown, how apathetic, how irritable! Nothing animates, interests, or arouses him; no generous, exalted, or enthusiastic ideas seem to occur for an instant to his altered mind. All that could conduce to an useful, brilliant, happy, honourable life was at his command. Now he cares for nothing—his country, his children, are of no consideration. He has fallen to be the *cavalier servant* of governesses, and is little better than their slave.

"I really believe that he holds to this woman (whom he has ceased to love at least these two years) because he fears that, once away from here, she would make his existence intolerable.

"It is strange; but I am convinced she attributes my pressing her dismissal to my love and jealousy of himself. He does not understand I now think only of my children. It flatters him; but I have no doubt that, if he had not believed my love inextinguishable, he would have treated me better. One might perhaps preserve a spark of love in one's heart for a man who, if harsh and cruel, is still capable of something great and honourable; nay, if he be but just and conscientious. But——

"Certainly there was good material in his heart and understanding, but the want of fixed moral and religious principles has been fatal to him; and his mental indolence gave the material passions way.

"How lonely he has become! He has scarcely one real, sincere friend. He has only connexions formed for pleasure, bonds that become galling chains, because he has not the mental strength to fling them fairly aside. It is frightful!

"How weak, after all, are men! How strange! he has blamed, oppressed, humiliated, abandoned *me*, for the sake of one whom in reality he does not care for! *I* loved *him* only, and with an ardour that amazes me when I recal it *now*. It may be, I know not, but possibly in his heart he may yet prefer me to these women that he both disdains and fears, while I on my part am disenchanted with *him*.

"Our position is both strange and sad. He has had pleasure enough, but little love; and now the love he *might* have had is drowned in tears!

"How will it all end? I cannot think there will ever be a complete reconciliation, desirable as that must be for the children. He will shun me because he has done me wrong, and I shall only seek *him* through my devotion to our children. Some feeling within me revolts against making advances to a man, even my husband, while doubtful of his love.

"My God, Thou alone knowest all that I have suffered in hunger of the heart. If I have not fallen into temptation, glory to Thee, O Lord. Thou only art my stay. Oh, leave me not now, for, wanting Thee, I perish. My God, my God! support and guide me. I dread the future—the menaces he has uttered (*j'ai peur de l'avenir—des menaces qu'il m'a fait*)—the difficulties which every day arise.

"But Thou art at hand, and I have trust in Thee, that Thou wilt support the poor mother fighting this hard battle for her children. *Lord, help me!*"

These were the last recorded words of one whom we have called, we think not inaptly, the

MARTYR-WIFE.

THE END.

www.ingramcontent.com/pod-product-compliance
Lightning Source LLC
Chambersburg PA
CBHW021323110726
47900CB00005B/1334